I0633133

Murder Exit Stage Right

Mabel and Violet Mysteries, Volume 5

Joan Havelange

Published by Brown Wolf Publishing, 2025.

Published by Brown Wolf Publishing
Saskatchewan, Canada

Dedication

To my dear Wolseley Thespians, "I'm so glad we had this time together."
And Kim, thanks for the hair-raising advice.

Chapter One

The mud-spattered sports car turned into the Community Theatre Hall parking lot. Driving past the front of the hall, the car lights momentarily lit the theatre's large main doors. Parking the car at the side of the hall, the driver quickly killed the motor. Did anyone see the car lights? Was anyone about? The late-night visitor smirked. It was unlikely. Little prairie towns like Glenhaven Saskatchewan, rolled up the sidewalks long before midnight. But one could never be too careful. The black-clad figure closed the car door, shivering. It was April, but the night felt cool. Or was that nerves? Flashlight in hand, the prowler quietly crept up to the side of the hall, shoes crunching on the frozen gravel.

The intruder came prepared with a set of burglar tools bought off the internet but found no need for them. It was ridiculously easy to open the old side door. The interloper chuckled; who would ever want to break into this old hall? The renovated theatre held nothing of value except for the midnight caller.

Once inside, the trespasser found the light switch and flicked the lights on. Another bonus was the theatre had no windows. The lights were startling after the darkness. The intruder waited until their eyes adjusted, looking around the old hall, marvelling at Glenhaven's excellent job renovating the old movie theatre. The screen was long gone. But the sloped floor remained, and the ancient theatre seats looked newly upholstered. Heavy new burgundy curtains hung open, revealing the renovations had continued to the stage. New theatre footlights and the floor of the stage looked new as well. The old theatre was ready for the one-act drama festival to be held the following week. A small set of stairs on the theatre floor led up to the stage. The black-clad figure quickly ascended the three wooden steps, stepped onto the stage, paused, and grinned. Glenhaven had restored the old movie theatre to its former glory, but the town must have run out of money.

Flimsy flats flanked the stage. There were two openings in the black-painted wallboard, one on each side of the stage. The backdrop was a badly painted window on muslin. The stage was set for the Glenhaven Players. Stage left, a faded flowered loveseat that had seen better days. A green throw cushion hung precariously on the arm; a small oval-shaped coffee table sat in front of the settee. Stage right at the back of the stage, a brown cabinet made from chipboard, a blue and white vase crammed full of various plastic flowers set on top of the cabinet. The intruder's eyes sparkled with amusement. What a shabby set, as shabby as the Glenhaven Players.

The midnight visitor chuckled and exited stage right; it was time to leave a little surprise.

It was seven in the evening when Violet Ficher parked her late-model hybrid car in the empty parking lot beside the Glenhaven Community Theatre Hall. Turning to her good friend, Mabel Havelock, she said, "We're early, or the rest of the cast are late."

"They're not late. We're early, as usual." Mabel looked out the car window at a small, dirty snowbank that stubbornly refused to melt. "You're always in such a rush for rehearsals. I barely had time for my dessert." She ran her tongue over her teeth. She should have brushed them after her meal.

"You could always drive yourself if you don't want to be on time like me," refuted Violet. "Oh, wait, you can't drive in the evening because you refuse to get your cataracts taken care of. You big chicken."

Violet and Mabel, two retired nurses, were chalk and cheese. Despite their differences, they were fast friends. Mabel was barely five feet tall, chubby, with short, snow-white hair. Violet, a tall, six-foot, thin, athletic woman with fiery red hair from a bottle, was a three-time divorced woman. And a stickler for cleanliness that bordered on a phobia. She never bent the rules. Unlike Mabel, a widow who thought rules were more of a suggestion.

"I'll have you know I have an appointment with a cataract surgeon the week after the drama festival," defended Mabel.

"Oh, good at last, so you're going for a pre-op consult."

"No, I'm going for an interview."

"If you remember correctly, the term is consult, not interview." Violet pulled down the visor, checking her image in the mirror. She tucked a stray lock of her short red hair behind her ear.

"Violet, I know what the correct term is. But I'm going to have an interview with this ophthalmologist and ask for references. No one is tinkering with my eyes until I'm sure of their qualifications."

"Seriously." Violet's forehead furrowed, and she flipped the visor back up. "You're going to interview the ophthalmologist?"

"Yes, seriously. I'm not letting just anyone take a laser to my eye. It's my eyes," defended Mabel. "I'm employing him to do the surgery. So, I'm checking his credentials."

"What if it's a woman?"

"Don't be silly. Of course, I don't care what sex the doctor is, but I do want references."

Violet chuckled. "I should like to sit in on your interview."

A small red Volkswagen pulled up next to Violet's car, the tires crunching on the frozen gravel.

"Ah, Helen is here at last."

"You mean on time. I don't know how I got conned into helping with this darn drama festival?" Mabel grumbled, stepping out of the car, a stiff breeze ruffling her snow-white hair. She tugged the zipper on her jacket up to her chin.

"You don't fool me. I can tell you're having fun prompting. I bet you know everyone's lines." Violet reached into the back of the car for her script.

Mabel's short, chubby legs raced to keep up with her friend's long stride.

Helen Graham, the director of the Glenhaven Players, a small, nervous little woman with iron-grey hair, got out of her car, buttoning her blue padded jacket over her heavy woollen sweater. Helen was always cold. She wore a down-filled vest in July. "Do you think we'll be ready for the festival? The last rehearsal was a little shaky," the middle-aged woman asked as she tugged a big white plastic bag out of her car. The bag fell to the ground, and sheets of paper with handwritten stage directions slid out of the bag onto the gravel parking lot. A bright green pen rolled under her car.

"It's a one-act play," Violet said, stepping on a sheet of paper that threatened to fly away. "I think we'll be ready." She stooped, gathering more papers and stuffing them back into the plastic bag.

Mabel, crouching beside the Volkswagen, guffawed.

Helen looked down at Mabel, a worried frown on her face. "Do you think there is a problem? I know some of my actors forgot a few of their lines."

Violet stood up, offering the plastic bag to Helen. "I'm sure by now everyone knows their lines."

"Some do, some don't," contradicted Mabel. Kneeling, she peered under Helen's car.

"I do hope nothing goes wrong with the rehearsal tonight," Helen fretted. Ignoring the offered bag, she hurried to the side door of the hall. Fumbling in her purse for her keys, she smiled nervously. "I've got too much stuff in here."

"I can see your pen," Mabel called, "But I'm not crawling under your car for it."

"That's okay. I'm sure I can borrow a pen," Helen said as she continued to rummage in her purse.

"I've got pens. I'll give you one," Violet said, joining Helen at the door.

Mabel stood, wiping the icy gravel bits off her hands on her jeans. "I forgot my script," she said, jogging back to Violet's car.

"Ah, here it is." Helen inserted her key into the lock. She turned it, but the door remained shut. "Darn it." She turned the key again in the opposite direction. This time, the door opened, and she hurried in, followed by Violet. The lights were on in the hall. "Oh, no, Mike has left these lights on. Just imagine what the power bill will be," worried Helen as she accepted the bag with her notes and a pen from Violet.

Violet, removing her jacket, folded the red fleece coat and placed it on a theatre seat, then mounted the wooden steps at the side of the stage. "I'll just pop up here and check my prop table." Her footsteps echoed in the hall as she disappeared backstage.

Helen took a seat in the middle of the front row, organizing her notes. The side door opened, and Mabel entered, followed by Helen's granddaughter, Jolene. The tall, slender girl shed her red leather jacket, tossing it onto the theatre seat on top of Violet's. Jolene's thick blonde hair cascaded down her back as she bent down to plant a kiss on her grandmother's cheek.

"I'm getting excited, aren't you, Granny? We have just a few days before the festival. Do you think I should try redder lipstick? Do you like my lashes? I just got lash extensions. Aren't they fabulous?"

Helen smiled warmly up at her granddaughter. "Jolene, sweetie, you're already beautiful. But if you want false lashes, that's fine with me."

Mabel rolled her eyes and tossed her jacket beside Jolene's. "I hope you've put as much effort into studying your lines as you have with your makeup. Last rehearsal, I constantly had to prompt you, particularly in the scene where you sit on the sofa with Beau."

"With who?"

"Who? Seriously? You've rehearsed for months, and you don't remember who Beau is? Rudy Sabatini, the guy who plays Beau, your boyfriend, in the play."

"Oh, yeah, Rudy." Jolene giggled. "I was just joking. Of course, I know who Beau is."

Mabel opened her playbook. "Glad to hear it. Have you studied your part? Do you have your lines down, memorized?"

"Oh, for sure, don't worry. I know my lines. I guess I do sometimes get kind of confused. But I can't help it." Jolene giggled again. "It's because of Rudy. I mean, Beau.

When he puts his arm around me, I get all fluttery and nervous."

"Oh, my, that's not good. I wonder if I can change that scene?" Helen said, flipping through her script.

"Oh, please don't do that, Granny. I mean, nervous in a good way."

Helen looked anxiously at her granddaughter. "In a good way?"

Mabel's eyes flickered with amusement. She could see why Rudy Sabatini set Jolene all a twitter. Rudy was a handsome man with a mop of brown curly hair, deep brown eyes, and a mischievous smile. Rudy, a young man in his mid-twenties, was just a few years older than Jolene. But a lot older in experience if Mabel was any judge. Speak of the devil, Mabel thought as the door opened, and Rudy confidently strode in. Jolene's blue eyes sparkled as she spun around to greet him.

"Hi, Mrs. H," he greeted Mabel. "I've been practicing my lines."

"Me too," Jolene said, fluttering her long lashes and flashing him a radiant smile.

"Were you born in a barn?" roared Mike, Helen's husband. "You're letting all the heat out. We're not trying to heat Saskatchewan. The power bill will be high enough as it is." The big, sloped-shouldered man with a pronounced Adam's apple lumbered through the open door. Slamming it shut behind him.

The door swung quickly open again, and Tommy Spears, a skinny young man with limp, lifeless, straw-coloured hair, entered.

"Never mind, Rudy. Mike left the lights on," reprimanded Helen.

"What? I didn't leave the lights on. I always make sure they're off." Mike's deep voice reverberated in the near-empty hall.

"Well, this time, you did forget because they were on when I came in."

"I don't know what you are on about. I always shut the lights off. Ask Tommy; before we leave, we always do a double-check. Tommy, tell Helen we shut the lights off last night."

"Oh, yes, yes we did," Tommy said earnestly.

"Then one of the members on the hall board must have been in here because the lights were on."

"Most likely our mayor. He's always poking around," growled Mike, hitching his trousers over his potbelly.

"Never mind. It's not important," Helen said, spreading her notes on her knee. A handwritten note of stage directions fluttered to the floor.

Mike picked up the sheet of paper, read the notes, and smiled approvingly, then gave the paper to his wife. "You are a natural, Helen." He grinned. "You'll win the best director for sure at this festival."

Helen blushed, smiling back at her husband. "Thank you, sweetheart."

Tommy Spears sped to stand near Jolene. Shuffling his feet nervously, he said, "Hi. I hope I'm not holding you up." Brushing his lifeless straw-coloured hair away from his pale blue eyes, he added, "I'll get the stage lights on right away."

"You aren't late. We've all just arrived," Jolene said, giving the gangly young man a friendly smile.

Tommy's face flushed red as he beamed happily back at Jolene, blinking his long, thick white eyelashes.

Mabel felt sorry for the socially inept young man as she recalled someone unkindly referring to Tommy as a tall white rabbit.

Violet parted the heavy burgundy stage curtains and stepped to the edge of the stage. "Is everyone here?" she asked.

"We're still waiting for Alice, Sam, and Sherman. Oh, and Ned," Mabel answered.

"Come on, Tommy. You get the stage lights set, and I'll get the sound system going," Mike said, tromping up the aisle toward a ladder that led up to a small enclosed cubical that previously housed the movie projectors. The small booth now held the light and sound equipment.

Tommy, blinking his long white lashes, gave Jolene a bashful smile, turned and followed Mike, Helen's portly husband, up the aisle to the sound booth at the front of the theatre.

The door swung open, and Alice Woodstock dashed in. The small birdlike lady with a maid's cap pinned to the top of her frizzy orange hair shed her jacket, revealing a black dress and a frilly snow-white apron. She did a pirouette. "Well, what do you think? I had to make the apron myself. You would think someone in town would have an apron to lend. But no. So, I had to make this apron myself," Alice repeated, parading up and down in front of Helen.

"Very nice. It's a wonderful costume, but dress rehearsal is tomorrow night," Helen said, sorting through her notes.

Alice thrust her bottom lip out in a pout. "I try to be ahead of the game. And this is the thanks I get."

Helen, flustered, said, "Oh, thank you, Alice. You look wonderful."

Smiling, Alice grasped the ends of her apron and curtsied.

Mabel wrinkled her nose. Trust Alice to make a big deal out of a maid's costume. Mabel had little time for Alice Woodstock, the town gossip. Alice had previously maligned her friend Violet. And it stuck in Mabel's craw that the woman never apologized for the slander. Violet had forgiven Alice. But Mabel was not so generous.

Sam Peebles, a local farmer, sauntered in, followed by Ned Shwarts, a retired used car salesman. Sherman Mahan entered right behind them. Sherman, employed at the new potash mine, was a newcomer to Glenhaven.

Ned looked slyly at Mabel. Mabel tightened her lips. Her eyes darted left and right as Ned sidled up. The small bald man with a fringe of grey hair grinned a yellow tooth grin, his tongue flicking in and out of his mouth. He reminded Mabel of a snake.

"How are you tonight, dear lady?" Ned asked in his shrill, sharp voice.

His voice grated on Mabel's ears. "Fine," she replied, pasting a smile on her face. She wished he wouldn't stand so close to her. The man was emanating a sharp pine odour. The smell reminded her of the little pine tree deodorizer her father used to hang off his review mirror. Ned kept looking at her as he licked his lips, his tongue darting in and out. Mabel averted her gaze. Helen had cast the man as the villain in the play. And in Mabel's opinion, it was perfect casting.

"Are we ready to start?" Violet called from the stage apron.

Sam Peebles, a tall, gangly scarecrow of a man with a weather-beaten face, bounded up the side stairs. Appearing seconds later, on the stage beside Violet, he raised his baseball cap to scratch his thinning hair on the top of his head and asked. "Do you have my pipe?" His blue jeans were worn and patched, his bony wrists protruding from the sleeves of his faded red plaid shirt.

"Everything is on the prop table," Violet said, gesturing stage left.

"Thanks. I couldn't remember what I'd done with the darn thing at the last rehearsal." Sam's big, raw-boned hands tugged open the burgundy curtains. "Big Daddy has to have a pipe," he quipped, disappearing behind the curtains.

"You are not a big daddy," shouted Jolene after him. "You're my papa."

"He's called Big Daddy in the play," Violet called down from the stage.

"Oh, yeah, I guess he is," Jolene giggled.

Mabel looked at Helen's granddaughter and thought, and not for the first time, that Helen had let nepotism get in the way of casting. Jolene, who played Sam's daughter Bobbi Sue in the play, had trouble remembering her lines, and her acting was over the top, bordering on melodramatic. Sure, Jolene looked the part of the beautiful southern belle with her big blue eyes and long blonde wavy hair. But that was that. Plus, the girl never knew her cues.

"I see I'm not the only one dressed in proper attire," Alice said, looking at Sherman as he doffed his jacket.

Sherman, a man in his early fifties, had a shock of white curly hair. The handsome man in the black suit with tails was tugging on a pair of white cotton gloves. "Jeeves at your service," he said in a mock English accent.

"How come he's an English butler in a southern play? The rest of us have southern accents," asked Rudy.

"I think an English accent is best for a butler," Helen said, looking up from her script.

"Our play is set in the deep south. Don't you think an English accent will sound odd?" persisted Rudy.

Helen bit her bottom lip. "Oh, my, I guess maybe you're right."

"A fine time to point that out. I've learnt all my lines with an English accent. Helen, do you really want me to change my accent now?" Sherman asked.

"I don't know." Helen looked up at the cast. She had a worried look on her face. "Do you guys think it's too late?" The actors looked at each other and shrugged.

"Do you think you can try a southern accent, Sherman?" asked Mabel. "It's kind of up to you."

Sherman knitted his brow. "Yeah, I guess. But don't be surprised if I fall back on my original accent. After all, the butler is called Jeeves, which sounds English to me."

"Hey, when the heck is this rehearsal going to start?" Mike hollered from the sound booth at the back of the hall.

"Yes, please, everyone onstage," Helen urged.

The actors and Mabel trouped up the steps and disappeared off stage. Mabel went stage left to her stool, picked it up, and moved it so she could see and hear the actors. She climbed up on her stool and opened her script, grimacing. Mabel thought the play's plot was silly and convoluted. The play *Plantation Dilemma* was about a southern belle forced to marry the villain, Ned, to pay her father's debts or be evicted from the plantation. Beau, the gallant gentleman in love with Bobbie Sue, is rejected by Big Daddy, who does not think Beau is good enough for his daughter. Then Alice, the maid, confesses she is the birth mother of the southern bell. Ned, the villain, won't marry a maid's daughter, and Beau and Bobbie Sue run off to elope. The audience never discovers who the father is or what happens to Big Daddy and the plantation. But the play was a melodrama, and Mabel hoped the audience wouldn't care.

Chapter Two

The cast members took their positions offstage and waited for their entrances. Violet pulled the heavy burgundy velvet curtains open, and the stage lights came on. Standing in the opening stage left, Jolene flipped her blonde hair, took a deep breath, and entered. She paused, fluttered her eyelashes, fluffed her hair and sashayed across the stage toward the small loveseat. A spotlight followed her. "I do declare." She hesitated and looked offstage at Mabel. "Is it long? Or is it a long?"

"The line is. *It's a long and boring day*," prompted Mabel.

"A what?"

"Your line is *I do declare it's a long, boring day*," Mabel repeated in a louder voice.

"Oh yes, a long, boring day. I'll start again." The spotlight led the way as Jolene made her exit stage left. The tall, slender girl entered, paused in the spotlight, put one hand on her hip, flipped a long lock of golden hair with the other, and said, "I do declare it's boring."

"Tommy, sweetie," Helen called up to the engineering booth. "You don't have to put a spotlight on Bobbi Sue."

"I just thought since Jolene is the star, she should have a spotlight," defended Tommy, shouting down from the booth.

Jolene beamed up at him, giving him a wink.

"Did Helen tell you to put a spotlight on her?" growled Mike.

"Uh, no, I guess not," confessed Tommy, shutting off the spotlight.

"From the top, please," requested Helen.

Jolene sighed, pouted, and flounced offstage. Mabel whispered to her, "Remember your line is. *I do declare it is a long, boring day.*"

Jolene nodded and sashayed back onstage. She twirled, flipped her hair, and said in her southernmost drawl. "I do declare I'm bored; it's a long, long day." She stretched extravagantly and yawned.

Close enough, Mabel thought as Jolene swanned her way to the settee. Flinging herself down on the sofa, Jolene theatrically put her hand to her forehead.

"Overact much," Mabel muttered.

Jolene sat up, looked offstage at Mabel, and asked, "What? Did I miss my line?"

"No, you're fine," Mabel sighed. "Just keep going."

Jolene swooned back on the sofa. Her foot dislodged the green cushion on the arm of the couch, and the cushion fell onto the floor.

Entering upstage right, Sam, holding a pipe in his big bony hand, pointed the pipe stem at Jolene. The gangly man then loped across the stage to the couch and looked down at Jolene, sprawled across the sofa. "Booby Sue, what are y'all doing lying around? It is a splendiferous day." He kicked the pillow, sending it to the apron of the stage.

"Bobbie Sue, it's Bobbie Sue," prompted Mabel.

"That's what I said," Sam said, lifting his baseball cap and scratching his head.

"No, you didn't. You said booby."

"Oh, sorry," apologized Sam, his face turning red. He repeated his line, this time saying Bobbie Sue.

Sherman Mahan, playing Jeeves, the butler, entered and bowed. A tray balancing precariously in his white-gloved hand, he proceeded across the stage to Jolene. Green-coloured liquid splashed from a long-stemmed cocktail glass onto the tray.

"Please use both hands, Jeeves," instructed Helen.

"Right ho." The handsome silver-haired man tipped his head in acknowledgement and chuckled. And, then, with both hands holding the tray, he bowed to Jolene and asked in his best imitation of a British accent, "Would Madam like a mint julep?" Sherman then quickly held up a hand. "Wait, wait, I forgot." He bowed again and asked, "Would y'all want a little old mint julep?" Sherman and Sam broke into peals of laughter, Sam slapping his knee. Sherman looked down at Helen. "How is that? Too southern?"

"Oh, maybe a bit, too much," Helen replied timidly.

"Right, I'll tone down my accent." Sherman bowed again and said, "Would Madam like a little old mint julep?"

"I, I think that's much better," Helen said.

"Oh, mah word, I'm so delirious for a mint julep." Jolene sprang up from the sofa, taking the martini glass off the tray.

"Desirous," Mabel whispered from offstage.

"I said delirious," Jolene answered indignantly.

"Well, yes, you did." Mabel stepped onstage, script in hand. "It's desirous, not delirious."

Jolene stormed to the stage apron and called down to Helen. "Does it matter? Granny, does it really matter if I say delirious or desirous?"

Helen's hands flipped through her script. She read the line, then looked up at her granddaughter. "The script does say desirous, but maybe it would be okay if you said delirious. If that's all right with you, Mabel?"

"Sure, whatever, carry on."

Jolene gave Mabel a self-satisfied smile and pranced back to her place on the settee.

"Booby, Bobbie, Bobbie Sue, you are far too young for such a libation." Sam's big hand yanked the cocktail glass from Jolene's hand. He slammed the glass back onto the tray. The tray slipped from Sherman's hands, clattering onto the floor. The plastic cocktail glass rolled across the stage, coming to rest beside the green cushion.

"Oops, sorry," apologized Sam. "I kind of got caught up in my role as Big Daddy." "

No problem, old chap," Sherman said, picking the tray up from the floor and striding to the stage apron. He picked up the glass, tucked the pillow under his arm, and then, backing up, he bowed his way offstage.

Mabel sighed and turned a page of her script.

Jolene flung herself back on the settee with her hand palm upward on her forehead. "Papa, I'm not a little old child."

"It's Big Daddy," prompted Mabel.

"What?"

"Your line is *Big Daddy. I'm not a little old child.*" And please don't say '*what*' when I prompt you. Or it will be obvious to the audience that you have forgotten your line."

Jolene jutted her chin out, sighed loudly and repeated her line, this time saying Big Daddy.

Violet, holding a handheld mic, knocked on her prop table.

Sherman popped back onstage and asked. "Shall I see who is calling, sir?" Sherman grinned, held up his hand and started again, "I reckon I shall see who y'all is calling, sir?" he drawled in a mixture of accents; dipping his head, he pivoted on his heel, bowing his way offstage right.

Mabel rubbed her forehead. Sherman's new accent was not going to work.

"Yes, by all means, y'all see who is a coming calling," Sam said to the empty space.

Alice entered. "Oops too soon," she said, curtseying. She then turned and exited off stage.

Rudy bounded onstage. Removing an imaginary hat, the handsome young man made a sweeping bow. "Howdy, y'all." He brushed a lock of his curly brown hair off his forehead. With a cocky wink and a confident smile, he strode toward Jolene, who fluttered her eyelashes and giggled.

"Y'all are not welcome here. Get off my property, you scallywag." Sam stomped across the stage and grabbed Rudy's jacket, shaking him.

Rudy's eyes widened as his head flopped from side to side. He sputtered, "Hey, hey."

"Oh, my. Maybe try not to shake Rudy so hard," Helen called from the front row.

Sam, looking puzzled, released Rudy.

Rudy adjusted his jacket. "Yeah, man, not so hard."

Sam frowned. "Aren't I supposed to hate this guy? He's after my daughter, right?" He grabbed Rudy by the jacket, shoving the young man off balance.

"Hey, Sam, stop it. And besides, you don't grab me in this scene. That's my next entrance."

"Oh, yeah, right." Sam let go of Rudy's jacket. "Sorry, buddy," he said, patting the shorter man on the shoulder.

Alice entered, curtseyed, looked at the actors onstage, and said, "Sorry, not my cue." She ran offstage right, then immediately ran back on. "The wrong side," she called, exiting stage left.

"Bad dress rehearsal, good performance," Violet said, peeking over Mabel's shoulder.

"It's not the dress rehearsal, but I get your point." Mabel flipped another page of her script and was pleased. For once, the conversation between Jolene, Rudy, and Sam continued without a hitch. There was hope the play was not going to bomb.

The scene ended with Rudy being chased offstage by Sam. The only problem Mabel saw was Alice. She kept entering at the wrong cue, curtsying and exiting, only to pop on the stage moments later to repeat the process.

The play progressed. Sam exited, and Sherman entered and announced, "There is a gentleman caller to see y'all, miss."

Ned entered, cackled, and licked his lips. "Howdy, little lady," he screeched. "Is your?" Ned paused, then asked. "Is Big Daddy home?"

"My good sir... I mean, ah. Why do you want to talk to my good papa, my Big Daddy, good sir?"

Ned sidled over to the loveseat and leered down at Jolene. Sherman, bowing, exited stage right. Ned grasped Jolene's hand, his lips touching the back of her hand. Jolene shuddered. Mabel shuddered too. After a long pause, Ned and Jolene looked offstage at Mabel.

Mabel flipped a page of her script and prompted, "*My lovely, I am asking for your lovely little old hand in marriage.*"

Ned, kissing Jolene's hand, repeated the line. "My lovely, I am asking for your hand in marriage."

"My hand, mah dear sir?" Jolene pulled her hand away, wiping the back of her hand on her jeans.

Alice entered and strutted to centre stage, planting her hands on her hips, shouting, "You will never marry my little Bobbie Sue."

"Your Bobbie Sue?" Ned's voice rose to a shriek.

"Wait, wait, you guys, you've jumped a whole scene," Mabel yelled. "It's the scene where Ned threatens to evict everyone from the plantation if Bobbie Sue doesn't marry him."

"Oh right, because my papa owes money. Alice, you came in too soon," chided Jolene. "You messed us up."

"I did not. I followed your cue. You said my hand. That's where I come in," snapped Alice.

"People, people, please don't fight. Start from..." Helen rifled through her script.

Sherman entered stage right, stopped short, and asked, "Am I entering from the proper side?"

"We're not even close to your entrance. Alice has screwed everyone up," snarled Jolene.

"I have not. It's your fault," Alice defended. "Mabel, who screwed up? Not me, that's for sure."

A musical sound of a cell phone rang out. Sherman, looking apologetic, took his phone out of his pocket.

"Sherman, how many times have I told you to turn off your phone?" chided Helen.

"Oops, sorry, I keep forgetting." Sherman looked at his phone. "And I'm sorry, but I've got to take this. I won't be a minute. You guys sort out what scene we're in," Sherman said and exited stage right.

There was a slight pause, and then the loud accusations between Jolene and Alice resumed.

A blood-curdling scream cut through the air. The piercing scream came from stage right, followed by a loud crash. Then, dead silence.

Chapter Three

The dispute onstage abruptly ceased, the actors exchanging puzzled looks. Mabel jumped off her stool and dashed across the stage to exit stage right. Jolene, leaping up from the sofa, followed. She was trailed closely by Ned and Alice, who jostled each other, trying to leave the stage first. Rudy strode from backstage and took out his phone. Mike and Tommy, scrambling down the ladder, raced toward the stage. Tommy, tripping, stopped halfway down the aisle to tie his shoelace. Mike plodded past him and up the side stairs.

Helen, throwing down her script, stood. "What was that? What happened? Is someone hurt?" she shouted.

Mabel sped offstage and opened the small wooden door leading to the basement stairs. A musty smell greeted her as she stepped out onto the small landing at the head of the steps. She flipped the light switch on, and a row of yellowed fluorescent lights lit the dark, dank, windowless basement. The hall's basement was a storage area for a hoard of items used for plays and concerts. Boxes and tickle trunks containing old clothes and costumes. Nearby, an old artificial Christmas tree with faded decorations leaned against the basement wall by the landing. Tall red and white plastic candy canes piled up against black plastic chairs stacked on the other side of the basement wall. A tall grandfather clock with no hands leaned against a dusty old player piano. A stringless violin, broken ping-pong rackets, and a birdcage lay on an equally dusty bench. In the middle of the basement, curtains made from old bedsheets hung on a long, thin plastic line, makeshift dressing rooms for the drama festival.

A few feet from the steps, shattered makeup mirrors toppled over on a long wooden trestle table. Besides the table, face down on the cement floor, lay Sherman Mahan. Splinters of wood surrounded his motionless body. Wood from the broken railing. His arms flung out, one foot caught on the corner of the table. Blood was pooling around his head.

Looking down in horror, Mabel shouted, "Call an ambulance, and everyone, stay back." She stepped away from the gap in the handrail but was immediately pressed forward as Alice, Ned, and Jolene crowded up behind her, pushing and shoving, trying to see what lay below the broken railing. "I said stay back. There isn't enough room. Someone else is going to fall," Mabel yelled. "And please, for God's sake. Someone, call for an ambulance."

Despite Mabel's warning, Jolene elbowed aside the other actors, crowded on the small platform, attempting to peer over Mabel's shoulder. "Sherman, oh look, it's Sherman," Jolene said; with her hand on Mabel's shoulder, she stepped to the edge of the landing.

"Nooo," Mabel screamed. Her legs kicked in midair as she swung precariously over Sherman. "Help, help, help," she shrieked, clinging to a broken piece of the railing. The wood creaked and groaned, then cracked. The board broke, and Mabel fell. Frantically flailing her arms, she grabbed a branch of the tall plastic artificial Christmas tree, wrapping her arms and legs around it. The tree wobbled, bent, tilting from side to side.

The actors who were gathered on the landing watched in dismay as Mabel and the tree teetered, slowly collapsing onto the basement floor. Shaking, Mabel lay amid the branches, panting, trying to catch her breath. She looked across the cement floor and shuddered. Sherman's twisted body lay just a few feet away.

"You pushed her," Ned screeched.

"It was an accident," Jolene yelled defensively, backing away from the broken railing.

Violet pushed her way onto the landing and gasped, "Mabel, what are you doing down there? Good Lord, are you alright?"

"Never mind about me. It's Sherman. He's badly hurt," Mabel said, pawing at the tree's broken branches that covered her.

Violet, staying close to the wall, sped down the stairs. She rushed to Sherman's side, kneeling, searching for a pulse. Looking over at Mabel, she bit her bottom lip and shook her head. Sam, followed by Mike and Tommy, rushed onto the landing, brushing by Ned, Alice, and Jolene, who had started down the stairs. Unmindful of the broken railing, Sam took the steps down to the basement two at a time. He took off his baseball cap at the bottom of the stairs and crushed his cap in his hands. Mike lumbered past him and came to an abrupt halt, swearing under his breath as he looked down at Sherman. Alice, Jolene, Tommy, and Ned cautiously edged down the steps. The foursome crept by the two stationary men and formed a semicircle, gazing dumbfounded at Sherman. The dead man's white hair was turning dark crimson with his blood.

"Eww, yuck," cried Jolene, grasping Tommy by the arm; she laid her head on his shoulder. Tommy's face flushed as he awkwardly patted her on the back. Emerging onto the landing, Helen paused to look over the broken railing at Mabel, who was shaking synthetic pine needles out of her hair. "Are you okay?" Helen called. Before Mabel could answer, Helen spotted Sherman's body. "Oh no, no, no. Sherman. Oh my God, he's hurt. Poor Sherman, call an ambulance."

"An ambulance won't help Sherman," Mike yelled to his wife.

Helen gasped, put her hand over her mouth, and slowly descended the stairs.

"Mike's right. An ambulance won't help," Violet said, standing and looking down at Sherman, then over at the cast. "I'm afraid Sherman is dead. There is nothing we can do. We should all go upstairs. There is no need for all of us to be down here."

"Oh my gosh, you think he's dead," whispered Jolene. She stepped back. "I've never seen a dead person before."

"He can't hear you. You don't need to whisper," screeched Ned.

"Someone, do something," wailed Helen, bursting into sobs as she joined the cast, staring down at Sherman.

"Calm down, my love." Mike draped an arm around his wife's shoulders.

"Poor man, how on earth did that railing break?" asked Mabel as she joined Violet, looking down at the dead man.

Violet reached over and plucked a piece of blue tinsel from Mabel's hair. "You and the Christmas tree? What was that about?" she asked.

"I'll tell you later." Mabel tugged a sprig of artificial holly out of her sleeve and tossed the green twig over her shoulder.

Standing on the landing at the top of the stairs, Rudy called, "I phoned for the ambulance. The paramedics are on their way."

"The paramedics can't help Sherman now," Sam yelled back.

"Maybe he's not really dead. Maybe he is just knocked out," Jolene suggested hopefully.

"You mean the man that is lying here in a pool of blood?" Sam crossed his arms over his chest. "He's dead. I've seen dead men before, and Sherman certainly is dead. Poor guy. A hell of a way to die."

Tommy clumsily pat Jolene on her back as she wailed, "Oh, no!"

"Jolene could be right. Maybe Sherman isn't dead," defended Tommy.

"Sherman is dead," snapped Sam. "If you don't believe me, believe Violet; she said he was dead, and she's a nurse."

"She was a nurse. You're not a doctor, and neither is Violet." Alice tipped toed toward Sherman. "I'm going to take his pulse."

Mabel and Violet exchanged an exasperated look, and Sam rolled his eyes. Alice briefly touched Sherman's wrist, then leapt back, her lips curled down, rubbing her hands on her apron; she shuddered.

Ned snickered. "Better check that apron of yours, Alice. You might have Sherman's blood on it."

Alice's eyes widened, and her lips curled in disgust as she quickly checked her hands and examined her apron. Ned's high-pitched laughter grated on Mabel's ears, but she had to admit she enjoyed Alice's discomfort.

"A little more respect, people," shouted Alice. "The poor man is dead."

"Well, I'm glad you finally agree," sneered Sam.

"We should make poor Sherman more comfortable. The poor man's foot is hanging on the table," suggested a white-faced Helen.

Mabel gulped, "No, we mustn't interfere with, with—"

"We mustn't disturb the scene of the accident. The police will want to see things as they are," interrupted Violet.

Mabel gave Violet a questioning look. She wasn't going to say murder scene. But was this an accident?

"The police?" Helen gasped.

"That's how it's done; that is the proper procedure. The RCMP must be notified," Mabel said. "And we should call them now." The nearest RCMP Detachment was twenty minutes away in the town of Kipling.

"Oh, listen to miss know-it-all," sneered Alice.

Mabel glowered at Alice. Violet put a hand on her shoulder, and Mabel took a deep breath.

"Besides, he's dead. You can't make him comfortable," squeaked Ned.

Helen put her fist to her lips, tears streaming down her cheeks. Mike pulled a big blue and white hanky from his back pocket and gave it to his wife. Helen blew her nose. "Why did this have to happen to Sherman? A few minutes ago, he was on stage with everyone having fun rehearsing. And now this." Helen turned to her husband; he put his arm around her, hugging her.

"Come on, my love, we should go back upstairs," urged Mike. "In fact, I think we should all go back upstairs to the hall. We're not helping Sherman by standing around here gawking at the poor guy." He turned, leading Helen to the stairs. No one followed.

"Yes, yes, good idea," Violet agreed.

"I wonder how he fell?" asked Sam.

"The railing broke," Tommy said.

"I know the railing broke. But why did it break?"

"Sherman had a phone call, so he must have been leaning on the railing," Rudy said. "Yeah, I bet he was talking on his phone and leaning on the railing."

"I suppose that does make sense," murmured Mabel.

"How else?" Rudy mimed, leaning on the banister.

"Rudy, get back, don't be so foolish," Helen shouted.

Rudy gave a sheepish shrug and moved away from the gap in the railing. With his phone in his hand, he descended the stairs to stand with his fellow actors.

Mabel looked up at the broken railing, then down at the basement floor. "Where's his phone?"

Crossing her arms over her chest, Alice sneered at Mabel. "Stop trying to make a terrible tragedy into one of your so-called mysteries. And who cares where his phone is? This accident could've happened to any of us. It's just lucky it was Sherman."

Violet gasped. "Alice, what a thing to say."

"I mean, I mean, it's bad luck for Sherman. But any of us could have fallen. The washrooms and the changing rooms are down here. We all go up and down these stairs. It's shoddy workmanship. Whoever built these stairs should be sued."

"These stairs are old," Mike said.

"I wonder if Sherman's family will sue?" Jolene asked.

"They should have fixed the damn stairs when they did the renovations upstairs," growled Sam.

Mabel shivered. There was blood splatter on the steps. It could've been her. She could be lying dead beside Sherman.

Chapter Four

"Everyone, please go back upstairs," instructed Violet. "As Mike said, we're not helping Sherman by standing here. We'll only be in the way when the paramedics get here."

"Violet's right. And we must call the RCMP, and they won't be happy if we're still hanging about down here. Upstairs now," directed Mabel.

"Who died and made you the boss?" asked Alice.

"Sherman died, that's who."

"Don't be ridiculous. You know what I mean. Who are you to order us about? And I think it's just plain stupid to call the RCMP. No crime has been committed. Poor Sherman just fell."

"Somebody official has to determine the cause of death," Violet said.

"Yes, yes, come on, everyone," Helen called from the top of the stairs. "This is no place for us. And I can't bear the sight of poor Sherman lying here on this dirty, cold basement floor."

"Me either," agreed Jolene. Tommy trailed after her, followed by Rudy, texting as he mounted the stairs.

"Hey, stop looking at your damn phone and watch your step. There have been enough accidents," Sam muttered as he climbed the stairs.

"I can do both," Rudy replied, his fingers flying over the keypad.

Abruptly, Sam stopped on the stairs and turned to look down. "Shouldn't someone stay down here with Sherman until the paramedics arrive?"

"Why?" asked Ned in his raspy voice.

"I think it's kind of callous to leave the poor guy lying down alone," Sam answered.

"Sherman is dead either way," replied Ned. "But okay, who wants to stay down here with Sherman?"

"I'm not staying down here with a dead body on my own." Alice shivered and began to climb up the steps, hugging the wall as she did.

"Sam, I don't think anyone means to be callous. But we should all wait upstairs," Violet said.

Sam hunched his big shoulders and slowly mounted the steps.

"Come on, Mabel, let's go back up. There is nothing we can do for Sherman," urged Violet as she watched Sam and Alice leave through the door to the stage, following the rest of the cast.

Mabel paused, looking thoughtfully at the stairs, then at Sherman. There was something about the railing. Yes, the handrail was broken. But something else bothered her. She just couldn't put her finger on it. "There is one more thing we need to do. We need to phone the RCMP. Violet, will you call? Rudy called the paramedics, but I don't think he called the police."

"You don't think he did?"

"No, he's too busy texting."

"Alright, I'll do it. But have you noticed it's always me who calls the police?" muttered Violet, taking her phone from her pocket.

At the top of the stairs, Alice stepped back through the door, her phone in her hand.

Mabel heard a click. "Delete that picture right now!" she shouted.

Alice took another picture and shouted back. "People have a right to know."

"No, they don't."

"You're not the boss of me." Alice snapped another picture, then marched back through the door to the stage.

Mabel pressed her lips together. What could she do? Rip the phone out of Alice's hands? There was nothing Alice liked better than spreading the news. And knowing Alice, she'd probably try to contact the Regina Leader-Post with her grizzly pictures. She hoped the paper wouldn't print them.

With her phone to her ear, Violet paced in a circle, speaking in a sombre tone; she said, "I have, or I should say, we have a death on our hands again. And, of course, we certainly didn't have anything to do with it. The death, I mean. Sherman Mahan is our dead man. Well, he's not our dead man. But he is dead."

Mabel waited patiently as Violet paced. Violet tended to chatter when nervous. But when the chips were down, she knew her friend was always up to the task. Violet had saved her bacon in Russia.

Violet paused, listened, and turned to look at Sherman. "No, I don't suspect foul play. But of course, we can't say for sure, pending more investigation."

Mabel smiled and nodded approvingly. Violet was getting the hang of the lingo.

There was another long pause as Violet listened, then said, "The poor man fell from the landing onto the cement floor. We're at the old movie theatre down in the basement."

Mabel hurried to stand beside Violet. "Is that Robert you're talking to?" The ladies had a long history with the RCMP Officer Robert Shamanski. They'd always addressed the police officer by his first name. And Officer Shamanski had given up trying to change their familiarity with his name.

Violet put a finger to her lips. "Shush," she said in a whispered tone. "No, sorry, Robert, that shush wasn't meant for you. I was shushing Mabel."

"Tell him we've preserved the crime scene and ushered everyone upstairs."

"Shush, it's not a crime scene," disagreed Violet. "It's an accident scene."

"Maybe," replied Mabel

"No, sorry, Robert. I was talking to Mabel again." After another pause, Violet said, "No, Mabel isn't doing anything, I promise."

Mabel arched an eyebrow. "Oh, for goodness' sake. What does he think I'm going to do?"

"No, she hasn't, and we haven't tampered with a thing."

"Tampered," huffed Mabel. "Well, we might have investigated once or twice. But never deliberately... Okay, once."

Violet gave him the address and pocketed her phone. "Guess what? Our Constable Shamanski is now a sergeant. Isn't that great?"

"That is good news. Our Robert certainly deserves a promotion."

"Do you think we should address him as sergeant? Sometimes, he gets a little huffy when we call him by his first name."

"Oh, let's. I think that would make Robert happy. Is he coming? I hope we don't have to break someone else in."

"No, he's not, but he's sending someone."

"Darn, oh well." Groaning, Mabel knelt to look at the floor by the staircase. Then, going down on her hands and knees, she crawled under the stairs.

"Mabel, what are you doing? We should join the others onstage."

"I don't think this was an accident. Sam asked why the railing broke. His question has gotten me to thinking."

"Stop right there, Mabel Havelock. You have a nasty habit of always suspecting murder. Anyone can see the handrail gave way. The only worry I can see is. Workplace Health and Safety. Sherman's family might sue the hall board and maybe poor Fred Granger. He's the caretaker."

"I don't think Fred has anything to worry about." Mabel crawled out from under the stairs. She slowly stood, brushing her hands on her jeans. "Look at the handrail, then at the base of the landing. Do you see the screw holes? The ones at the base of the landing are perfectly clean. The screws weren't pulled out of the wood. But the railing. It's a different story. These screws have been ripped out. I think someone loosened the screws at the landing base but not on the handrail. This was deliberate."

"Really? Are you a carpenter? Please stop jumping to conclusions."

Mabel crossed her arms and stared thoughtfully at the base of the railing.

Alice, stepping out onto the landing, said, "Watch out. The handrail is broken. That's why poor Sherman is lying on the floor. I think Sherman is dead."

Two paramedics, carrying trauma kits, clomped down the stairs. Harvey Hanover, the tall, redheaded paramedic, said, "Thanks, Alice."

"Thanks for coming, but there's nothing you can do. Sherman is dead," Mabel said, stepping back as the two paramedics sped over to examine Sherman's body.

"Yeah, I can see that. It's a nasty way to die, poor guy. But we still have to examine him," Harvey said, crouching beside Sherman. "We have to record what we find. You know, procedure, rules, etc."

"I didn't know you were a paramedic. I thought you were a fireman," Violet said. "Your parents must be so proud. Mabel and I worked with your mom; we both liked her. She's an excellent nurse."

"Thanks, I'll tell her you said that," Harvey replied, bending to his task.

"Nasty way to die," said Connie Zhao, the small, dark-haired paramedic, as she joined Harvey.

"He fell through the railing," Violet said.

Mabel and Violet watched silently as the paramedics rolled Sherman over to examine him. His leg flopped on the floor, sticking out at a right angle. Sherman's forehead was crushed and bloody, and his white hair was now a mat of dark red congealed blood.

"Yeah, there is nothing we can do," Harvey said, closing his bag.

Connie's phone rang. She pulled off her gloves and stood with the phone to her ear; she listened, then said, "We have another call."

"We'll call the coroner. Have you called the RCMP?" asked Harvey as he and Connie raced back up the stairs.

"We did," Mabel yelled as they rushed out the door.

"I guess we really should go up to the stage and wait for them," Violet suggested.

Mabel took one last look at the dead man and the broken railing and joined Violet on the stairs. Alice, standing on the landing, held up her phone.

"Really, Alice? More pictures? Put your darn phone away!" yelled Mabel from the bottom step of the stairs.

Alice glared down at Mabel. "I'm phoning the police."

"No need, I'm here."

Constable Laurie Ohlerta, a tall, slender woman, stepped through the door. "Please go back to the stage and wait with the others," she said, putting on disposable gloves. Alice, pulling a face, reluctantly complied. With a camera in her hand, the constable began snapping photos of the broken hand-railing. Then, standing and leaning over the gap in the handrail, she pointed her camera down, taking pictures of the body lying below on the cement floor. Clotted blood had pooled around the man's head. There were splinters of wood from the banister strewn across the floor. And many bloody footprints. She tightened her lips, muttering, "What a mess. The world and his wife have tramped all over this accident scene."

At the bottom of the stairs stood Mabel and Violet. "Hi, my name is Mabel Havelock, and this is my friend Violet Ficher," greeted Mabel.

"I'm Constable Ohlert," the young officer answered briskly. "I will be conducting this investigation. Did you find the body?"

"Well, I guess Mabel was first, then everyone else came down to see," Violet answered.

The constable descending the stairs said, "Yes, that's pretty obvious. And what a hell of a mess you people have made!"

"Language, dear," scolded Mabel.

"Pardon me?" The constable's eyebrows rose at Mabel's rebuke.

"Don't apologize, dear. You're just a little upset with the crime scene," Violet soothed. "I mean the accident scene."

Constable Ohlert paused, frowned, and then sat on the bottom steps, pulling on blue paper booties over her boots. "I don't know why I'm bothering with these darn booties. There are bloody footprints all over the floor," she grumbled disgustedly.

"Sorry, I guess we all did crowd down here," apologized Violet. "But this time, it wasn't us who moved the body."

"This time?"

Mabel flashed a warning look at Violet. "She means we didn't move him. He was lying face down on the floor when we found him. It was the paramedics. They moved Sherman when they examined his body. By the way, his name is Sherman Mahan. He's the butler."

"The butler?"

"In the play," explained Violet.

"You're rehearsing a play?"

"Of course. Why else would we be here at the theatre?" Mabel realized too late she was being flippant. She needed to be more like Violet and keep her thoughts to herself.

Constable Ohlert briefly eyed Mabel, then began to circle the body, taking pictures as she went. "I know the paramedics were doing their job," she muttered. "But I wish I had seen how this man landed on the floor."

"Oh, I think there are pictures. Just ask Alice."

"Alice?" Pointing her camera at the stairs, the constable snapped more pictures.

"The maid you saw on the landing."

"The maid in the play?"

"Yes. We are, or we were going to perform our play in the drama festival."

"I see. Now, you two had better join the people upstairs. I'll take your statements when I'm finished here."

"I've spotted something interesting," Mabel said.

"Besides the dead body," added Violet.

"I think finding a dead man is interesting enough. I want you two upstairs onstage with everyone else."

The stage door opened, and Randolph Flegerler, the medical examiner, emerged. "Everyone, stay back," he ordered.

"Hi Randy, a bit of a grizzly one here," greeted the constable.

Randolph, ignoring the constable, yelled, "Hey, Mabel and you, Violet, get away from the body. Stay back out of the way."

"Randy, as you can plainly see, we are way back. We're not in anyone's way," answered Mabel.

The medical examiner stomped down the steps. "The name is Randolph. Use my proper name."

Mabel rolled her eyes. He didn't seem to mind if the constable called him Randy. She'd grown up with Randy Flegerler and saw no need to call him by any other name.

The skinny man with white-blond hair and washed-out blue eyes sat down on the last step, pulling paper slippers over his shoes and putting on gloves. "What a mess," he muttered, looking at the bloody footprints surrounding the dead body. "I don't know why I bother with these."

"I know. These bloody footprints are everywhere," the constable agreed.

"We apologized," defended Mabel.

"Ah, Mabel, I not surprised you had a hand in this calamity," Randolph said, donning a surgical mask.

Mabel fumed silently. Age had not improved Randy's attitude. He'd been a bossy little twerp when they were at school together and had taken great delight in tattling on her and her chums. Her private nickname for him had been Randy the Rat.

"This is not a calamity. It is a tragedy," rebuked Violet.

The medical examiner eyed Violet. "What are you two women doing down here? You shouldn't be here."

"Yes, ladies upstairs, please. I'll take your statement regarding the accident shortly."

"Accident? I have very important information that might say otherwise."

Randolph pulled down his mask and smirked. "Ah yes, Glenhaven's own Miss Marple." He barked out a laugh, pulled up his mask, and bent to his task.

Mabel scowled. Randy the Rat had not changed one iota.

"Forget him. Let's go back up to the stage," urged Violet, tugging Mabel's arm.

"Yes, fine," Mabel started for the stairs, then stopped and asked, "Aren't you going to check for fingerprints?"

Constable Ohlert put her camera in her bag. "Mrs. Havelock, you've been watching one too many TV detective shows. I must insist you go back and join your friends upstairs."

Randy stood, removed his mask and said, "Yeah, Mabel, you're not in an Agatha Christie novel." He gave her a superior smile, then turned to address the constable. "This man, of course, is dead. I see the damage to the railing. He obviously fell when the railing broke loose. The man died instantly when his head hit the cement floor."

Mabel paused on the staircase, muttering loudly, "And he gets paid for this?"

Randy turned, giving Mabel a dirty look.

Chapter Five

L oud voices greeted Mabel as she closed the door to the basement and entered onstage. The actors were gathered around Helen, voicing their opinions, each trying to drown out the other.

Mike, standing by his wife's side, was shouting the loudest. "Settle down, you guys," he ordered. "One at a time."

"Granny, we have to carry on. We can't cancel the play now," implored Jolene. "We just can't. We've been rehearsing for weeks."

Helen dabbed her eyes with Mike's blue and white handkerchief. Helen shook her head no and then nodded yes.

Rudy looked up from scrolling on his phone and said, "Listen to your granddaughter. She's right."

Jolene smiled broadly at Rudy and bobbed her head enthusiastically.

Rudy persisted, "Think of all the hours and all the hard work we have put in. And all the time we spent learning our lines and all those evenings we rehearsed. It will all be wasted if we don't perform our play. I'm sorry Sherman's dead. But the show must go on."

Scrunching the hanky in her hand, Helen nodded in agreement.

"Why? Who made up that stupid rule?" screeched Ned. The small man strutted up to confront Rudy. Rudy, ignoring Ned, continued to text on his phone.

Scowling, Sam crossed his arms over his chest and said, "A cast member is lying dead on the floor in the basement. We can't just carry on as if nothing happened."

Helen nodded in agreement again.

"Everyone just shut the heck up," roared Mike, dropping onto the loveseat, a leg on the couch wobbled. "Helen will decide what to do. She's the director."

The cast paused and looked in unison at Helen.

Helen sagged down beside her husband. The sofa leg wobbled again. "I don't know what to do. Everyone seems to have a valid point. But what is the right and proper thing to do?" Her eyes darted from actor to actor.

"Phone the mayor," suggested Mike.

Helen nodded vigorously, looking with gratitude at her husband.

"I'll phone the mayor for you, Helen." Alice pulled her phone from her apron pocket and scampered to the front of the stage.

Randy, the medical examiner, stepped onstage, followed by Constable Ohlert. "Can I please have everyone's attention?" requested the constable.

Alice waved a dismissive hand at the constable, puckering her lips. "I'm phoning the mayor," she said importantly.

"It's may I have everyone's attention," corrected Violet.

The constable shot Violet a curious look. "I need to take your statements."

Randy stopped centre stage. "I'll send my report."

"Thank you, Randy," the constable replied.

Jolene's eyes widened. She shuddered and asked, "You're not leaving Sherman down there, are you?"

"The funeral home is coming for the deceased," answered Constable Ohlert.

Jolene, exhaling a sigh of relief, perched on the arm of the small loveseat.

The coroner turned and waved. "Hey, Thomas, are you acting in this play?"

"No, just helping with the lights, is all." Tommy beamed. Turning to address the cast, he proudly said, "This is my uncle Randolph."

Mabel could see the resemblance. Both men were fair, with pale blue eyes and long white lashes. But where as Tommy was like a friendly puppy, Randy was like a pit bull.

"Well, good luck, everyone. I'm looking forward to the festival," the medical examiner said. Exiting stage left, he trotted down the steps to the hall floor and out the side door.

The constable stepped offstage, coming back with a chair, she said. "People, I have to take your statements."

Ignoring the constable, Jolene said, "You see, Granny, you heard what Tommy's uncle said. We have to go on with the show. I mean our play. Please, we can't disappoint our fan base."

"One fan isn't a fan base," cackled Ned.

Ned's shrill laughter got on Mabel's nerves. But she agreed with him. "Yes, Randy wants to come to the festival, but Randy is used to seeing dead bodies. But what will the public think about us hosting and performing in a drama festival when they learn Sherman died in the basement?"

"Randolph," Tommy piped up.

Mabel rolled her eyes. "Okay, sorry. Randolph is used to seeing dead bodies."

The constable shook her head and placed the chair centre stage. "Okay, people listen up. I now intend to start taking statements."

With a mutinous look on her face, Jolene got to her feet and said, "The funeral guys will take Sherman away. It's not like he's going to stay in the basement,"

"That's not what I mean. You're just being ridiculous. Of course, they won't leave Sherman in the basement," snapped Mabel.

"Jolene is not ridiculous," defended Tommy, glaring at Mabel.

Constable Ohlert, rubbing her forehead, took out her phone. "People, please pay attention. I am going to interview each of you, and I will record your statements on my phone. Does everyone understand?"

Jolene, her lips in a defiant pout, argued, "We should take a vote. I say we should perform our play. Us acting in a play won't make any difference to Sherman. He's already dead."

"That's extremely insensitive," rebuked Mabel.

"Jolene isn't insensitive." Tommy glowered. "She just wants to do the play. We all want to do the play."

"Not everyone," denied Sam, popping a candy into his mouth.

"Let's take a vote," suggested Tommy.

"Oh, for Pete's sake, shut up. I'm on the phone," yelled Alice.

The constable picked up her chair and thumped the chair down on the stage. The bang halted the debate. In a loud, commanding voice, she ordered, "Please, everyone, stop your quarrelling, sit down and be quiet."

"That's what I said," Alice said cheekily, rolling her eyes.

Constable Ohlert looked at Alice. "And you, please get off your phone. You can tell your friends later about this unfortunate incident."

"I guess unfortunate is one way of putting it," muttered Mabel.

"I'm not phoning my friends. I'm calling the mayor, it is essential that he hears this dreadful news from me. But of course, Mayor Hamilton is my friend." Alice smiled importantly, turned her back and walked offstage.

"Fine." The constable exhaled and turned back at the actors who were arguing amongst themselves as they milled around the stage. "And the rest of you need to settle down. I am now going to record your statements."

"What about voting? Are we going to vote?" asked Jolene.

"People," the constable said, rubbing her forehead. "This is not the time to have a vote for whatever it is you want to vote on. I am going to conduct the interviews, and you will all sit. And sit quietly, and you will give me your full attention. Is that clear?"

The side door to the hall opened, and Harold Hauke, the funeral director, entered, followed by two men carrying a black body bag. The men tramped up to the stage. The short, muscular man in a black suit asked, "Which way to the deceased?"

"Follow me," Mike volunteered, rising.

"Sit down, sir. I'll take these men downstairs," the constable said. She rose and led the men offstage.

Alice strutted back on stage, pocketing her phone, and announced, "The mayor and his wife are coming."

Rudy looked up from his phone. "His wife? Oh yeah, she's on the festival committee."

"Even if the mayor insists that we carry on with the festival. It will have to be without us. We don't have a butler," Helen fretted.

"Mabel knows everyone's lines by heart. She could do his part," volunteered Violet.

"Thanks a bunch, buddy. Sure, I know the butler's lines. But I'm not a man, as you can clearly see."

"We could change Jeeves to a maid," suggested Jolene.

"Jeeves is a butler," Mabel said.

"Change the name and gender," proposed Violet.

Mabel looked daggers at Violet. "No. The part is written for a man, and it would be just silly to have two maids," she objected.

Violet didn't meet Mabel's eyes.

"Yes, definitely silly. There is only one maid, and it's me," Alice agreed vehemently.

"You could dress up as a man," offered Ned.

"I thought you didn't want to proceed with the play?" Jolene asked, smiling at the little man.

"I never said that."

"Yes, you did."

"No, that was Sam."

"Whatever." Jolene tossed her head. Her blonde hair swirled around her shoulders.

"Those are all good suggestions. That is? If Mabel will do it," Helen said. "Will you?"

Jolene, Rudy, Tommy, and Ned looked at her expectantly.

Mabel shook her head and said, "I don't think it's a good idea."

"Well, perhaps it's not up to us to decide. I think it's up to the festival committee to decide what to do," Helen said, wiping her nose with the big blue and white hanky. "What do you think, Violet? You're on the committee."

Violet pressed her lips together, her eyes thoughtful. "Well," she said, "I can't speak for the festival committee. But for us, who were Sherman's friends. I think acting in the festival might look disrespectful to Sherman."

Helen nodded.

"I agree," Sam said, unwrapping a candy.

"I wasn't his friend," Jolene said.

"Jolene," rebuked her grandmother.

"I'm just being honest. I wasn't," Jolene said, pouting.

"On the other hand, everything has been arranged. We have all the little theatre groups from the surrounding towns participating in the festival. And Mandy Swan has accepted our request to be the adjudicator for the festival. I believe it's a feather in our cap to have Miss Swan. She is a distinguished theatre director from Regina. I guess the committee should hold a meeting to decide," finished Violet.

Helen's forehead creased, and she nodded again.

Sam's lips set in a grim line; he sighed and popped a candy into his mouth, chewing vigorously.

"You mean it's up to Gloria, our esteemed Mayor's wife," Mabel said. "She's the chairperson of the festival committee."

"No, no, we all have a say," contradicted Violet.

Constable Ohlert stepped back onto the stage.

"Where's Sherman?" Jolene asked. "Aren't they taking him away?"

"They will be bringing his body up directly. In the meantime, everyone, please take a seat. I'm ready to take statements from you."

Alice rushed up to the constable and said, "I was the first one on the scene of this tragic accident. I saw poor Sherman laying face first on the cement floor."

"No, you weren't first. Mabel was," contradicted Jolene.

"Oh yeah, right, and you pushed her. Mabel almost ended up like Sherman," accused Alice.

"I did not," denied Jolene.

"You did. I saw you."

"Oh no, don't go blaming me. I never laid a finger on her. It was you."

"People, people." Constable Ohlert turned to Mabel. "Is this true? Were you pushed?"

"It was an accident. No harm done."

"See, I told you," Jolene mocked.

Alice snickered. "Yeah, Mabel is a bit of a clumsy clod. She's always tripping over her own feet."

"Mabel is not a clumsy clod," defended Violet.

"Enough," shouted Constable Ohlert. Then, taking a deep breath, the constable said in a quiet, commanding voice, "Everyone, just sit down. I will now take your statements. And we will do this in a calm and orderly fashion. Is that clear?" She cast a stern look at Alice, who was smirking contemptuously at Mabel. And at Mabel, who was glaring back.

Jolene plopped down on the oval coffee table in front of the loveseat and turned to smile at her grandparents. Her blue eyes lit up, fluttering her long eyelashes; she beamed at Rudy as he joined her. Rudy momentarily returned her smile before reading a text on his phone.

Dragging a black plastic chrome chair from offstage, Violet placed the chair facing the front of the stage. Mabel, following her, carried her prompting stool. She plunked the old wooden stool beside Sam. Sam, the tall, gangly farmer, had his arms folded across his chest, sucking on a candy. He leaned against the set's back wall. The wall swayed, and Sam moved, leaning against the brown chipboard cabinet. He dug in his pocket, producing a small bag of candy. He opened the bag and offered candy to Mabel and Violet. Violet declined, but Mabel took one.

Ned, darting backstage, appeared moments later, carrying a backless wooden chair. As he set the old wooden chair beside Mabel, the skinny little man looked up at her, licking his lips and giving her a gap-tooth grin. Mabel smiled briefly back at him, then quickly looked away, wishing he'd picked somewhere else to sit.

Standing centre stage with her hands on her hips, Alice asked, "Where am I supposed to sit?"

"Tommy, would you please get a couple of chairs from the back? And Rudy, please help him?" requested Helen.

Rudy stood, put his phone in his pocket, and walked offstage. Moments later, he returned carrying two faded old orange plastic chairs. He plunked them down onto the floor and returned to sit on the coffee table beside Jolene.

Alice, sighing loudly, picked up an orange chair and placed it near the front of the stage. Tommy put a chair beside Ned, sat down, sniffed, then picked up his chair and plopped it down beside Violet.

Violet turned to Mabel. "Were you pushed? Is that how you ended up sitting on the basement floor surrounded by that tree? I'm so sorry. I asked before, but you didn't say. I should have insisted you tell me."

"We had bigger fish to fry. What with Sherman lying dead on the floor and all."

"But were you pushed off that landing? You could've been killed."

"I was fine. The tree broke my fall. Me and the tree kind of came down together," Mabel said, trying to blot out her terrifying feeling as she flew onto the Christmas tree.

Ned leaned in and asked, "Did Alice, that little Ronald Macdonald goblin, push you?"

Mabel wrinkled her nose. The pine smell was overpowering. "No, it wasn't Alice. And I'm not naming names. Everyone, including you, Ned, was pushing and shoving, trying to get a look at Sherman. I felt a hand on my shoulder, and the next thing I knew, I was clinging onto that Christmas tree."

"Thank goodness for the tree." Violet squeezed Mabel's hand.

"Thank goodness for Christmas," joked Mabel.

Violet pressed her lips together. Her eyes glistened as she smiled fondly at her friend.

"Attention, everyone." Constable Ohlert sat centre stage facing the actors. She took out her phone and said, "I will record your names first and then take your statements."

Dragging her chair beside the constable, Alice said, "My name is Alice Woodstock. I'm the maid, and you may interview me first."

"Alice, please, let's not get into the argument of who was the first again," Helen pleaded.

The corners of Alice's lips turned down. "Irregardless—"

"Irregardless is not a word," corrected Violet.

Alice pursed her lips and wrinkled her nose.

The constable's eyes darted to Violet, an irritated frown on her brow. She paused and turned to Alice. "Tell me, Mrs. Woodstock—"

"Miss Woodstock, but you can call me Alice."

Constable Ohlert eyed Alice for a long moment, then asked. "How did you know Mr. Mahan had fallen?"

"We all heard his scream," volunteered Mabel.

Constable Ohlert inhaled deeply, then slowly released her breath. "Mrs. Havelock, I said we will do these interviews in an orderly fashion. I'll take your statement all in good time."

Alice looked at Mabel, smirked, and drew her chair closer to the constable. "As I said, I was almost the first person out on the landing where this terrible accident happened."

"In my opinion, the railing broke because of sloppy maintenance," piped up Ned.

The little sofa rocked as Mike jumped up and shouted, "Ned, keep your stupid opinions to yourself." Looking around at the rest of the cast members, he added. "And anyone who says my friend Fred does sloppy work. Is a damn blasted liar."

"I'm entitled to my own opinion," Ned stood shouting back.

The constable rose from her chair and raised her voice. "Quiet down." She waited until Ned resumed his seat; he gave her a gap-tooth smile. The settee wobbled as Mike plopped down on the loveseat beside his wife.

"Alice, we will need your address and contact phone number. And I'd like to see your phone, please," requested Constable Ohlert.

"My phone?"

"Yes, and if anyone else has pictures of the accident, the body of Mr. Mahan, I want them. Unfortunately, the paramedics moved the body during the examination. These pictures could help to determine how the man fell."

Alice smiled importantly and handed her phone to the constable.

Chapter Six

The constable continued the interviews, ending with a question. "What can you tell me about Mr. Sherman Mahan?"

All eyes turned to Alice.

"Why look at me?"

"Because, Alice, sweetie, you have your finger on the pulse of Glenhaven," Helen said diplomatically.

Mabel grinned. That was a nice way of saying Alice was the town gossip.

"Well, I guess I do." Alice smiled proudly. "Sherman moved here when the new potash mine opened south of town. He is in management, I think, and he's not married, but he has a girlfriend. I see her car parked in his driveway on weekends. She's pretty. Younger than Sherman, I think. I have seen her around, but I have never actually met her. They live in that big, swanky house two doors down from Violet. Have you seen her?"

"Yes, I have. Sherman's girlfriend's name is Crystal Harrison. She seems like a nice girl. She told me she's the workplace health and safety officer at the mine where Sherman works. Pardon me, worked."

The funeral home men carrying the black body bag entered the stage. Sam stood, took off his baseball cap, and placed his hand over his heart as the men carried their burden across the stage and down the stairs. Harold Hauke, the funeral director, called over his shoulder. "Good luck with the play; my wife and I have tickets."

Jolene looked at her grandmother. "See, Granny, we have fans. We really have to do this play."

The side door to the hall opened, and Mayor Mathew Hamilton and his wife Gloria entered. The mayor, a big barrel-chested man with chubby reddish cheeks and a bulbous nose, held the door open as the three men carrying the heavy black body bag exited. "Terrible business," he said solemnly as Harold Hauke passed. "Oh, I don't mean the funeral business. I mean the unfortunate death of poor..." his voice trailed off. "Who died?" he whispered to his wife.

"Sherman Mahan."

"The untimely death of Sherman," the mayor shouted to the trio as they approached the hearse. He ran a hand through his hair, his eyes darting skyward, then turning, he looked at his wife and asked. "Sherman, who?"

Gloria, the tall blonde-haired woman with an elegant straight nose, her blue eyes fringed with thick dark lashes, rolled her eyes and said, "I told you, Sherman Mahan."

"Mahan," yelled the mayor at the men, closing the door to the hearse.

Gloria undid the buttons of her long black coat as she mounted the side stairs to the stage. "I must tell you that my husband and I are devastated, just devastated."

Helen rose from the loveseat and clasped Gloria's hands. Thank you for coming. We're all extremely upset."

"I was the one who phoned you," Alice said.

Helen, ignoring Alice, gave Gloria a hug. Gloria awkwardly patted Helen on the back and then quickly disentangled herself.

Mayor Hamilton, bounding up the stairs, strode over to Constable Ohlert. "Terrible, just terrible," he said, shaking the constable's hand vigorously. "I'm Mathew Hamilton, the mayor of this lovely little town. Have you determined what happened?"

"I'm Constable Ohlert," she said, greeting the mayor. "Our investigation is ongoing."

"Is there anything you can tell me about this unfortunate accident? As I said, I'm the mayor."

"I'm sorry, but not at this time."

"Well, I can tell you this much. This hall is well maintained. I heard the poor fellow fell down the stairs to the basement. It is a terrible thing, but it was a freak accident."

"As I said, the investigation is ongoing,"

"May we proceed with the festival?" asked Gloria.

"We're done here. But before anyone else goes down to the basement. Repairs to the stair's railing must be done and inspected."

The mayor patted the constable on the back. "Good to know, good to know. I'll have the repairs done tomorrow."

The constable, taken aback by the pat on the back, said, "Yes, well, I'll leave you to it." She pocketed her phone and exited the stage.

The mayor ran a hand over his dark, slick-back hair, bending to shake Helen's hand, then proceeded around the stage, repeating, "Terrible, terrible." To each cast member as he shook their hands.

Gloria took the chair vacated by the constable and carefully draped her long black coat over the chair's back. "Now, let me walk you through what we are going to do."

"You mean the drama festival?" Helen asked, regaining her seat beside Mike.

The mayor strode across the stage. "I'll take a look at the stairs. Then I'll call Fred Granger. I hope to hell the family of this guy Mahan doesn't start a lawsuit."

Gloria cast her husband an impatient look and turned her attention to Helen. "Yes, well, Helen, the drama festival is my concern. Of course, this terrible accident is regrettable. But the show must go on."

"That's what I think. The show must go on," Jolene said enthusiastically.

"It's regrettable for Sherman, that's for sure," muttered Mabel.

Gloria gave Mabel an impatient look. "Please don't interrupt with your nattering and pay attention." There was no love lost between Mabel and Gloria Hamilton. When Gloria's husband, Mathew, had taken office, she decided the town needed to move with the times, as she put it. First on her agenda was to make changes to the local fall supper, from turkey and homemade pies to a wine and cheese party. Mabel had been the most vocal opponent, and although the rest of the townspeople were against Gloria's innovation, Gloria blamed Mabel for the opposition when her improvements for the fall supper were voted down in favour of the traditional turkey supper.

Mabel bristled at the term nattering. She was about to issue a scathing retort when she felt Violet's hand on her shoulder. Her friend's hand on her shoulder signalled her to let Gloria's snarky response go. She knew Violet was right. Sherman had died. And this was not the time to get into a petty, pointless argument with the mayor's wife. So she bit her lip and remained silent.

"As I was saying, the drama festival must go on. The drama groups that have entered this competition will be devastated if we cancel. Not to mention our patrons. Many of them have bought advance tickets."

"Really. How many?" Mabel asked. "I heard tickets weren't selling."

Gloria cast a disdainful look in Mabel's direction. "Well, not all the tickets have sold. But the ones who bought it will be very disappointed. My committee has worked very hard, putting posters up all over Glenhaven, Kegworth, Maryland, Insinger, Berryman, and Perm, as well as all the towns with drama groups coming to our festival. More tickets will sell, so don't you worry about that."

"Ticket sales hardly matter now," Helen murmured.

"What did you say?" Gloria stood, hands on her hips. Helen flinched.

The mayor stomped back onstage. "It's a gruesome sight in the basement. Don't go down there. There's a great pool of blood, and I bet there are brains on the floor. It's ghastly, just ghastly."

Gloria screwed up her face, shuttering. "Eww, Mathew, do you have to be so graphic?"

"We've all seen the blood. We were all down there," screeched Ned. "Who do you think found him?"

"Oh, yes, of course. I meant my wife. Sweetheart, don't go down there."

"Don't worry; I've no intentions of going."

Helen stood, her face drawn. She took a deep breath and said, "Gloria, are you sure you want the drama festival to continue? You know we can't possibly participate."

Gloria strode to centre stage; turning to address the cast, she said, "Yes, the festival will go on. And, of course, The Glenhaven Players should participate. There's no reason not to. It will only take a little soap and water."

"Soap and water?" asked a confused Helen.

"Fred can clean the basement floor."

"And fix the railing," added the mayor. "We have to get that darn railing fixed." He took his phone from his pocket and descended the stairs to the main floor.

"Yes, of course, fix the railing, and no one will be the wiser," Gloria said impatiently.

Sam, striding to centre stage, popped another candy into his mouth. "No one the wiser?" he scoffed. "Everyone will know Sherman is dead and that he died in the basement of this theatre. It's a small town. If you sneeze in your living room, someone in the town will say gesundheit."

"And more importantly, someone should inform Sherman's family," Violet said.

"I'm sure the RCMP has," Alice said, importantly.

"But what if they didn't?" worried Helen.

Gloria sighed. "Mathew," she called down to her husband, whose foot was resting on a seat in the front row. "Find out who Sherman's family is and let them know."

Holding his phone to his ear, Mathew waved a dismissive hand at his wife.

Jolene smiled gleefully. "Oh, Mrs. Hamilton, I'm so happy you want us to perform our play."

"Yes, of course I do. My committee and I have worked very hard arranging this festival."

"I don't know. Do you think we should? I think it might look disrespectful," Helen said, wringing her hands.

"Please, Granny."

"The town is depending on you, Helen. You, your brave granddaughter, and this wonderful, valiant band of actors. You can dedicate the performance to Sherman. It would be a wonderful tribute to the poor man." Gloria put an arm around Helen's shoulders. "You do see, don't you, how disrupted this would be for The Glenhaven Players if you pulled out of the festival at this late date? We have a reputation to uphold. And think of how disappointed the people of Glenhaven will be. I think our dear departed Sherman would want the show to go on. Don't you?"

Jolene clapped her hands, Alice and Tommy joining in. After a pause, Rudy, Ned, Sam and Violet added their applause. Feeling left out, Mabel clapped, too. Mike looked at his wife, tilted his head and nodded.

Helen walked to the front of the stage and turned to face the actors. "But how can we? We don't have a butler."

"Mabel," said a course of voices from the cast.

"We've been through this before. I'm not a man, so how can I play a butler? And I'm the prompter. And heaven knows this cast needs a prompter."

"Costume and make-up will fix that," Gloria said. "You do know Sherman's lines?"

"Mabel knows everyone's lines," Violet said.

"Thanks a bunch. Okay, yes, I do know the butler's lines. And I would take Sherman's part; I really would. I want to help. But we still need a prompter. And Violet can't do it. She is busy with the props, costumes, and make-up."

"I could do it," volunteered Violet.

Mabel made a face at her.

"No, I will do the prompting," Gloria announced. "How hard can it be? Good, now that's settled. We should have another rehearsal as soon as possible."

Mabel felt she was being railroaded, so she asked, "What if the RCMP declares this a crime scene? Then what?"

"Don't be silly. Sherman fell; it was an accident. A tragic accident. But an accident nonetheless," Gloria stated firmly. "Besides, I did ask that officer if we could go on with the festival. And she said yes." Gloria began strutting back and forth across the stage. "Now, Mabel, get a costume rigged up as soon as possible."

"I haven't said I would do it," protested Mabel.

Gloria turned on her heel and strode back across the stage. The tall, blonde-haired woman's eyes narrowed as she looked down her elegant nose at Mabel. The imposing woman crossed her arms over her chest. She didn't say a word, but her eyes drilled into Mabel's. Mabel began to squirm under her intense stare. Then Gloria's eyebrows rose, and a small smile appeared on her lips. Lifting her chin, she turned to address the actors. "It's a sad turn of events when one person can destroy dreams. Destroying everything you and my festival committee have worked so hard for. And the dreams and hopes of all the other drama clubs who have also worked very hard."

"Are you talking about Sherman? That's just despicable," snarled Sam.

"No, no, Sam. I certainly meant no disrespect toward Sherman," hastened Gloria. "I meant, someone here can save us from this unfortunate disaster. And we all know who that is." Gloria turned and looked at Mabel. Tilting her head, she tapped her toe. "Which is it to be, Mabel? You can dash these people's dreams or make them come true."

The actors crowded around Mabel, looking expectantly at her.

Mabel knew when she was beaten. What the heck? It was one night. She knew Jeeves's lines. "Okay, I'll do it," she said.

"Yes." Jolene made a fist pump.

Ned gave her a gap-tooth smile. "Welcome aboard," he said in his screechy voice.

Violet, looking guilty, caught Mabel's eye. 'Sorry,' she mouthed. Mabel shrugged and smiled. Violet, looking relieved, smiled back.

Rudy held up his phone. "Come on, everyone, gather around. Tommy, take a picture of us with our new cast member."

Mabel, encircled by the actors, felt uncomfortable. "Don't you think this is kind of ghoulish? Sherman just died."

"It's not like we are celebrating. I'm documenting history. Besides, the show must go on." Rudy handed his phone to Tommy.

"If I hear the show must go on one more time, I'm going to puke," grumbled Sam. But he stood behind Mabel with the rest of the cast as they posed for their picture.

"I will have no more debates. We are going ahead as planned. We'll have a dress rehearsal tomorrow night. I want to see everyone's costumes. It is so important to get the ambiance right. Set the scene, so to speak. Mabel, look in one of the tickle trunks. I'm sure you'll find an outfit there. And make sure it's a butler's attire." Gloria turned to face the other actors. "Right, you all may go. But please be on time tomorrow night. I will accept no excuses for tardiness." Gloria then turned to Helen, her mouth curving into a condescending smile. "Oh, are these arrangements I have made alright with you, dear?"

Helen, looking bewildered, nodded.

"Good, everything is working out." Gloria spread out her hands, looking very pleased with herself.

Mabel, feeling mulish, muttered, "Not for Sherman." She'd been intimidated into taking Sherman's role. But that didn't mean she approved of Gloria's callous attitude.

"Don't be morbid," reprimanded Gloria. "Now, the next thing to work out is how we can get down to the changing rooms in the basement."

"No problem, no problem, my dear friends. Your mayor has fixed everything," Mayor Hamilton announced, bounding up to the stage and rubbing his hands together. "I've called Fred. He and a crew of men will mend the railing tomorrow. And this drama festival will take place as advertised. Your mayor is not called Mr. Fixit for nothing.'

Chapter Seven

M abel closed the side door to the hall. Only a few cars remained in the parking lot. Most of the cast had left. But not Violet, who stayed behind to confer with Gloria about the arrangements for the festival. Mabel had declined the ride offers from her fellow actors, needing time alone to process the terrible events of the evening.

She crossed the dark parking lot toward the street, gravel crunching under her feet. The only light was from the stars in the night sky and the moon on the wane, casting little light. In the distance, a door slammed, and a dog barked. A stiff breeze sprung up; Mabel zipped up her fleece and dug her hands into her pockets. But the chilly night air was welcome after the stifling smell of the varnish and the fresh paint in the hall.

And most of all, the memory of Sherman lying dead at the bottom of the stairs. And her near-death experience. She shivered, but not from the coolness of the evening. Her thoughts went back to how narrowly she missed ending up like Sherman. That Christmas tree had saved her.

Stumbling on a rock, Mabel paused, wishing she had a flashlight. Head down. She carefully made her way across the loose stones on the parking lot toward the sidewalk. The next time she saw Mr. Fixit, the mayor, she'd make sure to tell him the town needed to put up more streetlights. As she left the parking lot, she tripped again, this time on the sharp edge of the sidewalk. Regaining her feet and remembering Alice's comments about her being a clumsy clod, she dusted the grit off her hands. A car honked as it sped by, and Mabel waved. She couldn't see the driver of the car. But in a small town, you didn't ignore a greeting, even if the greeting was just a car horn.

Her thoughts kept going back to the accident. But was Sherman's falling down the stairs an accident? Mabel stopped under a lone streetlight, waiting. A vehicle was speeding down the street toward the intersection, its lights blinding her. She fanned her hand above her eyes, shielding them. Mabel wasn't sure if the vehicle had high beams on or if it was a new model with halogen lights. In her opinion, the halogen lights were just too darn bright. Did the car owners really need to see the hairs on a squirrel's back?

The vehicle sped up, swerving up onto the sidewalk. Mabel gasped in terror; the speeding car was coming down the sidewalk directly at her. She leapt back, throwing herself into a caragana hedge. Squeezing her eyes shut and praying the car wouldn't hit her, she flattened herself against the branches, a sharp twig digging into her back. Mabel screamed. She could smell the exhaust and feel the wind from the car as it sped inches from her, then the car roared off down the street into the night.

Mabel's breath came in big gulps, her heart pounding as if it was going to jump out of her chest. Entangled in the hedge, she lay shivering. The prickly branches began to break off as she slowly sank onto the cold cement. Twice in one night, she almost shook hands with death. Mabel pulled dried leaves out of her hair with trembling hands and tried to stand. But quickly slumped back down. Her legs were shaking. Wrapping her arms around her chest, Mabel took a deep breath. In and out, she instructed herself as she watched more cars drive past, unaware that she was sitting on the sidewalk. You can't sit here all night, Mabel told herself. Trembling, she stood. The car was long gone. Whoever the idiot was, didn't know they'd almost hit her? It couldn't have been deliberate, could it?

Chapter Eight

"Good Lord, Mabel, you just told me you were almost run over last night. Why didn't you call me?" asked Violet. She was sitting on Mabel's bed, watching as Mabel tugged on a pair of black trousers.

"Why? There was nothing you could do. I wasn't hurt."

"I don't care. You should have called me. And you don't know whose car almost ran you down?"

"No," sighed Mabel. "It was too dark. And everything happened so fast. One minute, I was standing on the sidewalk, and the next minute, a car was almost on top of me. Then the car sped off and was gone."

"And you didn't get the make or the model of the car? Or the license plate number?"

"No, like I said, it happened so fast. It was dark, and the headlights were so bright I couldn't see a thing."

"You should report it. This is a hit and run."

"I wasn't hit. So, no, it's not a hit and run. And anyway, what good would it do? As I said, I don't have a clue what kind of car it was that nearly hit me, except the car had those really bright lights."

"Halogen lights?"

"Yes, or the driver had the high beams on."

"I still think you should report it. You could have been hit." Violet held up a black suit jacket. "It must've scared the living daylights out of you."

"Yeah, it did. I was scared spitless," admitted Mabel. "But there is no point in reporting it. I told you I don't know the make or model of the car or who was driving." Mabel said, stuffing long white shirttails into the slacks. "I'm not sure the driver even saw me."

"Didn't see you! That's ridiculous. Of course, the driver saw you. You don't drive up on a sidewalk and almost kill someone and not see them."

"But no harm done. I'm fine." The less they talked about it, the better. She didn't want to dwell on the near miss. The near miss that came right on the heels of Sherman's tragic fall. But who would want to hurt her? It had to be a coincidence, didn't it? It couldn't be deliberate. But Violet was right; the driver had to have seen her. No, she mustn't dwell on it. It had to have been some drunk or an idiot on their phone. "I can't do up the button on these trousers. Let's get on with this stupid costume. Look at my slacks. They're so tight. They fit the last time I wore them. I think they have shrunk?"

"Just suck in your tummy." Violet held up the black suit jacket by the shoulders. "I'm not happy with this jacket. It's a different shade of black."

"Black is black."

"No, not at all. There are different shades of black."

"Whatever. This jacket will have to do." Mabel sucked in her tummy and fastened the button on the slacks. The button popped off. Bending down, she picked up the fallen button, complaining, "Well, that takes care of that. The suit jacket is the wrong shade of black, and I don't have another pair of black slacks. This is a stupid idea."

Violet laid the jacket on Mabel's bed. "Don't be silly; just sew the button back on."

"Oh, sure, no problem, but with my luck, the button will probably pop off again when I'm onstage."

"This defeatist attitude is so unlike you. You dismiss a hit and run, and yet, you worry about a little button." She handed Mabel a brown leather belt. "Are you worried about acting on stage?"

Mabel pulled the belt through the loops on her trousers. "It wasn't a hit and run, and I don't have stage fright if that's what you mean. It's the dressing up like a man. What if I look like a clown?"

"You'll look fine." Violet held up the jacket.

Mabel reluctantly donned it, flapping her arms. The jacket sleeves swallowed up her hands. "Who did you borrow this from? It's miles too big."

"We'll pin up the sleeves. And speaking of pins. You'd better pin your slacks. Just in case you do pop that button."

"Oh, great, I go onstage with pins holding this suit together. What are the odds one will come on done and poke me?"

"Stop worrying and put this tie on." Violet handed Mabel a long black tie.

"How do you tie this thing? Is there a special way a butler wears a tie?"

"I don't know, but I can do a Windsor knot. Here, let me do it." Violet tied the tie.

Mabel tucked the long tie into her waistband. "This is bizarre. Here we are playing dress-up. And poor Sherman is lying dead in the morgue."

"I know, poor guy. Last night in bed, I thought of those screw holes you showed me. Maybe someone did unscrew the screws. But who on earth would want to hurt Sherman?" Violet took a black wig out of a bag. "Intentional or an accident? The thing is. It could've been any one of us lying dead in that morgue. We all use those stairs to go to the washroom in the basement. I've gone down looking for props. And so have all the actors. I really doubt Sherman was targeted unless that phone call Sherman took was deliberate, a way to get him offstage. And even if it was, how would the caller know Sherman would lean on the handrail? That's a leap."

Mabel raised her eyebrows, a half-smile on her lips.

Violet rolled her eyes. "Yes, I know, a bad turn of phrase. But, like I said, how would the caller know he'd lean on the railing?"

"But there is a discrepancy with the screws."

"Yes, I know," Violet said, shaking the wig and placing it on Mabel's head; she adjusted it. The curly black wig parted in the middle hung over Mabel's ears.

Mabel preened in front of her mirror. "Hey, I look good. Maybe I should dye my hair black." She picked up a hand mirror, admiring the side and the back of her head.

"I think that ship has sailed. And I think maybe we should rethink this wig."

"No, I like it. It suits me."

"I'm not liking it."

"Well, I do, and I'm the one wearing it."

"I'm still not a fan, but if you're sure."

"I am."

"Okay, it's up to you." Violet looked at her watch. "Oh, sorry, I've got to rush off. Gloria has called an emergency meeting of the festival committee."

Mabel followed Violet out to her kitchen.

"You know, Mabel, if you wanted to do a little spruce up of your kitchen, I'd help. I'm pretty good with a paintbrush."

"Why? What's wrong with my kitchen?"

"Nothing, I'm just offering." Slipping on her jacket, Violet stood with her hand on the door handle and said, "Think about it. Anyway, I have to go. Gloria is a stickler for punctuality."

Chapter Nine

Excited to tell her mom the good news about her acting debut, Mabel picked up her cell phone and punched in her mother's number. She pulled out a kitchen chair and sat, waiting for her mother to answer. Mabel looked around at her comfortable, old-fashioned kitchen. To heck with what Violet thought. She loved her kitchen. Sure, the old oak cupboards could do with a sprucing up, but there was nothing wrong with her chrome table and chairs. The grey-topped chrome table with the red chrome chairs was as good as the day she bought them. And she loved the bright red and white floral curtains that hung over the old white porcelain sink. She thought they matched perfectly with her red laminated countertop.

"Hi, Mom," she said cheerfully.

"Really, Mabel, I almost didn't answer. I thought you were a scammer calling. Why aren't you calling on your landline? Did you get rid of it? I wouldn't advise that."

Mabel rolled her eyes. She wondered how old she would have to be before her mom stopped telling her what to do. "No, I still have my landline. I just thought I'd use my cell."

"I see. Well, never mind, what's new?"

"Since you asked, I do have some news for you. Do you remember me telling you I was helping with the play for the drama festival?"

"Yes, dear, I do. You're painting sets or some such thing. Oh, wait a minute, the oven timer is ringing. I've got cookies in the oven." Sophie, her mother, was known for her delicious chocolate chip cookies.

Mabel hunched her phone to her ear and undid the belt and the black suit jacket buttons, letting her tummy relax. Her orange tabby cat, Gertrude, sauntered across the white and black tile kitchen floor. Stretched, then jumped up on Mabel's lap. Mabel scratched the orange cat under her chin. "I should really rename you. Call you, Sandy, or something. Would you like that? But it's probably too late now. You like your name, don't you?" Mabel continued to pet the cat, this time behind her ears. "Not that you ever come when I call you."

"What? Come when you call me? I'm not your cat."

"I was talking to Gertrude."

"You're not getting a little senile, are you dear?" teased Sophie.

"Anyway, Mom, I was going to tell you my news."

"I know all about it, dear. You said you're helping with the play, painting flats."

"No, I was the prompter."

"Was? Oh, no, did they let you go? What did you do? You sometimes are a little too sarcastic. Not everyone appreciates your humour."

"No, I wasn't let go. I was the prompter, but now I have a part in the play."

"How nice for you, dear. Did someone drop out?"

"No, sorry to say someone died."

"Oh my, is it someone I know?"

"I don't think so. The victim was Sherman Mahan. He's new in town. Well, I guess I should say he was new in town. Anyway, the man worked out at the potash mine."

"How did he die?"

"Accident, I guess. The poor man fell down the basement stairs last night."

"Where?"

"I said at the theatre."

"No, you didn't?"

"Oh, well, anyway. We rehearsed last night at the theatre, and Sherman fell down the basement stairs and died."

"I'm sorry to hear, poor man. But back to this acting of yours. Do you have any lines?"

"Yes, I do," Mabel said proudly.

"That's nice, dear. I hope you can remember the lines. It would be terrible for you to draw a blank onstage. So, what is your part?"

"I play Jeeves, the butler. It was the part Sherman was playing."

"You can't mean you're taking this dead man's part in the play?"

"It's not a big part, and I know all his lines."

"You're playing the part of a dead man?"

"Not in the play, honestly, Mom. I told you it's the butler role, and the butler is very much alive."

"Well, I'm glad to hear that. But really, the part of a man? That's silly. How can you play a man?"

"I have a costume."

"A costume. Really, dear, do you think you should? You will end up looking like a clown."

Mabel's heart sank. That was what worried her.

"You don't want to look like a fool?"

"Violet helped me with the costume, and I have a wig. I think it will be okay." Mabel yanked off her black wig and scratched her head. The darn thing made her head itchy. "I have to do it, or there will be no play."

"I think you are very unwise, dear."

"There is no one else. I can't let the cast and Helen down."

"Tell these people no. The idea of you dressing up as a man is ridiculous."

"I promised."

"Well, don't say I didn't warn you."

"Thanks for the support."

"Oh, I support you, dear. I'm just afraid you will look silly. But if you're determined, then I'm all for you."

Mabel supposed this was as much support as she would get from her mom. Her mother never minced words, and she never measured up to her mother's expectations, unlike her brother, the golden child, except when she'd solved the murder of her mother's best friend. This thought gave her confidence as she asked, "Are you going to come to the play? You can see then if I'm a clown or not."

"I didn't say you would be a clown, dear. I said I'm afraid you might look like one."

"Whatever. Are you coming to the play? It's this Friday."

"Oh, I'm sorry, dear. A bunch of us are going to that new bingo place out at the lake."

"You're going to play bingo."

"Yes, dear, we go by bus, and the food is included in the fare. And I sure don't want to miss the entertainment after. They're featuring an Elvis Presley impersonator. Or is he an impressionist? Anyway, it doesn't matter. I'm so looking forward to his performance."

Mabel sighed; she guessed her impression of a butler didn't compare to an Elvis impersonator.

Chapter Ten

Mabel walked briskly down a tree-lined street, brushing dried leaves off her jacket. The dry leaves that had clung to the branches all winter now fluttered down from the trees, giving way to the new growth. Enjoying the sun's warmth on her face, she unzipped her fleece. She grinned; Herbert Muggridge, a small rotund man, was yanking on the rope of his lawnmower and swearing. "Sorry, Mabel," he called out apologetically.

"No worries, Herbert, I've heard worse. It's annoying when the darn things don't start."

Herbert waved and went back to yank on the cord of his lawnmower, and Mabel continued down the street. She stopped in front of Sherman Mahan's house. A red Porsche was parked in the driveway. Was that snazzy car Sherman's car or his girlfriend's? And what was the girlfriend's name? She plucked another dried leaf from her hair, trying to remember the name. "Ah," she said aloud. Digging her phone out of her pocket, Mabel pressed Violet's phone number. As she waited for her friend to answer, she heard Herbert's lawnmower start, sputter, then quit, followed by more cursing.

"Hi, what's up?"

"I'm in front of Sherman's house. But I can't remember what his girlfriend's name is."

"Why are you at Sherman's house?"

"I want to talk to his girlfriend."

"Oh, that's so nice. I'm glad you're there to offer your condolences."

"Well, yes, that too."

"That too? What do you mean? What are you up to?"

"Well, I am here to offer my sympathies. But if Sherman's death wasn't an accident. She might know who had a reason to kill him."

"Oh, Mabel, can't you leave well enough alone? The police will have talked to her. Besides, it's only you who are suspicious." Violet sniffed. "Like that's something new."

"Never mind, I've been right before. Please, just tell me the girlfriend's name."

"Mabel, you can't barge in on this poor girl and ask her a whole bunch of questions while she is grieving. That is extremely insensitive."

"I'm a sensitive person," Mabel said indignantly. "I'm not just going to barge in on her. I'm going to offer my sympathy. I was a friend of Sherman. Okay, maybe not a friend, but I knew him from the play."

"No matter what I say, you're going to do it. But for goodness' sake, don't ask the poor woman who would want Sherman dead."

Mabel looked up at the sky and shook her head. "Of course, I won't ask that."

"Okay, but promise me you'll be subtle. Sherman's girlfriend's name is Crystal Harrison,"

"Thanks, and don't worry, I will be the model of sensitivity."

"I sure hope so," Violet said, ending the call.

Mabel followed the curved driveway toward the attached two-car garage and mounted the steps to ring the doorbell. The big, newly built two-story red brick house with white trim looked imposing beside the old one-story bungalows on either side. Mabel stood under the covered portico, waited, and pushed the doorbell again. She leaned forward, and with one hand on either side of her face, she peered through the frosted glass window in the door. The door swung open, and Mabel stumbled forward.

"Yes, can I help you?" asked the young woman dressed in a baggy orange sweater and grey sweatpants.

"Crystal Harrison?" Mabel asked, her cheeks red in embarrassment.

The attractive young woman ran an agitated hand through her brunette hair. "Yes," she said in a no-nonsense tone.

"I'm sorry to intrude. My name is Mabel Havelock. I was a friend of Sherman. I was there at the theatre when he died. I just want to offer my condolences."

Crystal's face softened. "You were there when, when Sherman had his accident, and, and died?"

"Yes, I'm so sorry for your loss."

"Please come in." Crystal stood back, letting Mabel enter the large hallway. Hardwood floors gleamed, and the sun shone through the frosted glass, making rainbow patterns on the cream-coloured walls.

"I'll take off my shoes," Mabel said, pausing on a small oatmeal-coloured mat.

"No, please don't bother; just come in."

"It's okay. It won't take a minute." Mabel kicked off her shoes and followed sock-footed into the spacious living room. A large green, rust, and gold Persian rug partly covered the hardwood floor. Vibrant prints of prairie landscapes depicting the four seasons, some with stunning sunsets, hung on the cream-coloured walls. A tall ebony and gold cheetah figurine sat in the corner of the room. Two plush armchairs in pastel greens flanked a grey fieldstone fireplace.

"Please sit down. Can I get you something to drink?" The young woman picked up an empty crystal glass from the long oak coffee table.

"No, thank you." Mabel sat on a mustard-coloured loveseat under the window. Crystal refilled her glass from a whiskey bottle set on an oaken drinks cabinet. Above the cabinet hung a print of a golden harvest. She added ice from a silver bucket, and in one fluid movement, Crystal flopped on a striped, pale green and gold armchair. With one leg curled under her, the woman dressed in the oversized sweater and sweatpants somehow managed to look elegant.

Crystal lifted the glass to her lips, took a deep drink, and swallowed, tears shimmering in her eyes. "You said you were there at the theatre. You were there when it happened." She paused, her voice shaking. "When, when it happened."

"Yes, unfortunately, I'm so sorry."

"The police came and told me Sherman fell. And that Sherman was dead," her voice caught on a sob.

Mabel watched as Crystal wiped her eyes with the sleeve of her sweater. She felt guilty. Violet was right. It was insensitive of her to barge in on this woman in her time of grief.

Crystal took another swig of her whisky. "The constable didn't say much else. Or maybe she did. I was in shock. All I can remember is her telling me Sherman was dead." She drained the glass, wiped the tears from her cheek and asked, "What can you tell me? Was it quick? Did he suffer?"

Mabel, a retired nurse, had experience telling loved ones about their spouse's or parent's passing. But it had never gotten easier. "I can tell you Sherman didn't suffer. It was very quick." It also was very violent and messy, but his girlfriend didn't need to know that.

Crystal took a shuddered breath, stirring the ice cubes around her empty glass with her finger. "How could he have fallen at the theatre? It doesn't make sense."

"Unfortunately, he fell down the stairs leading to the basement."

"I know he fell down the stairs," Crystal's voice trembled. "Did he trip? It's just so weird. Sherman was steady on his feet. He never had a problem walking."

"The railing on the stairs leading to the basement broke."

"That old railing broke! Oh, Sherman." Chrystal's voice trembled, and tears rolled down her cheeks. "How could this happen?"

"I'm sorry, I don't know." She did have her suspicions. But Crystal was right; the banister was old. She might be completely wrong. And this certainly wasn't the time to voice them, especially not to the grieving girlfriend.

Crystal wiped her tears with her hand, picked up her glass, went to the cabinet, and refilled it. "Are you sure you don't want a drink?"

Mabel wondered how much the woman had to drink before she came. "No, thank you. Is anyone coming to stay with you?"

"Yes, Sherman's mom and dad. They live in Winnipeg." Crystal sank back in her chair.

"Have you known Sherman long?"

"We met at work. Sherman made me feel welcome the first day I stepped into the office. And our relationship went from there. It was almost love at first sight." Tears streamed down her cheeks. "Some people I know thought our relationship was an unlikely one." Chrystal wiped the tears from her cheek with her hand. "Because of our age difference. But Sherman was young at heart.

We had so much in common. We both loved skiing, golf and travel." She smiled weakly. "We bought a place in Mexico. We were there just a few months ago." Crystal's voice broke. She took a deep drink of her whisky, then continued. "It's so hard to believe we'll never be able to do those things together again."

Mabel eyed the black and gold cheetah in the corner. "Did you pick up that beautiful statue on your travels?"

Chrystal smiled briefly. Using the sleeve of her sweater, she wiped tears from her cheek. "Yes, not my favourite thing. Sometimes, our tastes differed."

"Did Sherman tell anyone at work he was in our play?"

Sniffing, Crystal gave a small chuckle. "Oh yeah, he told everyone in the office. He was so proud of it. He bought tickets for everyone in the office to the festival."

"Everyone, wow. Did Sherman get along with all his coworkers?"

"Why do you ask?"

"Just wondering, is all," Mabel said hurriedly. "That's a lot of tickets."

"Sherman was a great guy and a good boss. He got on with everyone. Except for Jason, he made fun of Sherman's acting. But Jason Greenwood is a jerk. Sherman called him a lazy doofus. I think if Sherman had his way, the company would fire Jason's ass. Anyway, to hell with Jason. I don't want to think about him. Sherman was happy acting." Crystal looked down at her glass and then over at Mabel. "Did all the actors in the play like Sherman?"

"Oh yes, we, that is, everyone loved Sherman."

The young woman tilted her head, her brown hair falling over her forehead. Brushing the strands of hair off her face, she looked at Mabel. "A woman came by this morning. She said her name was

Alice Woodstock. She told me the festival was going to take place. And the Glenhaven drama club was going to perform the play. Without Sherman." Crystal's eyes welled up with tears. "I think her exact words were. 'The show must go on.' I believe this woman thought I would find that comforting. I didn't! I'm afraid I was a little sharp with the woman. In fact, I shut the door in her face."

Mabel suppressed a grin. Alice had the door slammed in her face. Alice, the town gossip, would have been looking for tasty tidbits for Coffee Row. But was she any better? She had come in the pretense of offering sympathy. She, too, was prying for information. But, she told herself, not for gossip but for information. "I'm sorry about Alice," she said. "But the cast really did like Sherman; he was such a friendly man. And Sherman was very good at playing the part of Jeeves, the butler. He will be missed. We all liked him. A lot."

Crystal sprang out of her chair and returned to her drinks cabinet, pouring herself another glass of whisky. This time, she didn't add ice. "I just can't believe they are still going ahead with the play. It's so disrespectful to Sherman."

"Ah, ah, yes," stuttered Mabel.

"Did you know some insensitive creep is taking Sherman's part? I'm appalled." Crystal took a big drink and slammed the glass down on the coffee table.

"Um, yes, ah, yes." Mabel's face flushed in embarrassment. "I just wanted to express my condolences. I should be going."

Crystal walked her to the door and waited as Mabel slipped on her shoes. "Thank you for coming. None of the other actors from the Glenhaven Players have bothered to come by. Except for that nasty little woman, Alice."

Mabel tried to push back the feelings of guilt about her reason for visiting Crystal. She told herself it was important to find the truth behind Sherman's death. Was Sherman's death an accident, or was it murder? And if it was murder, did that mean someone driving that car targeted her too? "Did you, by chance, phone Sherman at the rehearsal? I mean, the night he died?"

"No, the police asked me the same thing. Do you know if Sherman's phone has been found? I asked the RCMP officer, but she said they didn't find it. I'd like to have his phone. I guess it isn't important. But still," Crystal choked back a sob.

"I don't think so. But if we find Sherman's phone, we will be sure to give it to you."

Mabel walked down the driveway, mulling over the information she'd learned from Crystal. People from the mine knew Sherman was in the play. And she bet most would have his cell phone number, particularly this Jason guy. There appeared to be a grudge of some kind between the two men. But enough to want Sherman dead?

Chapter Eleven

"Somehow, your slacks look different," Violet said as she opened the side door to the hall, stepping aside for Mabel. Mabel was wearing a black baggy suit jacket and pants. Covering her grey hair was the curly black wig that was parted in the middle.

"I had to borrow these slacks from Wonda next door. Those pants of mine must have shrunk."

Violet grinned. "Yes, I'm sure they did. But I have to tell you. These trousers look a little baggy on you."

"Wonda is a little taller and a little stouter than me," Mabel said, hitching up her trousers. "But I have a belt holding them up. These slacks will have to do. At least I don't have to worry about a button popping off or a pin sticking into me."

As Violet closed the door, the sound of hammering and sawing echoed through the near-empty hall. The noise was coming from the basement.

"Good, good you're here," gushed Gloria, waving her arms. She was fluttering about the stage, adjusting the vase on the cabinet, rearranging the artificial flowers, and stopping at the sofa to fluff the cushion.

Sitting in the middle of the front row, Helen raised her hand and timidly called out, "Gloria, I've got a question."

"Yes?" Gloria asked, stepping back to view the positioning of the green cushion on the loveseat.

"The mayor. I mean your husband."

"I know who my husband is, dear." With a condescending smile, Gloria asked, "What is your question?"

"Oh, sorry, I'm wondering. I wonder if the mayor, your husband, thinks everything will be ready in time for the festival. Fred and his crew are still downstairs. And the steps will have to be inspected." Helen nervously concluded.

"Not a problem, I assure you. Mathew has everything well in hand." Gloria turned back to face the stage and clapped her hands. "People, people, gather round. I want to see you in costume."

Violet nudged Mabel and whispered. "Poor Helen. It looks like Gloria has taken charge."

The actors, dressed in costumes, entered the stage from both sides. The first to enter was Sam, the lanky, raw-boned farmer who was playing Big Daddy, Bobbie Sue's father, a southern gentleman. Sam was sporting a greyish wig and beard. Outfitted in a white suit and white shirt with a black string tie, he looked like a skinny Colonel Sanders. Alice was next. A lacy white headband held her frizzy orange hair in place. She pranced past Sam to the front of the stage. Holding the hem of her frilly white apron, Alice curtsied. Rudy entered onstage, tucking his cell phone into his pocket; he strode confidently to stand centre stage. And despite being dressed in a powder blue suit and a polka-dot bowtie, the tall young man somehow still managed to look handsome. His brown eyes twinkled as he bowed and tipped his Panama hat. Jolene's long blonde hair swirled around her shoulders as she twirled across the stage. The twirling revealed the white crinoline beneath her bright yellow dress. Last to appear was Ned, attired in a brown houndstooth suit and green and red-flowered tie. Twisting the ends of his fake black mustache, he giggled in a high-pitched tone.

Mabel took a deep breath and self-consciously clambered onstage to join the actors, hoping her outfit didn't look silly.

Helen beamed up at the cast. "Oh, I'm so pleased. You all look just the way I imagined. Good job, everyone."

"Yes, yes, you all look the part," Gloria said, taking centre stage. "But before we start, there is something I need you to remember. What you need to remember is that we have a reputation to uphold. But of course, we aren't performing this play just for the glory of winning. Although I'm sure our play will win. The most important thing for you to remember is our performance is a tribute to our dear departed friend Sherman. It's our chance to shine and make Sherman proud of us." Helen, along with the cast, applauded. Smiling, Gloria waited until the applause had stopped, clapped her hands and announced in a clear authoritarian voice. "Places everyone." The actors quickly disappeared offstage. Violet lowered the curtain, then raised it again. The stage lights came on, and the play began.

Jolene swanned across the stage, paused in front of the loveseat, and gracefully took her position on the couch. Her yellow dress billowed out, the crinoline beneath hiding her face. She pressed the skirt down with both hands and said her lines. "Oh, I can't hear you," called Helen. The sounds of a drill and sawing from the basement drowned the actress's voice.

"Oh, for God's sake," yelled Gloria. "We can't hear a thing with that racket coming from the basement. Sam, go tell them to stop."

Sam, the tall, gangly farmer, tromped onto the stage, grumbling, "Why me? Why don't you tell them to stop?" He stuck his pipe in his mouth, grimaced, quickly removed it, and popped a candy into his mouth.

"I, I'm not comfortable going down there," stuttered Gloria.

Ned snickered, "Scared of Sherman's ghost."

"Don't be ridiculous. Of course not, it's, it's. I think Fred would better take direction from a man than a woman."

"Little Fred Granger? Fred's a pussycat. If you want the work to stop, you tell him." Sam grinned, rolling the candy around in his mouth.

"I'll go," Mabel volunteered. She didn't think Gloria was superstitious but maybe squeamish. The woman was probably afraid she might see Sherman's blood.

"Fine, please do it now. We are losing valuable rehearsal time."

Mabel trotted offstage and out the small door. The smell of fresh, newly cut lumber filled the air. It was a welcome difference from the last time she had ventured out to the landing. A reddish stain on the cement floor below was the only reminder of Sherman. Fred was using a hand-held circular saw to cut a length of wood. An oldish man with a yellow hard hat dressed in blue coveralls was drilling holes into another section of lumber. A younger man, also in blue coveralls minus the hardhat, had a handful of screws in his hands. His long brown hair was hanging down untidily. He looked up, and Mabel waved. "I need to speak to Fred," she called.

"What?" the young man yelled back.

"I need to talk to your boss?"

"Fred?"

Mabel raised her eyes to the ceiling, shook her head and hollered, "Yes, Fred, your boss."

The sawing stopped, and Fred removed his earmuffs and ran his hand down the cut on the board he had just made.

"Fred, Gloria needs to talk to you," shouted Mabel.

"No need to shout. I'm not deaf." Fred sauntered over and looked up at her. "What the heck are you dressed up as?"

"I'm Jeeves, the butler in the play."

"Seriously?"

"Yes, seriously." Mabel's forehead puckered. She looked masculine, didn't she? She screwed up her mouth and said, "Anyway, Gloria wants to talk to you."

"Okay, guys, take a break. This shouldn't take long. But remember, no smoking down here." Fred clumped up the stairs to follow Mabel back on stage.

"Well?" asked Gloria. "Are you going to stop this racket?"

"Racket? We're fixing the railing." Fred lifted his baseball cap and ran a hand through his sandy hair. "We can quit if you like. But I can't come back to finish until next week. I've got a list of jobs to do as long as my arm."

"Oh, for God's sake, Fred, we can't wait a week. The banister on those stairs must be repaired now. We have the drama festival on Friday. Can't you repair them quietly?" Gloria asked.

The corners of Fred's eyes crinkled. Smiling, he said, "No, sorry. Hammers and drills do make a sound. But we're almost finished. Then we just have the cleanup. But no worries; my guys clean up real good." The sandy-haired man snickered. "And cleanup doesn't involve any hammering or sawing. So, do we finish the work tonight? Or next week?" Fred crossed his arms, waiting.

Gloria's lips tightened; she took a deep breath and exhaled loudly. "We have no choice. Of course, finish the work tonight." She looked up at the sound booth. "Tommy," she called. "Go down to the basement and help those men finish the repairs. The sooner they are out of here, the sooner we can get on with rehearsals."

Grinning good-naturedly, Tommy loped down the aisle and followed Fred to the basement, and the actors filed off the stage one by one to the ground floor. All except for Violet, who remained onstage, checking her prop table.

Ned took a package of cigarettes out of his pocket and went outside. Sam slouched in a theatre seat, his long legs stretched out. His beard slipped down under his chin as he chewed on a candy. Rudy scrolled through pictures on his phone, sharing them with Jolene. The young girl hung over his shoulder, giggling and squealing in appreciation. Gloria strutted up one aisle and down another. Alice followed her, peppering her with suggestions on how to improve the play. Helen, looking forlorn, sat with her hands folded on her lap. The script, unopen, lay on a seat beside her.

Mabel tramped backstage, watching her friend rearranging items on her prop table for the umpteenth time. Bored, she strolled over to examine the contents of Violet's makeup box. She rummaged around, coming up with a small mustache. Her eyes sparkled; the little fat black mustache reminded her of a paintbrush. "What style would you call this little furry guy?" she asked.

After appraising her prop table one more time, Violet looked over at Mabel. "That, I think, is a mini walrus mustache. I did think of Sam, but the grey wig and beard seemed to suit his character."

Mabel picked up another package containing a small black mustache; she read the label aloud. "This little black mustache is called a toothbrush. It's kind of cute." She took it out of the package.

"You're not thinking of wearing that, are you?"

"Absolutely." She pasted the little black mustache over her upper lip. "This little guy will be just the thing to complete my costume. I will look more manly." She looked up at her tall, red-headed friend. "I do look more manly, don't I?" Mabel stood before the long mirror propped up against the back wall. She turned from side to side, admiring her black suit. Sure, the suit was a little on the baggy side. But at least she wouldn't burst a button. She liked her shaggy black wig and the little black toothbrush mustache. She thought she looked quite dapper.

Violet wrinkled her forehead, eyed Mabel's costume, and said, "You sure don't look like yourself. And you definitely look like a man. You remind me of someone. I'm just trying to remember who. An actor from the silent movies." Violet gasped. "Oh, Mabel, maybe not—"

"Good, I like it, and I'm wearing it."

Violet shook her head and said, "I don't know Mabel. You had better ask Helen if the mustache suits Jeeves, the butler."

Mabel gazed into the mirror, admiring the effect. "Yes, it's perfect. Helen will love it. Now I look like a Jeeves."

Violet, with a worried frown on her face, followed Mabel back on stage as Fred and his workers entered stage right.

"We're done. You have your nice quiet theatre back," Fred said as his workmen stomped across the stage and down the stairs carrying their tools.

Tommy, following the workers, darted over to join Jolene. "Hey," he said timidly, smiling hopefully.

Jolene was posing for Rudy, who was using his phone to snap her picture. She glanced at Tommy momentarily, then flashed a dazzling smile at Rudy.

"Guess what I found," Tommy said shyly.

"Not now, Tommy. I'm busy," Jolene replied, tilting her head, her blonde curls swirled around her shoulders. She fluttered her eyelashes at Rudy as he took another picture.

Tommy's smile sagged as he trotted back up the aisle to the sound booth, where Mike was snoring loudly.

"Thanks, Fred, for your speedy work," Gloria said. "Mathew will be so happy. As am I, of course."

Fred tipped his baseball cap. "No problem, all part of the service. I'll send in a bill," he added cheerfully.

As soon as Fred and his men had left and the door was closed, Gloria ushered everyone back onto the stage.

FOR ONCE, THE PLAY went smoothly. All the actors knew their cues, entered onstage at the proper time, and knew their lines. Although her part was small, Mabel was a hit with the cast; even Alice had good things to say about her performance. She felt confident as they rehearsed their final bows.

"Great job, everyone," praised Helen.

"Yes, well done, people," Gloria said, adding. "Now, before you go, I have information that I need to share with you. I've gotten emails from some of the drama clubs. They are asking if we can help them backstage. Most of the clubs are short of support staff. So, I've volunteered our Glenhaven club to help. Because we are the hosts of this drama festival, I feel it is our duty."

"Really, should we? We want to win. I don't think we should help them," Alice objected.

"Of course, we should help. It's only proper," Helen said.

"Helen is right," Gloria said. "We'll look very petty if we don't offer. And helping backstage has nothing to do with the drama club's acting abilities. The plays aren't judged on the placement of props."

"What do they need?" asked Mike.

"I'm not sure. Perhaps helping set the stage, as in moving props. Maybe the lights and the sound. And I'm sure the other clubs will be on hand to help each other."

"I'll help," confirmed Mike.

Mabel, Violet, Tommy and the other cast members volunteered. Even Alice reluctantly agreed.

"Good. Now, let me walk you people through what is taking place tomorrow. I want all of you to be at the Lions Hall for the welcome. Miss Swan and the participants in the festival will be there. My committee has arranged for an informal luncheon. And you, my dear Glenhaven Players, are the hosts. So, no excuses. Everyone has to be there."

"I've got to work. I can't be there," stated Rudy. He was an accountant for the local implement dealer.

"Nor me. My boss is away." Jolene added. "And I'll have to take her appointments at the hair salon."

"I doubt that. You're just making an excuse," scoffed Alice. "You're only a trainee. You aren't a real hairdresser."

"Hairstylist," corrected Jolene. "I'm doing my apprenticeship with Flo. And she trusts me completely."

"The more fool Flo." Alice tossed her frizzy orange hair. "I also have a lot of things I should be doing. But I'll make an exception for the festival."

Mabel's eyes crinkled in amusement. Alice was retired. Her main focus in life was gossip. She spent most of her time hanging out in restaurants and stores, picking up tidbits of news.

Gloria, arms folded across her chest, looked coldly at the cast. "Great, just great. I'm extremely disappointed in all of you."

"Oh, I'll be there," Helen nervously interjected.

"Me too," squeaked Ned.

"I can't. I have to work," Tommy said. "They are short-staffed at the lumber yard. I can't get away."

Sam also begged off, explaining he had work to do on his farm.

"Violet, you better be there. You're on the committee." Gloria gave Violet a stern look.

"Oh yes, of course."

Mabel ripped off her wig, scratched her head and said, "And I'll be there too. But relax, Gloria. It's not the Academy Awards. It's just a drama festival."

Gloria sniffed and pursed her lips, laughing disdainfully. "My dear, you just don't understand etiquette. I don't know why I'm surprised."

Chapter Twelve

Mabel's fingers were numb. She was carrying her tray of hors d'oeuvre pigs in a blanket into the Lions Hall. Mother nature was playing tricks. Yesterday was a warm, balmy day. Today, it felt like March. She followed Violet across the worn grey tile floor of the Lions Hall to a long trestle table. The Lions Hall had been closed all winter, and the hall had a damp, stale smell. Three long rows of fluorescent lights lit the auditorium. Two lights near the front of the hall buzzed and flickered on and off. Facing a podium, rows of hard black plastic molded chairs. Two members of the chamber of commerce and three town councillors, all still wearing their coats, were sitting in the front row. Mabel wondered if they were drama fans or if they were here at the mayor's behest.

Six festival committee members sat a few rows back, and they were also wearing their jackets. Mabel thought the women looked unhappy. They seemed to be arguing and casting sullen looks at Gloria, who was rushing around at the food table giving orders.

Standing at the podium, arranging his speech notes, the mayor tapped on the microphone. Behind him hung a long banner. '*Glenhaven Drama Municipal One Act Drama Festival*' was printed in gold on a blue background. The high school band, all decked out in red jackets with gold braids, began warming up. A tuba blared, clarinets, saxophones tooted, and cymbals rang out. One small boy with a snare drum was doing his best to drown them out. The parents of the band smiled encouragingly at their children. Mabel, hoping their playing would be worth the noise, zipped her jacket back up. Why was the hall so cold? Was the furnace on the fritz?

To the left of the podium, Gloria stood directing two ladies who were arranging trays of homemade hors d'oeuvres on long trestle tables. The tables were laden with assorted vegetables on tiny skewers, bacon-wrapped chestnuts, apricot turkey pinwheels, savoury crackers, and plates of various cheeses. Baskets of chips, bowls of salsa, and dips crammed in beside the cheese plates. Mabel's stomach rumbled as she spied deviled eggs. The eggs were her favourite. She hoped the welcoming speeches were short. A tray of tall plastic fluted wine glasses sat next to sparkling white wine bottles. Since the hall was so chilly, Mabel had no doubt the wine was well chilled.

The first drama group to arrive was The Kegworth Players. The threesome stood in the doorway, perusing the room. Mayor Hamilton left the podium and hurried to greet them. "Welcome, welcome." The band, tuning up, overpowered his voice. He turned, bellowing at the band. "Stop, stop."

The band began to play a mixture of *Pomp and Circumstance and Oh Canada*. The bandleader, the buttons on his red jacket straining against his corpulent belly, bent to fish sheet music from his briefcase, looked up briefly, then continued his search.

Gloria marched over to the band and raised her hands, palms facing them. "Stop, stop this instance." The band played on. Clenching her jaw in frustration, she tapped on the bandleader's shoulder.

He looked up in surprise. "What?" he yelled.

"Make them stop," Gloria yelled back.

"What?"

"For the love of God. Make these kids stop playing. Right now. And I mean immediately."

The portly man waved his hand, making a cutting motion in the air. The girl playing the cymbals stopped mid-clang. The drummer did likewise. But the trumpet and the tuba player continued unabated.

"Stop, stop, for God's sake, stop this racket," screamed Gloria at the top of her lungs just as the horn section ceased. Gloria's last words, 'Stop this racket,' echoed throughout the hall. The bandleader stood up, giving Gloria a ferocious look.

The mayor's face flushed. "Sorry about the." He paused, smiled brightly and said, "The ah commotion. The band, of course, is very talented. We'll have the pleasure of listening to them later."

"Yeah, I can't wait," chuckled the tall man with thinning black hair, his eyes sparkling behind the round, wire-framed glasses perched on his nose. "We're the Kegworth Players, and I'm Max Woodard, the director. And you are?"

"I'm Mathew Hamilton, the mayor of this beautiful little town." The mayor grasped Max Woodard's hand, pumping it.

Over at the buffet table, Mabel greeted her friend Mary Woodhouse and gave her the platter of pigs in a blanket. Violet bustled, rearranging items on the table to make room for theirs. Mary smiled indulgently; Violet was well known for her compulsive neatness. Mabel turned in time to see Helen step forward to greet the Kegworth director, only to be shunted to the side by Gloria. Mabel nudged Violet, who was still reorganizing the trays. She set her dish of sausage wontons on the table. "What? I'm only making things look nice, well nicer," she said, straightening the trays and pressing the plastic clingfilm on a salsa dish.

"No, not you," Mabel said. "It's Gloria. She is, as usual, taking over. Poor Helen is being left out. This is not right. I distinctly remember Gloria telling us we were the hosts. And Helen is the director of our play." With a determined look on her face, she marched over to Helen and took the woman by the arm. "Come on, Helen, the Glenhaven Players are the hosts."

With one last look at the food table, Violet joined Mabel and Helen. The two women had taken positions beside the mayor. Helen shyly put out her hand. "Hello, I'm Helen Graham, the director of The Glenhaven Players."

Mayor Hamilton brushed Mabel to the side. He stepped in front of Helen and put an arm around the Kegworth Director's shoulders. "Let me introduce you to my darling wife, Gloria, who has almost single-handedly organized this drama festival."

Gloria, grinning ear to ear, preened. "Thank you, Mathew. I've done my best."

Mabel glanced at Violet. Didn't she feel slighted? Gloria was taking all the credit. Mabel knew Violet and the committee members had worked diligently to get the festival up and running. But Violet just smiled and shrugged. Mabel rolled her eyes.

Determined, Mabel quickly sidestepped in front of the mayor. "Welcome to the festival. I'm Mabel Havelock, one of the Glenhaven actors."

A youngish man with an arresting smile, his blue eyes sparkling, introduced himself. "I'm Martin Hendrix. I'm with the Kegworth Players. Me and Craig."

A solidly built man with a florid face and a big grin put a muscular arm around Martin's shoulder. "Hi, I'm Craig Bannon. Martin, my good buddy and I are the Kegworth actors. We're doing *Hockey is Life.* Are you familiar with the play?"

"No, sorry, do you know it, Helen?" Mabel asked.

Before Helen could answer, Mike lumbered over to join his wife. "I'm Mike, and I'm Helen's husband. I look after the lights at the theatre. If you need help, just ask me, and I'll do what I can for you." He grasped the man's hand, shaking it vigorously.

"Thanks, Mike. We are a little short. I was hoping we could get someone to do the lights," Max, the director, said. "Oh, and the sound." The director pushed his glasses up on his nose and grinned. "And someone to raise the curtains. I guess you could say we are a lot short."

"No problem," Mike said. "Young Tommy does sound. He'll help out."

"Yes, well, thank you, Mike." Gloria placed a hand on Max's shoulder. "Don't you worry, Max. I'll arrange everything. Now, please take a seat." She turned to Violet. "Violet, show these gentlemen where they should sit."

"Any chance we get heat?" asked Mabel as she stuck her hands in her pockets. "It's freezing in here."

The mayor's eyes narrowed, forcing a smile said, "We're doing the best we can. The furnace is acting up. The darn thing was working yesterday. But don't worry. The furnace will be fixed momentarily."

"Ah, yes, our mayor, Mr. Fixit." Mabel grinned at the mayor; the mayor bowed. Mike, guffawing loudly, followed the Kegworth players to their seats.

The door opened, and a tall, middle-aged woman wearing a long burgundy cashmere cloak entered. The woman's platinum blonde hair was elaborately braided to form a crown atop her head. She undid a large gold broach depicting comedy and tragedy. Her cloak fell open to reveal a white and green leaf-patterned dress.

"Oh, it's Mandy Swan," Gloria said breathlessly. "Go help Violet," she ordered over her shoulder to Mabel and Helen as she sped to the door to welcome the newcomer. Helen bit her lip and obeyed.

Mabel crossed her arms over her chest and waited for an introduction. She was not going to be shunted aside. Someone from the Glenhaven Players should be on hand to welcome the adjudicator.

"Hello, you must be Mandy Swan," greeted Gloria.

Long gold earrings glittered as the handsome woman nodded her head. "Yes, I am she."

"I'm Gloria Hamilton, the coordinator of the drama festival. We've spoken many times on the phone. I can't tell you how happy I am that you agreed to come and adjudicate our little drama festival," gushed Gloria.

The woman's lips twisted in a half-smile. "I'm sure."

"I have everything organized, and I think you will be pleased."

"Really? Is this where the festival is going to take place?" The woman curled her lips as if tasting something sour.

"Oh, no, this is the reception hall," Gloria said hurriedly.

"Some creature at the gas station told me to come here." Her voice had an artificial tone as if she was speaking from a stage.

"We are only using this hall for the welcome ceremonies. We have a newly renovated theatre for the festival. The theatre is charming. You'll love it," Gloria said, smiling warmly.

"Yes, I'm sure," replied Mandy Swan, sniffing; she pursed her lips.

Mabel surged forward, outmaneuvering the mayor. "Hello, welcome to Glenhaven. Our theatre is charming. But I have to tell you that our theatre has a sad history. A very recent, sad history."

Gloria's forehead furrowed. "Mabel, my dear, please take a seat. You'll get a chance to talk to Miss Swan later." The mayor's wife's lips formed a tight smile. "Mabel is one of our actors," she explained to Mandy. "And this handsome man is my husband, Mathew. He's the mayor of Glenhaven."

The mayor took Mandy Swan's hand, a hand which she quickly withdrew. The mayor, taken aback at the adjudicator's reaction, plastered a smile on his face. "Delighted to meet you. I'm sure you will enjoy your time in our little town."

"Really? You think so?"

"My name is Mabel Havelock. As Gloria pointed out, I'm one of the actors with The Glenhaven players."

"How nice for you," Mandy said, wrapping her burgundy cloak tightly around her body.

An Uncertain smile hovered on Mabel's lips. Was that a slur? "I expect you have adjudicated many drama festivals. It's so nice you could come to adjudicate ours."

"Indeed. I'm an accomplished actor and an experienced director. I've had a great deal of experience from both sides." Mandy's lips turned down as she looked down her nose at Mabel, "And I've adjudicated many drama festivals. But never one this small."

"I could tell you are a woman of experience," Mabel said.

"Oh, really." Mandy Swan smiled smugly.

Mabel, detecting a snobby attitude from the adjudicator, said, "Yes. Oh, and I like your hair. The way you braid your hair reminds me of my grandmother. She used to braid her hair just like you do."

Mandy's eyes widened, and Gloria cast Mabel a scathing look and took the adjudicator's arm, ushering her away.

Mabel grinned.

Chapter Thirteen

Still wearing their coats, the crowd stood as the high school band played *O Canada*. Then Gloria, holding up a huge silver goblet, marched proudly down the aisle to the band's rendition of *Pomp and Circumstance*. The trophy, awarded each year to the Municipal One Act Drama Festival winner, was almost as big as the NHL Stanley Cup. Gloria stood with the cup, looking around for a place to set it. With her brows furrowed, Gloria eyed her husband. The mayor looked at the council members. The councillors, shrugging their shoulders, looked at each other, then back at Mayor Hamilton. A member from the chamber of commerce, a chubby man with a double chin, stood. He swivelled his head one way, then the other. Shaking his head, he threw up his hands and sat back down. The crowd began to titter.

Mike, who was sitting in the second row, picked up a black plastic chair and tramped to the front. Making a show of dusting off the chair, he daintily set the chair in front of the podium. The crowd applauded, and Gloria placed the trophy on the chair, turning the cup so that the name of The Glenhaven Players engraved on the cup was facing the audience. The crowd applauded again, and Mike bowed. Gloria, with a flushed face, twisted her lips into a smile. "Thank you, Mike."

"You're welcome," Mike replied, giving the trophy a wipe with his sleeve.

Gloria tilted her head impatiently, motioning for him to take a seat. Mike grinned and slowly lumbered back to sit with the Glenhaven Players.

Mayor Hamilton stood, removed his coat, and rubbed his hands together, striding across the floor to stand beside the silver goblet, smiling at the drama participants gathered for the introductions. With one hand on the trophy, Gloria held her ground, forcing her husband to walk to the other side of the trophy chair. Her husband raised an eyebrow, then laughed, "My wife, as usual, has the place of honour."

Gloria, forcing a smile, let go of the trophy and took two steps back.

The mayor bowed to his wife and continued. "I think many of you here know that The Glenhaven Players have a long and proud history. Glenhaven has won best play three years running in this festival." The mayor beamed as the hometown crowd applauded enthusiastically. "Would The Glenhaven Players please come up here and take a bow and introduce yourselves?" the mayor requested, clapping his hands.

The audience joined in as Ned, Helen, Alice, Violet, and Mabel trooped to the front. Ned, bowing and bobbing, scooted up to stand by Mabel, winking at her. Mabel frowned and inched away.

Beaming, Mayor Hamilton shook Helen's hand. "Ladies and gentlemen, for those who don't know this lovely lady. Let me introduce her. Helen Graham is the director of The Glenhaven Players. And the winner of last year's drama festival. Congratulations, Helen, on last year's best play award. I'm looking forward to this year's play." The mayor flashed a toothy smile at the crowd and chuckled. "And, of course, I'm looking forward to all the plays."

Helen smiled timidly and took a deep breath. "I, I wasn't the director of last year's winner. Cindy Glover was the director. Dear Cindy has passed on. Our Cindy has gone to that drama stage in the great beyond."

Alice bowed her head and folded her hands as if in prayer.

Mabel shifted her feet uneasily. Cindy, an avid fisherman and hunter, died in a Northern Saskatchewan hunting accident. But she guessed the term passed on fit.

Helen swallowed nervously. "Dear Cindy was the director of the Glenhaven Players for all these many, many years and, of course, the winner of last year's festival." A tear trickled down Helen's cheek. She took a deep breath. "It is a great honour to continue Cindy's work. This year, our cast is new. And we hope we can do justice to Cindy's great legacy." A big round of applause followed Helen's speech. She blushed and stammered, announcing the name of their play and explaining how most of this year's cast members couldn't make it to the ceremonies, ending with introducing Alice, Mabel and Ned. "Oh, and we could not do this without our dear Violet. She's not acting, but we can't manage without her." There was more applause as the cast returned to their seats.

Gloria motioned for her husband to do the same. She opened a printed program and said, "This lovely lady sitting here is Mandy Swan, who has graciously agreed to adjudicate our drama festival." Gloria then read off a list of Mandy's accomplishments. Mandy rose from her chair and bowed to the polite applause. Gloria waited for the adjudicator to sit, then announced the names of the drama clubs participating in the festival. "And now I ask each drama club to come up and introduce yourselves and the play you will be performing. Starting with The Kegworth Players."

The Kegworth Players left their seats and filed up to the front. Max, the director, bowed. "Our play is *Hockey is Life*. I wrote it," he said proudly and waited, but no applause accompanied his statement. Looking a little uncomfortable, Max then introduced his two-man cast. Martin Hendrix and Craig Bannon. He finished with. "The play I wrote is about hockey and the meaning of life." There was polite applause from the crowd and the other participants.

Mabel groaned inwardly. "Good Lord, the meaning of life, shoot me now," she muttered to Violet. Violet shushed her.

Next was the Berryman Drama Club. Audrey Marson, the director, a dark-haired, full-figured woman with a ruddy complexion, called for her actors to introduce themselves. A slim, round-faced man with deep-set brown eyes grinned at his director. "Thanks, Audrey. Our intrepid director is shy, except when she's directing. Let me tell you; she's not shy then." Good-natured laughter followed his statement.

Mandy Swan nodded approvingly. A good sign for the Berryman club thought Mabel. The round-faced man grinned at his director and continued. "My name is Eric Ko. And the play we are going to perform is *Never Again*. I play a guy who is getting a divorce from..." He gestured toward a petite woman with a pert nose and flyaway blonde hair that hung down over her eyes. She introduced herself as Ivy Feinstein. Then, a solidly built woman with a ponytail and bad teeth said, "My name is Vera Devon. I play the lawyer." Her voice had a no-nonsense quality to it. Mabel thought the woman could play a top sergeant in the army or a crime boss. The club filed off to applause.

The Maryland Musers: four actors and the director paraded up to stand next to the silver drama trophy. The director, Sheeran

Maier, a dowdy woman with sparse blonde hair, cleared her throat and announced, "*Not Again* is a drama. This play is very relevant to our troubled times. It's about a self-help group of divorcees. And these are the talented actors who will perform it for you." She nodded to the actors. Each actor, one by one, stepped in front of the trophy, bowed, and introduced themselves.

Levi Sindanoi, a square-jawed, dark-eyed man, was first. The attractive man in his mid-forties saluted the crowd. Next was Grant Middleman; he had a shaved head, bushy dark brows, and deep-set eyes. Then Magdalen Kaminski took a bow. A pretty girl in her early twenties, she was a tall, auburn-haired girl with a tiny voice. Mabel wondered if they would have to mic her up. The theatre did not have the best acoustics. Fortunately, each group had a time slot scheduled so that they could rehearse before their evening performances. The fourth actor, Daryna Melnyk, also twenty-something, had a shock of red hair. A short man with a small potbelly jumped up from his chair as the cast sat. The man had pale blue eyes and a double chin. "The name is Adam Kaminski, father of Magdalen, and I do the props and the prompting. These guys couldn't get along without me. I take care of everything. I'm the fixer." He sat down to laughter and applause.

The last drama club to introduce themselves was The Moose Creek Little Theater. Each cast member wore a matching sweatshirt with a big brown moose, sitting on a director's chair holding a bullhorn. The director, Romelu Abbott, a sharp-faced man with piercing blue eyes, his long grey hair tied back in a ponytail, bowed. "I have the honour of directing these wonderful, talented actors. This young lady is Adele Janssen. She plays the lead in our mystery." Adele Janssen, a thirty-something woman with closely cropped black hair and a brilliant smile, waved at the crowd.

"Our other lead actress, or should I say, actor?" Romelu grinned. "Regardless, this is Britney Riter, and I am very lucky to have her in our cast." Britney, a short middle-aged woman with a shock of red hair, blushed. "And this handsome man is Novak Simms; he plays more than one character in our mystery. And it is a mystery to me how he learned two parts, each so different from the other." The director clapped his hands as a tall, dark-haired man with a Van Dyke beard made a deep bow. "And now, but certainly not least, these two lovely young ladies make up the rest of our cast." With a sweep of his hand, Romelu indicated the two pudgy grey-haired ladies, who looked exactly alike.

Chapter Fourteen

Mandy Swan drove her car down the main street of Glenhaven, muttering to herself. "What was I thinking? I should've never accepted the offer to adjudicate this clodhopper in the sticks festival." She gave a mocking laugh. She couldn't wait to tell her friends about the welcoming ceremony and the oversized trophy cup paraded like an academy award. And that tiresome woman, Gloria. The woman actually gave her the grand tour of Hicksville. What a joke. As Mandy drove past the library, a sign caught her eye. *Cut Up* printed in bold red letters flanked on either side by silver scissors. Pulling her car to the curb, she recalled the nasty little woman, Mabel, something or other, telling her that her hair looked like her grandmother's. Mandy lifted one hand from her steering wheel and ran her fingers over her braid. There was nothing to do until the night's performances by the country bumpkins. So maybe she should get a shampoo and a set. A small bell tinkled as she opened the red metal door. The salon smelled of perfume and perms. Striped red and white wallpaper covered the walls with pictures of attractive women modelling hairstyles. In front of a long mirror were three red leatherette salon chairs. Sitting in one of the chairs, a young girl filing her nails looked up. "Hi, have you an appointment?"

Mandy raised her eyebrows. An appointment here? Really? "No, but I would like a shampoo. And well, I'm not sure." She ran her hand over her braid. "Maybe it's time for something different. I've had this hairstyle for a long time." Her thoughts returned to the rude woman's comments about her grandmother's hair. "Yes, it's definitely time for something different."

The girl jumped up from the chair. "You're in luck; we have an opening right now." Mandy eyed the attractive girl's beautiful blonde hair, which was styled in a fashionable cut.

"Good, and I happen to have the time," she said, hanging her bag and cloak on an old-fashioned wooden hat stand.

"I'm Jolene."

"Yes, I'm sure you are."

Jolene looked uncertain as she shook out a red-flowered plastic cape.

Mandy gave her a condescending smile. "My name is Mandy Swan. I'm here to adjudicate the drama festival."

"Oh wow, awesome, I'm acting in the festival. I have the lead in our play," Jolene said excitedly, leading Mandy to a row of sinks at the back of the salon.

Mandy raised her eyebrows and sighed. The last thing she needed was for this girl to prattle on and on about her amateur acting. "In that case, we will not talk about your play or the festival. I must remain impartial."

Jolene wrapped a small white towel around Mandy's neck and placed the plastic cape over her clothes. "Oh, yes, of course." Jolene beamed, nodding enthusiastically, as she unbraided Mandy's hair. "You have beautiful hair and lovely texture. Is the colour natural?"

Mandy smiled. "Yes, of course."

Jolene, humming a tune, began shampooing Mandy's platinum locks. "I'm not a dog, please, a little gentler," admonished Mandy.

"Oh, sorry." Jolene finished the shampoo and began to rinse Mandy's hair.

Mandy turned her head, causing the water to trickle down her neck. "Hey, hey, you're getting me wet."

"Oh, sorry," said Jolene, wrapping a fluffy towel around Mandy's head.

"You had better not have gotten my collar wet," warned Mandy.

"No, it's just your neck. I'm sorry; I don't know how that happened," apologized Jolene, leading the disgruntled woman to one of the salon chairs.

"Fine." Mandy ran a finger around her collar.

"What would you like? A cut or a perm?" Jolene asked as she combed Mandy's long platinum blonde tresses.

Mandy looked in the mirror. Maybe her long hair and braids did make her look old. "A cut, but not too much, mind you. And maybe a perm, yes, a perm."

"Okay, awesome, just tell me when you are satisfied with the length." Jolene picked a pair of scissors and began to cut. Long locks of hair fell to the floor as she chatted to Mandy, who nodded occasionally and muttered one-word answers to Jolene's inquiries. Satisfied with the length, Jolene turned the chair and held a mirror for Mandy to look at the back of her hair.

"Yes, I think that's short enough. Can you perm hair this short?"

"Oh, for sure. You said your beautiful colour is natural; you don't dye it?"

Mandy preened. "Yes, it's natural. I'm lucky that way," she lied, smiling at her image in the mirror. As Jolene wrapped her hair in small perm-rods, Mandy decided to spread her natural charm, becoming chatty. She even made herself talk about the weather as Jolene mixed and applied the perm solutions to her hair wrapped around the tiny perm rods. Then, placing a plastic cap on Mandy's head, Jolene led her to one of the hair dryers. Mandy sniffed; she disliked the smell of the perm. Her nose, wrinkling in distaste, she checked her watch. This was taking a lot of time. But since there was nothing else to do in this one-horse town, she might as well relax.

"I've set the timer for twenty minutes. Would you like a cup of coffee? We have instant decaffeinated and regular."

"God, no," Mandy said, closing her eyes.

A hand shook her shoulder, and Mandy realized she must have dozed off.

"It's time to rinse your perm solution out," Jolene said, leading her to one of the sinks.

"How long have you had this salon?" Mandy asked as Jolene sprayed her head with warm water. "You are very young to own your own business."

"Oh," laughed Jolene. "Flo owns the salon."

"Flo?"

"Yes, I think it's short for Florence."

"Where is this, Flo?" Mandy felt a ping of unease.

"She had to take her mom to Regina. So, I'm looking after the shop for her. Answering the phone and, you know, taking care of her customers," Jolene said as she applied neutralizer to the perm-rods in Mandy's hair.

"You are a hairstylist?" Mandy asked, looking worriedly at her reflection in the mirror.

"I'm doing my apprenticeship. But don't worry, I'm fully qualified to do cuts, styles and perms." Jolene removed the perm rods from Mandy's hair and rinsed out the neutralizer. The little bell tinkled over the door, and Tommy entered, smiling shyly at Jolene.

Jolene's face paled, uttering a small, faint eek sound. She put her hand up, covering her mouth, and stood momentarily, staring down at Mandy's head. Then, shaking out a fluffy white towel, she quickly wrapped the towel around Mandy's head. "I'll be right with you," Jolene said, her voice cracked, rising an octave. "My buddy Tommy looks like he has something for me."

Mandy returned to the red leatherette salon chairs as Jolene sped over to Tommy standing by the door. Mandy's brow wrinkled as she sat in front of the long mirror, looking at her reflection. Don't worry; she told herself the haircut looked good. And how could you screw up a perm? They were factory-made. And after all, didn't people do home perms? Didn't they? She swivelled her chair, watching the skinny young man with lifeless, pale straw hair hold out a cell phone.

"See what I found," he said proudly.

"Oh, Tommy, I don't want some old broken cell phone. It's no good to anyone. Why bring this broken piece of junk to me?" asked Jolene, casting a nervous glance back at Mandy.

Tommy shifted his feet, his cheeks flushed. "I wasn't going to give it to you. I found this phone in the theatre basement while I was helping Fred and the guys fix the banister. The thing was under the steps. I think this may be Sherman's phone."

"Of course, it's Sherman's. No one would toss a phone under the steps?"

"Do you think I should take the phone to the police?"

Jolene bit her lip nervously as she looked from Tommy to Mandy. "What would they want with it? I really don't have time for this. Just throw it away." Then, taking a deep breath, she returned to Mandy, unwrapping the towel from her head. Mandy's hair was a thin mass of white frizz. She looked like an albino chia pet.

"Oh my God," shrieked Mandy. "What the hell! You little bitch, you've ruined my hair. I'll sue you and your employer for everything you've got."

"I'm sorry, I'm sorry. I don't know how this happened. I followed all the instructions. I've done this tons and tons of times." Tears coursed down Jolene's cheeks.

Mandy watched in horror as a terrified Jolene, sniffing back tears, began drying her ultra-curly, frizzy white hair with a handheld blow-dryer. Spotting Tommy standing by the door, Mandy screamed, "This isn't a freak show! Get the hell out of here!"

Glaring back at her, Tommy hurriedly left, slamming the door behind him.

"You bleach your hair, don't you?" accused Jolene, switching off the blow-dryer.

"What if I do? What business is it of yours? How I colour my hair has nothing to do with this disaster you've created," snarled Mandy. "What the hell am I going to do now?"

"It has everything to do with what's happened to your hair. And, and, this is not my fault. You should have told me the truth. If you had, I would have set the timer for bleached hair," sobbed Jolene.

Mandy threw the plastic cape onto the floor and marched to the hat rack, grabbed her cloak and bag, and turned to scream at a sobbing Jolene. "When I'm done with you. You won't get a job washing dogs."

The distraught woman slammed the salon door, strode to her car, threw her purse in the passenger seat and started the car. Still seething, Mandy pulled out onto the street and heard a loud bang, followed by a sudden jolt. She was thrown forward, then blasted back as the airbag deployed. Seconds later, the car stopped, and the bag deflated. She sat stunned. Was she hurt? What the hell happened?

Mandy lay her head back and sat for several minutes in her seat, breathing in and out. The car was shut off. Did she do that? She didn't remember. But the main thing was that she was okay, maybe not the car, but she was. Wasn't she? Mandy felt a sudden rage. Some clod-hopper idiot had rear-ended her car. Good God, these imbeciles didn't even know how to drive. She opened her car door and stomped back to survey the damage to the back of her car. "You bastard, you didn't even stop," Mandy screamed, looking down the street. There was no sign of the vehicle that rear-ended her car.

"Are you okay?" a man's voice asked.

Mandy swung around. It was Tommy, the Huckleberry Finn from the hair salon. "Yes, I am, but not my car, as you can bloody well see," she snarled. The back bumper had folded like an accordion. "I need a garage. If there is such a thing here?"

"Yeah, Rusty's Auto Shop?"

Sauntering up to view the car, Mike Graham lifted his baseball cap and scratched his head. "That's nasty. Your bumper is a mess. What the hell happened here?"

"If you have eyes, you can plainly see some moron rear-ended my car," snapped Mandy.

Mike, ignoring Mandy's outburst, looked curiously at the dishevelled woman. "Hey, I think I know you. Are you Miss Swan, the adjudicator?"

"Yes, I am, you idiot."

"No need to get so het up about it. You look different, but yeah, I do see some resemblance. What the hell happened to your hair?"

"Please don't ask her that," pleaded Tommy.

Mandy put her hand to her hair, her eyes blazing with anger. "Never mind my hair, you halfwit. Look at my car. One of your local yokel inhabitants of Hicksville rear-ended me."

Unfazed by her slurs, Mike bent down to examine the bumper, scratched his head again, and said, "Yep, your car is a hell of a mess. It's going to cost a pretty penny to get this fixed. I hope you got insurance?"

"Of course I do," snarled Mandy.

"Then it might be a good idea to get yourself checked out by a doc. You know, for insurance reasons."

It only took Mandy a few seconds to consider Mike's advice. "Yes, you're absolutely right," she said, raising her hand to the back of her neck. "Take me to the emergency. I hope to God you have a hospital." She felt okay, but insurance money would go a long way to help her out of her money woes. Things had been tight, that was the reason she had accepted the adjudication at this dreadful drama festival.

Chapter Fifteen

Mabel crept up to the heavy burgundy stage curtains. Standing in the middle behind the curtains, she peeked through a tiny slit. Peering out to look at the audience. Maybe her mother changed her mind and came to the play. She scanned the crowd and saw friends and relatives of the Glenhaven Players in the audience. Mabel's heart sank; there was no sign of her mom. I'm being childish, she told herself. I'm a grown woman, so what if Mom doesn't come to see me act. She suddenly felt butterflies in her tummy, remembering her mother's warning about looking like a clown. And she cringed as she remembered what Crystal said about an insensitive creep taking Sherman's part in the play.

Violet came to stand beside Mabel, peering over her shoulders to have a look. "It's a full house," she said.

"The festival has a sell-out crowd on the opening night. Gloria will be pleased. Who knew there were that many drama fans in Glenhaven? You don't think they are here because of the unfortunate death of Sherman?"

"You mean morbid curiosity?" Violet nodded.

"I hope not," Mabel said as she continued to scan the crowd. She wondered if Jason Greenwood was in the audience. Sherman wanted the man fired. Could he have arranged Sherman's fatal accident? But how? There was no sign of a break-in. And even if he was here, she didn't know what the man looked like. And there were a lot of faces she didn't recognize, as there were people from the neighbouring towns who were friends and relatives of the other drama clubs.

It was a two-night drama festival. Because The Glenhaven Players hosted the festival, they were the first to perform. After them, The Kegworth Players. In the morning, a workshop conducted by Mandy Swan would take place for all of the participants in the festival. On the final night, performances from the Maryland, Moose Creek, and Berryman drama clubs. Then, Mandy Swan would announce the best actor and director and present the trophy for the best play.

Mayor Hamilton, tapping on his cell phone, sat in the front row centre with the ladies from the festival committee. On the right-hand side of the aisle, the mayor's special guests, town council members, and their spouses were in the front row. Behind the mayor, a row of empty chairs roped off from the audience, where the Glenhaven cast would come after their performance to watch The Kegworth Players. When both plays were over, the adjudicator would take the stage and judge their performance. Mabel spotted Mandy Swan wearing a neck brace and a pale-yellow turban on her head. She was reading a script at a small table strategically placed in front of the seats to the left of the stage.

"Mandy's wearing a neck brace. I wonder what happened to her?" Mabel whispered to Jolene, who had crept up to stand beside her.

The starched crinoline under Jolene's full-skirted bright yellow dress brushed against Mabel. Violet and Mabel stepped aside to make room for the girl to peek through the curtain's small opening. Jolene peered, then quickly let the curtain drop. Her face paled. "She's wearing a turban," she moaned. "I did her hair this afternoon." Jolene bit her bottom lip. "Her hair didn't turn out well. I hope she doesn't hold that against us."

Helen tip-toed up to the group that was gathered behind the closed curtains and put an arm around her granddaughter's shoulder. "Oh, sweetie, I can't imagine you ever giving anyone a bad hairdo."

"You don't know," Jolene wailed. "She called her hair a disaster. And she's right. It is. But honestly, it's not my fault."

"Of course, it's not," Helen said, hugging Jolene; Jolene's skirt encircled Helen.

"I doubt Mandy Swan is concerned with a hairdo. The woman is wearing a neck brace," commented Mabel, lifting her wig and scratching her head. She settled the wig back on her head and pressed her hand to the little black mustache on her upper lip. Mabel hoped the darn thing would stay put. She wanted to look masculine, but was the mustache too much? Her tummy was doing flip-flops. Breathe, she told herself.

"It's bad, very bad," Jolene said. She licked her lips, red lipstick smearing her front teeth.

"Nonsense, sweetie, you are worrying about nothing. Miss Swan's hair can't be that bad," Helen said reassuringly to her granddaughter.

"Oh, it is, it is," Jolene wailed; she spun around and sped offstage.

Helen peeked out between the curtains. "Poor Miss Swan," she said, stepping back, she let the curtains close.

"Are you worried about her hair?" asked Mabel.

"No, of course not. Jolene is just being silly. There is no way she did a bad styling for Miss Swan," replied Helen, her eyes flashing indignantly.

"Then why poor Miss Swan?" Violet asked as she brushed orange cat hair off Mabel's jacket with a small brush.

"She's wearing a neck brace," Mabel said.

"What happened to her?" Violet motioned for Mabel to turn.

Mabel did. "Does anyone know?" she asked as Violet vigorously brushed more cat hair off her black suit jacket.

"This afternoon, Miss Swan was driving downtown, and someone rear-ended her car," explained Helen.

"Good golly, that's terrible," Violet said. "Hold still, Mabel." She sunk to her knees, tackling Mabel's trousers.

"Yes, the poor woman's car rear-ended. And in our town," Helen said, outraged at the idea.

"You should try parking at the post office when the mail arrives," snickered Mabel.

"I suppose. But at least dear Tommy was a good Samaritan. He came across the poor woman just moments after the accident," explained Helen. "And it was fortunate Tommy came along when he did. He and Mike took the poor woman to the emergency in Kipling. Mike told me the doctor said she has whiplash, so now, poor Miss Swan is wearing a neck brace."

"Did Tommy see who rear-ended her car?" asked Mabel.

"No, I don't believe he did."

"Enough gossiping ladies, it's time to get to your stations. The show is about to begin." Gloria Hamilton waited until the trio backed up. Then, with notes in her hand, she took a deep breath, parted the curtains, and stepped out to the stage apron. Rudy, Jolene, and Alice crept up to join Mabel, Helen and Violet. The cast quietly stood behind the closed curtains, listening to Gloria's opening remarks.

"Ladies and gentlemen, welcome to the opening night of the Municipal One Act Drama Festival. And a warm welcome to our guests." Consulting her notes, Gloria rattled off the names of the drama clubs. Applause from the audience followed her presentation. She waited until the applause died, then with a fixed smile on her face, she resumed her introduction. "And a special welcome to Miss Mandy Swan from Regina. Miss Swan has graciously agreed to adjudicate our little drama festival."

Violet nudged Mabel, pocketing her small brush, whispering, "Miss Swan has graciously agreed for a hefty fee." Mabel grinned back.

Mandy stood with a hand on her neck brace and bowed to the applause. Gloria put a hand over her heart, paused, looked down from the stage at Mandy, and, with a curious smile on her face, continued. "Miss Swan, as you can see, has suffered an injury. But in the great tradition of show business. She has bravely insisted that we go on with the festival." More applause followed. Beaming, Mandy bowed.

Gloria clapped along with the crowd. But she was inhaling and exhaling impatiently. She tapped her toe on the floor, waiting for Mandy to sit. When the adjudicator finally took her seat, Gloria sniffed and announced, "And now, without further ado. Let us entertain you." The audience applauded again.

As Gloria parted the curtains to join the cast, Helen stepped out. Gloria looked taken aback. Helen cleared her throat, nervously wringing her hands. "Before we begin, I want to say a few words."

Gloria, looking puzzled, forced a smile onto her face.

"Some of you may have heard about the terrible accident that happened to our little drama family," Helen's voice faltered; she gulped and continued. "To those who haven't heard. I want to tell you about Sherman Mahan. He was a dear and valued member of our cast." Helen took a deep breath. "Our dear Sherman died here in this theatre." Some members of the crowd gasped; others nodded knowingly.

Gloria shot Helen a furious look. Her fists clenched at her side.

Helen waited until the audience quieted down, took another deep breath, and continued. "It was a tragic accident. The cast and I want to acknowledge Sherman. He was a fine actor and a good friend. Tonight, we are dedicating our performance to Sherman." Helen clasped her hands in front of her as if in prayer. "Would you all please stand and bow your heads and join me and our cast in a moment of silence?"

The audience stood, bowing their heads. Gloria also bowed her head. But looking out the corner of her eye at Helen, her lips formed a thin, tight line.

"Thank you," Helen said, quickly parting the curtains; she darted back behind them.

"That was so nice, Helen," Mabel said, joining the cast as they gathered around their director, giving her a group hug.

"People, people, places, please," Gloria urged impatiently. The cast obeyed, chattering in hushed tones as they scattered offstage.

Sam, chewing and smiling, strolled onstage. "What's up?" He had a handful of colourful gummy candies, which he popped into his mouth.

"I said, get off, get off the stage. We're finally going to start," Gloria snapped.

Rudy took Sam by the arm, ushering the grinning man offstage. "You better slow down on those things."

"These candies are great. You should have some. I think chewing on these little gummy guys is calming me down. I've got to say I was a little nervous. But now I feel great. I just don't feel great. In fact, I feel absolutely great. I couldn't feel better."

Rudy gave Sam a curious look, then shrugged, and took out his phone and snapped a picture of Jolene. She smiled coyly, batting her eyelashes, picking up her skirt, swishing the yellow fabric in a cancan fashion.

"Put that phone away. We're almost ready. And please, everyone, make sure your phones are off," warned Helen.

Rudy grinned, winking at Jolene; he stuffed it into his pocket. At the mention of the phone, Mabel's thoughts returned to Sherman's lost phone. Was that a text he got? Or a phone call? If it was a text, that would be a bonus. A clue. But where was it? Was it still in the basement? Then, all thoughts of Sherman, the phone and the accident fled from her mind. Violet was raising the curtains.

Chapter Sixteen

The house lights went off, and the stage lights came on. After a moment of silence, Jolene, who played Bobbie Sue, the southern belle, entered. A spotlight followed her as she flounced across the stage to sit on the loveseat, her yellow dress puffing up around her.

"I do declare..." Jolene said in her best southern drawl, paused and looked offstage, beating her skirt down, repeating, "I do declare?" She waited, then stood with the palms of her hands upward in a helpless gesture.

Gloria, backstage, frantically flipped pages back and forth.

"Have you got the script back to front?" Violet whispered.

"No, I bloody well don't," hissed Gloria. "This isn't my script. It's not even our play."

Jolene circled the sofa to stand centre stage. The spotlight followed her.

"You're bored," Mabel whispered offstage.

Jolene turned to face stage right. She squinted, blinked, cupped her ear and asked, "What?"

"You're bored," Mabel said loudly.

Jolene, smiling broadly, revealing a smear of red lipstick on her front teeth, said in a very loud, unsouthern drawl, "I do declare. I'm bored as hell." The audience tittered.

Jolene, following the spotlight, sashayed her way back to the settee. She laid herself down on the sofa. As her skirt billowed up, she theatrically flung her hand on her forehead. The green cushion fell off the arm of the couch, and a settee leg wobbled.

Sam, who was playing Big Daddy, Jolene's father, entered upstage right, a pipe in his hand; he pointed the pipe stem at Jolene. "Bobbie booby Sue, what are y'all doing lying around? Y'all are like a splendid dish." Loud laughter erupted from the crowd. Sam turned to face the audience, and with a broad grin on his face, he bowed.

Mabel entered with a tray and bowed. Sam sauntered over to her. He placed a big hand on Mabel's head and rotated her wig. As more laughter followed his actions, Sam beamed. Mabel's eyes widened; her face flushed, cursing silently. She knew what had happened. She'd taken the itchy hairpiece off to scratch her head and had put her wig on back to front.

Heart pounding, Mabel stood still, frozen to the spot. Her hands shook as she stared out over the footlights at the audience. She opened her mouth and closed it. What was her line? What was she supposed to do? Sam and Jolene looked at her expectantly. The silent pause lengthened. And the audience snickered. Mabel stood shaking, clutching the tray, her mouth a gap. She felt weak in the knees. She was going to be sick.

Mabel looked down at the tray in her hands. Yes, the tray, she knew what to do. She gulped and took a deep breath, then carefully walked over to the loveseat, the tray shaking in her hands. Kicking the pillow out of the way, she bowed and licked her dry lips. "Wot madam like a mint julep?" she asked in her best imitation of a British accent, her accent sounding more like a Cockney fish seller than an upper-class butler.

"Oh my, I'm so delirious for a mint julep," Jolene drawled, springing up from the sofa, looking at the empty tray, then at Mabel.

"Desirous," contradicted Mabel.

Backstage, a horrified Violet pressed her hand to her mouth, whispering, "What the heck? Where is the glass?"

Onstage, Jolene asked in an unaccented voice, "Where is it?"

"Where is...oh," Mabel sputtered.

"Booby, Booby, Sue, you are far too damn young for liberation," Sam said in a sing-song voice. Sam then paused, looked puzzled, and asked, "Libation?"

Mabel stood gaping at the empty tray in her hand. Damn it; she forgot the glass? Now what? Was she supposed to exit?

Sam, nudging her, said in a stage whisper, loud enough for the audience to hear. "Bugger off." Sam then ran a hand over his grey beard. Raising his bushy eyebrows up and down, he pulled the fake beard down under his chin. Eyes twinkling, he pulled his beard back up. The crowd laughed and applauded. Grinning, Sam bowed.

Mabel looked at Sam in astonishment, bowed, and backed up. Stumbling over the cushion, she turned and ran for the exit. Jolene flung herself back on the settee with her hand on her forehead, palm upward. The settee leg gave out, and the loveseat collapsed onto three legs. Jolene slid off the loveseat, landing on her bum. Her yellow skirt flew up, covering her face and revealing her white crinoline.

The audience clapped and roared with laughter.

Gloria, Violet and Helen watched helplessly as things went from bad to worse. The broken settee leg forced Jolene to do her swooning on the arm of the couch. Jolene continued to miss her cues, forgetting her lines and looking offstage at Gloria, who had no script to prompt. Ned, who played the rejected suitor in the play, had trouble standing still while delivering his lines. Ned lifted his feet as if standing on hot coals, ending each sentence with his shrill, nervous laughter. Alice, the maid, kept ducking on and off the stage like a jack-in-the-box. Rudy, who played Beau, the love of Bobbie Sue, was the only actor who appeared on his mark and knew his cues. Even when Sam, the usual brusque strait-laced man, made ab-lib comments that had no connection to the play, Rudy was able to keep the play somewhat on track. His overtures to Bobbie Sue and Big Daddy's rejection went well. The women felt hopeful until Rudy's second entrance.

Mabel regained her composure, her confidence grew, and her performance improved as Jeeves, the butler. Unfortunately, her English accent did not. Mabel continued to sound like a Cockney fishmonger. "Mistuh Beau is ere ta see ya," she said.

Fortunately, regardless of the accent, Rudy knew his cue. And Beau bounded on stage, swept off his Panama hat, and knelt at Bobbie Sue's knee. Jolene, perched primly on the arm of the sofa, swished her yellow skirt and laughed nervously.

"Mah, dear darlin' Bobbie Sue, I can not take our estrangement any longer. I can not stay away from you, mah darlin'. Will you do the honour of taking my hand in matrimony?"

As Rudy held Jolene's hand, she struggled to remember her lines and giggled. Mabel, who was about to exit stage right, turned, padded back to stand behind Jolene, and whispered. "Mah, dear darling Beau, y'all must ask Big Daddy for permission."

Jolene smiled and said, "We must ask Big Daddy for permission."

Sam heard his cue and stomped onstage. He put his hands on his hips and yelled, "Scallywag, get away from mah, daughter."

Rudy jumped up and turned. "Big Daddy, I wish to ask for your daughter's hand in marriage."

There was a pause as both men looked at Jolene. Jolene looked at Mabel. Mabel whispered. "Please, Big Daddy, I truly love Beau, and I want to be his bride."

"Sam, I mean please, Big Daddy. I truly love Beau, and I want to be his bride."

"Over mah, dead body." Sam strode over and grabbed Rudy by his jacket lapels, lifting the man up and shaking him like a rag doll.

Rudy struggled to get out of Sam's grip. Sam shoved him to the floor. Upset by Sam's overacting, Rudy bounded up, fist clenched and took a swing at Sam. Rudy missed. Both men batted their fists in the air, circling around each other. The crowd cheered and applauded as the men dodged and weaved, avoiding being hit by the other.

Ned, entering stage left, came to an abrupt standstill. His mouth fell open as he watched Sam and Rudy swing their fists at each other. He looked at Mabel and then dashed forward at the same time as Mabel. Ned grabbed Sam by the arm. Sam flung the small man aside. And Ned landed on the couch beside a stricken Jolene. The couch's last legs gave out. Ned giggled, and Jolene screamed as the sofa crashed to the floor.

Sam and Rudy continued to circle each other, punching the air. Mabel ducked into the melee just as Sam took another swing at Rudy. Mabel dodged the blow, but her wig came flying off. The hairpiece soared out to the audience, landing on a festival committee member's lap. The chubby little woman in a polka dot dress picked up the curly black wig with two fingers as if it were a rat. "Eek, eek," the woman screamed, throwing the rumpled toupee across the aisle. The wig fell onto a man's knee; laughing, the man held it up, waving the hairpiece like a flag. The crowd cheered.

Sam, astonished at Mabel's grey head, put an arm around her. Mabel looked warily back at him. But she remained standing between Sam and Rudy, who still had his clenched fists poised in the air. Rudy's eyes darted between Mabel and Sam. Mabel gave him a little headshake, and Rudy dropped his hands. She looked offstage to see a white-faced Helen, her hands covering her mouth.

Alice popped onstage and skirted around Sam. "Get away from my daughter, you scallywag wag," Alice said, shaking a finger at Ned.

Sam, looking dazed, giggled and said, "Hey, that's my line."

Alice glared back at him and said, "You scallywag, get away from Jolene. I mean, Bobbie Sue is my daughter."

Ned, jumping up, shrieked in his high-pitched voice, "A maid's daughter? I'm a gentleman. I will not lower mah self to marry a maid's daughter." He then giggled shrilly.

Rudy, rushing over, knelt in front of Jolene and said, "Mah darlin' Bobbie Sue. I do not care if you are a maid's daughter. Will you give me your hand in marriage?"

"Why yes, I will, mah, darlin' man."

Rudy grabbed Jolene by the hand, and they dashed offstage. The crowd cheered, and Violet lowered the curtain.

Chapter Seventeen

There was enthusiastic applause from the partisan hometown crowd as the Glenhaven Players took their bow. But the only one smiling was Sam. The rest had pasted fake smiles on their faces. The smiles dropped as they gathered onstage behind the curtains, and the actors looked somberly at each other, except for Sam, who was still grinning from ear to ear; he was excitedly patting his fellow actors on the back. "Great job, great job," he kept repeating. "Guys, we're a hit."

Helen, wiping her tear-stained face, emerged from backstage.

"Sorry, Helen. We let you down," Mabel said, hugging her.

Gloria strode onstage, scowling at the cast. "You were all just dreadful, an absolute catastrophe. I'm so disappointed in all of you. What happened on this stage tonight is beyond belief. A total nightmare." She cast a look at Helen. "Can you imagine what Cindy Glover would say if she were here? As the director of the Glenhaven Players, she won the best play for three straight years in a row. You were obligated to honour her memory. Instead, you let her down."

Helen hung her head and said, "I know, I know." Her voice broke; taking a hanky from her pocket, she wiped her nose.

"You are being way too harsh. What happened on stage isn't Helen's fault. We were all to blame. And some more than others." Mabel looked over at a grinning Sam.

"Well, I'm not taking any blame. I did my part perfectly," exclaimed Alice.

"Yeah, right. The on-again, off-again maid. You ran around like a chicken with its head cut off," snickered Ned.

"Did I miss an entrance? I darn well don't think so."

"No, you didn't miss any. You were always entering."

"You don't have any room to talk, Mr. Hotfoot. Dancing around like a cat on a hot tin roof."

"Alice, Ned, please stop bickering," Helen said. "I can't bear it. What's done is done." Helen sighed. "We need to get our stuff off the stage. The Kegworth Players are waiting in the wings."

"I can't believe the couch fell down like that and crashed to the floor," Violet said. "Why, oh why didn't I see that coming? I should have checked the darn thing. And I'm so sorry about the misplaced prop," she apologized. "I can't understand it. I'm usually so careful."

"Oh, Violet, the lost prop wasn't your fault. I should've noticed that I was carrying an empty tray onstage. But I had such an attack of stage fright I didn't even notice my wig was on the wrong way," lamented Mabel.

"Yes, but where is the darn thing? I looked all over for that glass, and I still can't find it. I'm usually so careful," fretted Violet, carrying the coffee table offstage.

"This play was an absolute failure. And you're all to blame, a disaster from start to finish. I'm so ashamed for you all," Gloria said, her lips in a grim line. "I just can't believe it. Glenhaven, the winner of the drama festival three times running, has sunk to these depths." She crossed her arms, watching as the cast hurried to get the stage clear of their set.

"You were no help. You're the worst prompter of all time," complained Jolene, picking up the green cushion.

"I had the wrong script, but the wrong script wouldn't have mattered if you knew your lines," snarled Gloria, snatching the pillow from Jolene. Punching the cushion, she stomped offstage.

Pouting, Jolene turned to Rudy. "That woman is darn right mean. I did my best."

"Your best? Gloria is right. You missed more lines than I can count. In fact, it would be a heck of a lot easier to count the lines you did remember. Didn't you even study your lines?" questioned Rudy.

"Yeah, at least I didn't get into a fight."

"Well, I think old Sam losing it onstage was probably the best part of the play. The audience loved our sparring scene," Rudy chuckled; grabbing the broken loveseat, he hauled the old broken piece of furniture offstage.

Jolene tossed her head and flounced across the stage to Sam, who was struggling with the brown cabinet. She took hold of one side of the cupboard and Sam the other. Jolene pushed one way, and Sam shoved the other. The cabinet rocked, and the blue vase on top of it wobbled and then fell, the plastic flowers flying across the stage.

"Oopsy a daisy," giggled Sam, bending to pick up a flower.

Mabel picked up the plastic vase. "Sam, why in the heck did you drink? Today of all days? Was it stage fright? Is that why you got drunk?"

Sam crouched beside her, picking up a blue plastic rose. He sniffed it. "Mabel, Mabel, Mabel," he said in a sing-song voice. "I'm not drunk. I swear. I don't know what's the matter with me. I was on top of the world. And now I feel so very, very sad. Sad for the world." He sunk to the floor.

"Never mind, Sam, come with me." Helen tugged at the gangly man's arm. "I think you need to change out of your costume."

Sam stood, gazing with adoration at Helen; he handed her the blue rose. "You are the very best woman I know."

"Thank you," Helen said, smiling sadly at the plastic flower.

Mike tromped onstage. "Sam, you darn fool. Come with me. It's time you sobered up." He put his arm around Sam's shoulders, ushering him offstage.

Sam giggled. "No, no, I'm not drunk, old buddy."

"What a jerk," exclaimed Jolene, gathering the rest of the plastic flowers from the floor. "To think I looked up to Sam."

"It's not all Sam's fault. Things were destined to go wrong," Helen said, wiping her nose with her frilly lace hanky. "We should never have gone on with the play," she murmured. "I feel Sherman's ghost was watching us. He didn't like us disrespecting his memory."

"But Granny, we did the play in honour of Sherman's memory," Jolene said.

Mabel grimaced, ghost or not. There was no honour in this calamity.

Chapter Eighteen

Mabel filed down the aisle to sit with her fellow actors in the row behind Mayor Hamilton. The cast was seated away from Sam. The gangly farmer was grinning happily, sprawled back in his theatre seat, his feet propped up on the back of the empty seat in front of him. Helen unhappily shook her head and sat beside him. "Sam, feet down," she scolded.

"Right on, Y'all," Sam drawled. Swinging his long legs down, he sat straight, his knees almost touching his chin.

Alice, sitting next to Ned, sniffed. A strong pine scent was wafting up, mixing with the perfume of his aftershave. Alice wrinkled her nose and got up, moving to sit beside Mabel.

Mabel placed a hand on the theatre seat and said, "Sorry, Alice, I'm saving this seat for Violet."

"Really? Where the heck is she? If she wants to sit with us, she should be here."

"Violet is manning the curtains."

"Ah, yes, Miss Goody-two Shoes, always helping. I suppose those who can't act must find ways to make themselves useful."

Mabel bristled. "Violet could act if she wanted to. And Alice, I wouldn't talk about acting if I were you. Remember, I was on the stage with you."

Helen leaned over and whispered, "Please, ladies, I've had quite enough wrangling for one evening. Squabbling amongst ourselves is not helping anything."

"Sorry, Helen," apologized Mabel.

"Me too," Alice said begrudgingly.

"Thank you, girls. And Alice, you must remember that Gloria asked our club to help the other groups. And that is exactly what Violet is doing. Max, the director of the Kegworth club, asked her to man the curtains. And Tommy and Mike are doing the light and sound."

"Oh, yes, sorry, I remember," Alice said, looking a little contrite. She sat beside Sam, and Sam grinned cheerfully at her. Alice, compressing her lips, did not return his smile.

Rudy, next to Jolene, took his phone out, stood, turned to take pictures of the audience, and then sat back in his seat, giving Jolene a broad smile. Jolene glared back at him and looked pointedly away. "Don't try to get back into my good books," she said.

"What did I do?"

"If you don't know, I'm not going to tell you." Jolene lifted her chin and pouted. Rudy shrugged and took a selfie; Jolene scowled.

"Congratulations, I thought your play was really funny," the mayor said to his wife as she dropped into the seat next to him.

"That fiasco was not my play," Gloria responded sharply. "It was a disaster from start to finish. I could just sink into a hole and pull it in after me." Her fingers tapped a rapid tattoo on the armrest of her seat.

"Why? The audience laughed. Weren't they supposed to? After all, the play was a melodrama, wasn't it?"

"Oh, for God's sake, Mathew," she spat. "The laughter was in all the wrong places." Looking at the ceiling, Gloria laid her head back and moaned, "This drama festival was supposed to be a feather in my cap."

"And for the town of Glenhaven."

"Yes, of course, for Glenhaven. And look how that is turning out."

"You're Making a mountain out of a molehill. Wait and see how the evening progresses," Gloria's husband said, gently squeezing her hand.

Gloria jerked her hand away. "Seriously, a mountain out of a molehill? You saw that debacle. And damn it all to hell. We're hosting all these horrible people at our house for after-drinks. My position in this town means something, and now I've been humiliated because of that stupid play."

"Now, now, sweetheart."

"Don't now, now me. You have no idea of what I've been through. And I've had to put on a good face and pretend everything is just fine." She exhaled a long sigh, laid her head back, and looked at the ceiling again. "Good God. I can't bear the thought of these horrible little people lording it over me, us. I just don't know how I'm going to survive this evening with them and that dreadful woman, Mandy Swan." Gloria spat out her name and gave a very un-lady-like snort. "I gave that pretentious woman a tour of the town. And can you believe it? She stuck her nose up at absolutely everything. And I was gracious enough to take her to Mary's Bed and Breakfast. Can you believe it? That snob acted like I was asking her to stay in a mud hut. She's lucky I didn't book her into The Last Chance Motel, where everyone else is staying. By the way, that motel is a disgrace. Mathew, you should really do something about that place."

"Darling, I'm just the mayor. I can't regulate the motel. Besides, it's not that bad. Travellers stay there all the time."

"Well, I certainly wouldn't." Gloria compressed her lips into a tight, disapproving line. Her husband raised an eyebrow and sighed.

"This whole weekend is a mess. The play is an absolute failure. And to top it off, the stupid woman goes and gets whiplash. I expect, somehow, she will blame me. What a catastrophe."

"Sweetheart, Miss Swan was in a car accident. Why would she blame you?"

"My only hope is the rest of the festival goes off without a hitch. As you know, I was the driving force to get the damn thing here. If this festival succeeds, that will be at least something." Gloria clasped her hands in prayer mode.

"Darling, I'm sure the festival will be a success."

Gloria looked at her husband. "It just has to be a success. It is the only way for me to save face after the failure of that ridiculous play."

"You're working yourself up. Relax. I bet Miss Swan doesn't think your play is that bad. The crowd loved it. I'm sure she won't be too harsh."

"I told you, Mathew, that disaster was not my play," snapped Gloria. "It's Helen's. And it's her fault. I blame the committee. Why on earth did the committee select Helen to direct?"

"I thought Helen was your candidate?"

Gloria glared at her husband and snapped, "Shush, the play is about to begin."

Chapter Nineteen

The curtains parted slightly, and the director of the Kegworth Players, Max Woodard, stepped out. The tall black-haired man adjusted his round wire-framed glasses on his long aquiline nose and bowed. "Greetings, ladies and gentlemen, guests and fellow actors. The play you are about to see is my play. I wrote it. My play is titled *Hockey is Life.*" He paused for the polite applause, smiled appreciatively and continued. "The inspiration for this play came to me after my team's humbling loss in the playoffs. So, instead of becoming depressed about the loss. I wrote this play. I'll set the scene for you. The goalie is sitting alone in the locker room after the rest of the hockey players have left. The team has just suffered a humiliating loss to their rivals." After receiving another warm round of applause, he bowed and slipped back behind the curtains.

The theme music, *Hockey Night in Canada,* played, and the curtains opened. Sitting near the front of the stage on a long wooden bench, a hockey goalie sat in full gear. The all-white mask covered the goalie's face. The mask looked like Jason's eerie mask in the movie *Friday the 13th.* The goalie ripped off his mask and slung the mask to the floor. The goalie, Craig Bannon, looked at his goalkeeper's hockey stick and chucked it to the floor beside the white mask. He then stripped off his hockey gloves and threw the gloves down onto the stick. Craig hung his head down, shaking it from side to side. He then began unlacing his rollerblade skates.

He stopped and raised his head, his lips turned down, and with a dejected look, he gazed out at the audience.

"The first period was full of promise," he lamented. "I stopped a lot of shots on goal. Sure, a few pucks got in. But I was in command." The big man's shoulders sagged, and he tugged the skate off his left foot. "The second period was awful. And it was not all my fault, you understand. There is no 'I' in team. The defence sucked, and I had no help. If only the forward line would've scored a goal. But we were doomed. And the team blames me."

He slammed his skate on the floor. There was a long, awkward pause. Craig, looking left, fiddled with the skate laces on his right foot.

Finally, after a lengthy delay, Martin Hendrix, wearing a hockey helmet and dressed in a blue and white hockey uniform, skated onstage on rollerblades. He did a pirouette, then skated in a circle around Craig.

"What a game, what a game," Martin chanted, twirling again, then stopping to lean on his hockey stick. The stick slipped, and Martin tipped and teetered. Regaining his balance, he folded his hands on the pommel handle of his hockey stick, grinning and giggling.

Craig looked befuddled; his eyes narrowed.

Martin tilted his head and looked out the corner of his eyes at Craig. Tapping his stick on the floor, he asked in a sing-song voice. "Buddy, buddy. Are you awake, old buddy?"

Craig frowned, then resting his forearms on his knees, he said, "I thought everyone had left. The team is blaming me for the loss. It's so unfair."

"Not me, old buddy." Martin tossed his blue and white helmet to the floor and stick-handled the helmet, shooting it toward Craig.

The hockey helmet hit the leg of the bench, rolling to the front of the stage. "Nice save," he giggled.

Craig looked at the helmet, then back at Martin. "Yeah, the game. What a lousy loss. Just like my life."

Martin skated up to his helmet, grinned at the audience and flipped the helmet up with his stick. Catching it, he popped the helmet onto his head.

Mabel applauded along with the audience. She expected a long, tedious, drawn-out drama about the meaning of life, but this looked promising.

Martin beamed and bowed to the audience, then skated back to Craig. "Yep, you're lousy like your hockey," he said.

"What the hell?" Craig barked, then regaining his composure, he asked, "What do you mean hockey is like life?"

Martin skated away from the bench and spread his arms as if flying. Stretching one leg out behind him, he soared across the stage. The audience clapped and roared with laughter.

"What do you mean, hockey is like life?" Craig yelled as Martin flew past him.

Martin skated back to centre stage, then, holding his hockey stick close to his body, he spun around. After two revolutions, he stopped, swayed, and planted the stick on the floor. His lips twitched, and he grinned. "Damn, that's harder than it looks. I'm dizzy as hell. How the hell does Kurt Browning do this?"

"Hockey is like life," Craig said in a stage whisper, veins popping out on his neck. He stood, one sock-footed, the other still encased in a skate; he limped toward Martin.

Martin, snickering, pointed to the hole in Craig's sock. "I can see your big toe," he taunted, skating backward, away from a red-faced Craig.

"What do you mean, hockey is like life?" Craig roared for the fourth time.

Mabel felt that everything was not going as it should. If Martin was improvising, it sure didn't look like Craig was in on the act.

Martin stopped just before crashing into the stage flat. He spun around and said, "Phew, I was almost a goner."

"For God's sake, hockey is like life. It has its ups and downs," shouted a voice from offstage.

Martin turned and skated to the front of the stage, spinning the hockey stick in his hands like a baton and reciting, "Hockey is like life. It has an up and a down." The stick spun out of his hands and fell to the floor. Chuckling, Martin bent to pick up his stick. Limping up behind him, Craig grabbed the younger man's hockey jersey, pulling the sweater over Martin's head. Martin, escaping his clutches, skated away, guffawing. "Stick to goaltending, old buddy. That's what you're good at. Oh, wait, you were a sieve." Skating in a circle around the hapless man, Martin laughed as Craig kept reaching out to grab him.

A voice from offstage shouted. "Stop acting like an ass. Sit the hell down and get back on the script."

Mabel listened in shocked silence as the audience erupted in laughter. Things were falling apart. Maybe Glenhaven's silly farce wasn't that bad. At least compared to The Kegworth Players.

Craig scowled at the audience's laughter, and Martin beamed.

Chapter Twenty

When the curtain fell, Mabel's reaction was one of relief for the luckless Craig. The play had continued at a chaotic pace, with Martin playing to the crowd for laughs while Craig, bursting with anger, tried to keep the play on track. The curtain call was awkward. Craig, glaring at a grinning Martin, took a quick bow. Then he grabbed the young man by the arm, pushing and pulling the reluctant man, still grinning and waving to the crowd, back behind the curtain.

As Violet joined the Glenhaven actors in the second row, Mabel looked over at Mandy Swan. She was feverishly writing in her notebook.

"What happened, Violet? I gather the play was supposed to be a drama, not a comedy."

"Oh, Mabel, you have no idea. I couldn't believe what was happening on stage. And neither could Max. Martin's over-acting was even worse than Sam's. It was terrible. That boy was completely out of control. I feel so sorry for poor Max. Backstage, he was tearing his hair out as Martin kept hamming it up. I think the boy might have been drinking or something." Violet abruptly stopped speaking as Max, the director and Craig filed offstage to take seats next to the Glenhaven cast. Martin followed slowly at a distance, plopping down next to Gloria, smiling and winking at her. Gloria, screwing up her lips in distaste, looked away.

Mandy rose from her chair, marching up the steps to the stage, her long coral skirt swishing as she walked. She stood in front of the burgundy curtains, looked down at the actors, pressed her hand to her neck brace, and sighed loudly. "I can honestly say I've never witnessed two performances like this in all my years of acting, directing and adjudicating." The audience cheered and applauded enthusiastically.

The adjudicator frowned at the crowd, tapping her notepad against her leg. "I'm glad you enjoyed the performances. But I certainly did not!" There was an awkward silence from the partisan hometown crowd, quickly followed by loud jeers. Mandy's eyes narrowed. She waited for silence, then continued. "I'll start with the first play. Performed by The Glenhaven Players and performed very badly, I'm sorry to say. Helen, I know this is your first stint as a director. And I hope for the love of theatre. This will be your last. Your actors were a bumbling bunch of buffoons. And those actors and their performance are your responsibility. You, Helen, could win the award for the worst director ever."

Helen's face flushed. She bit her lip and hung her head, looking down at her hands, twisting her soggy lace hanky.

"Hey, lady, don't talk about Helen like that. Helen's a great director," Mike yelled from the back of the hall. Applause and cheers from the crowd followed Mike's outburst.

Mayor Hamilton stood and faced the crowd. "Please, everyone, let Miss Swan do her job. We may not all agree with her. But she is our guest, and we have invited her here to give her judgement."

"Thank you, Mayor Hamilton. And dear friends of theatre, let me tell you, it gives me no pleasure to give a bad review, just as it gave me no pleasure to watch what happened onstage."

Hissing and booing followed Mandy as she strode to stand at the stage apron, looking down at the Glenhaven cast. The mayor stood again and put his finger to his lips, signalling the audience to be quiet.

The adjudicator raised an eyebrow as she waited for the crowd to settle down. Then Mandy curled her lips as if tasting something sour and continued her critique. "The list of debacles is endless. But first, I have to comment on your shoddy set. The couch falling apart was a ridiculous spectacle. Who was in charge of props? No one? It is up to your stage manager to make sure all your props are on stage and in proper working order."

Violet, red-faced, ducked her head as Mandy paused to consult her notes. "And oh yes, let's not forget the missing cocktail glass, again sloppiness from your stage manager. But I have to say the most damning was the showboating. I'll get back to this gross and obvious overacting in a minute."

The Glenhaven cast's heads swung in Sam's direction. With a puzzled look, Sam nodded and asked, "Who is she talking about?"

"Like you don't know," hissed Alice.

"Shush, Miss Swan is talking," cautioned Helen.

"I will now bring your attention to all the missed cues and lost lines that were glaringly conspicuous. And yes, one actor stood out in the missed lines department. And I will get back to her as well." Mandy's eyes blazed with disdain as she looked down at Jolene. Jolene squirmed in her seat. "But all of you could have used some help. Did you even have a prompter?"

Gloria stood, face flushed, her nostrils flared. "I'll have you know I was the prompter, but none of this disaster is my fault. My script was misplaced, and I had a script from another play," she said, defending herself.

"That, my dear woman," Mandy said condescendingly. "Is entirely your fault. It's up to you to have the proper manuscript."

Glaring at the adjudicator, Gloria sat down. While her husband patted one hand, Martin reached over and patted the other. She quickly withdrew both hands, clasping them tightly in her lap, scowling at each man.

"As I said, the list is endless. Some of you didn't even bother to follow the script. And that juvenile improvisation. If that's what it was, the mock fight scene. And if it was improvisational, it was very badly done. It certainly wasn't in the script."

Another course of boos followed her critique. The mayor stood again to face the crowd. He held up his hands, waving at the people who had risen from their seats. "Please, please, this is not how the good citizens of Glenhaven act." He remained standing until the boos ceased and the crowd sat.

Mandy's eyes sparkled, and her lips twisted in a half-smile as she consulted her notes. It seemed to Mabel the woman was enjoying the audience's reaction. "And the butler, what a ridiculous spectacle. A woman dressed as a butler in a costume that was a cross between Charlie Chapman and Moe from the Three Stooges."

"Charlie and Moe, who?" asked Jolene.

Mabel's eyebrows rose. Charlie Chapman and Moe? Really? Okay, maybe the mustache was a mistake, but Moe?

"It couldn't be helped. Mabel had to step in and take the role of the butler. You may remember Helen telling you Sherman Mahan died. He died in this very theatre, just steps away from where you stand," Violet yelled, defending her friend.

Looking disconcerted, Mandy shifted her feet and said, "I'm sorry for your loss. But the costume was a farce."

"It may have escaped your notice," Mabel said, jutting out her chin. "But the play is a farce."

"Oh, that did not escape my notice. That whole pitiful performance was a farce in more ways than one. That accent of yours was the worst I've ever had the displeasure to hear."

Mabel pressed her lips together and crossed her arms.

"And as I said, this was a poorly acted. And a poorly directed play."

"I'm warning you for the last time. Do not talk about my wife like that," bellowed Mike.

Unfazed by Mike's threats, Mandy continued. "Oh, and let's not forget the many, many entrances by the maid. Which made me wonder if you even rehearsed." Alice opened her mouth to speak, then closed it, her eyes glaring up at the adjudicator; she elbowed Ned as he snickered.

"And now it's time to talk about booby Sue," Mandy smiled snidely down at Jolene. "I say booby because you were. Apart from the butler, you had the worst accent. You missed line after line, and when you actually managed to remember a line. You were totally unconvincing as a southern belle."

"You're not being fair. I Know why you're saying these awful things. It's because of your hair. And your hair isn't my fault. I was a great southern belle. And my accent was pure southern," Jolene said defiantly. "And the only reason I missed a few lines was that the leg on the couch broke."

Mandy reached her hand up to adjust her turban and glared down at Jolene. "If I were you, I would not even mention the word hair." Mandy inhaled and exhaled big breaths, then in an ice-cold tone, she said, "I am always fair. You did not know your lines. Your lame excuses don't count. And let's go back to your accent. I think yours was atrocious. And it's my opinion that matters. And you're acting, if you could call it that. Was the worst I've ever had the misfortune to sit through."

"That evil woman is taking revenge on me just because she didn't like how I styled her hair," Jolene pouted, muttering.

"You did miss a lot of cues," Rudy said as he put his arm around her shoulders.

"And if I did blow a line or two. It's all your fault," Jolene snarled, brushing his arm off.

"How is it my fault? First, you blame the couch, and now you're blaming me. How about Sam? He's the one who is high. Who's next? Poor old Sherman?"

Sam rubbed his chin, looking puzzled at Rudy and Jolene.

"Shush," hissed Alice.

"And one last note, and it's a very big note indeed. Big Daddy, played by." Mandy consulted her notes.

"Me, that would be little old me. I played Big Daddy," shouted Sam. He stood and waved at the adjudicator. "I thought we did a bang-up job."

"Sam, sit down," Helen said, tugging his sleeve. Grinning, Sam complied, sinking back onto his seat.

With a sneer on her face, Mandy shook her notebook at Sam. "Bang-up job? More like slap, dash, and crash. I don't know what you thought you were doing up there. You were a walking, talking disaster. You were the worst of the worst. It's a toss-up between you and the figure skating hockey player who was the worst scene-stealer. I have never seen anything like it in all my years of adjudication." A ring of boos followed her critique.

Sam looked puzzled. "I didn't miss a line."

The adjudicator sniffed, rolled her eyes, and walked back to stand in the middle of the stage apron. She paused to read her notes, then looked down at the Kegworth Players and said, "Now for the *Hockey is Life*. Apparently, it is not, as that phrase was repeated innumerable times. Yes, Helen Graham is a terrible director. But—"

"Hey, what did I tell you?" roared Mike.

The mayor stood and hollered. "Mike, settle down."

"Fine, but she better stop talking about my wife."

Satisfied, Mike was not going to interrupt again. The mayor sat down.

Gloria smiled at her husband and squeezed his hand.

"As I was about to say, Helen wasn't the worst. Max, you only had two actors to contend with. And why you cast that buffoon in your drama play is beyond me. I assume the play was supposed to be a drama. But it certainly was not."

"Yes," Max said sadly. "My play was supposed to be a drama."

"You jerk. We damn well know whose fault this is." Craig leaned over the seat, swatting Martin on the back of the head.

Martin rubbed the back of his head, a puzzled look on his face. "Me? What did I do?"

Max grabbed the big man, pulling him back. "Leave it. What's done is done."

"Yeah, I guess," Craig said, slumping back down onto his seat.

Martin leaned over to Gloria and said, "Craig is a little ticked at me because I got all the laughs."

"Get away from me." Gloria gave the man a dirty look, pushed him away and hissed, "Mathew, change places with me."

"Yes, dear," he said, swiftly changing seats.

Mandy waited until the mayor was settled, then continued with her critique of the Kegworth Players, blaming Martin for their play's failure.

Max and Craig kept nodding in agreement.

Martin, open-mouthed, had closed his eyes and snuggled up to the mayor. The mayor, uttering a disgusted groan, pushed the man's head off his shoulder. Yawning, Martin looked around wide-eyed.

The adjudicator looked out at the crowd. "I'd like to apologize on behalf of the actors and everyone involved in tonight's performances. This is an amateur drama festival. But there is a big difference between being an amateur and being sloppy. Tonight's performances were just plain sloppy."

Boos from the biased hometown crowd followed her statement.

Unfazed by the chorus of boos, Mandy continued. "I can only hope tomorrow night's plays will be an improvement. The bar is set so low. I expect they can't help but be better." She bowed to the silent crowd and strode across the stage to the small steps leading to the ground floor. As Mandy took her first step, the theatre lights went out. A piercing scream rang out through the darkness, followed by a loud thud.

Chapter Twenty-One

The lights came back on as suddenly as they went out. Mandy Swan lay in a crumpled heap at the bottom of the stairs. Her turban had fallen off, revealing her tight, frizzy white hair, making her look like an aged Orphan Annie. She moaned and swore, crying, "My leg, my leg."

Mayor Hamilton sprung up from his seat and rushed to her side. He was quickly followed by his wife Gloria, Mabel, Violet, and the cast from the Glenhaven Players. Actors from the other drama clubs pushed and shoved to get ahead of the audience members. Everyone was surging down the aisles to get a look at the adjudicator lying at the foot of the stairs.

The mayor knelt, offering a hand to the injured woman. "Here, take my hand, Miss Swan. I'm so sorry the lights went out. I don't know how that happened."

"No, don't, wait. Stop. She might have broken something," advised Mabel.

Mandy tried to stand, then collapsed back on the floor, shrieking in pain. "Yes, yes, it's my leg, it's my leg. Get away from me. My leg is broken," Mandy yelled, slapping at the mayor's hand. "Call a doctor, call an ambulance. Somebody, for God's sake, help me."

Mabel and Violet knelt beside the woman. "Don't move. Stay still," advised Mabel. "You don't know what is broken."

"I bloody well know what's broken; it's my leg. What's the matter with you people? I said get the hell away from me. This isn't a freak show. I'm injured. For God's sake, get the medics here. Surely, to God, in this one-horse town, you have medics?"

Mayor Hamilton stood, scanning the people crowding the aisle. "The Paramedics are here. They're coming," he said. The mayor puffed out his chest and turned to address the crowd. "Your mayor was, as always, prepared. I arranged for Connie and Harvey to attend."

Harvey Hanover, the tall redhead paramedic, and his partner Connie Zhao, carrying their EMS medical kits, were pushing through the crowd.

A pale-faced Jolene rushed up and picked up Mandy's turban, offering the yellow headdress to Mandy, who lay on the floor. The adjudicator's coral skirt had ridden up, revealing her long, white, lacey bloomers.

"Get away from me," Mandy shrieked, swatting the turban. "Damn it. My arm, my arm."

The turban twirled and spun, unravelling as it flew across the floor, landing in front of the stage. Jolene scooted over, picking up the scarf and bunching it in her hands. "I don't think your hair looks that bad. Do you?" she asked worriedly.

"My Hair? Can't you see my leg is broken? And my arm. I think I've broken my arm. Someone get this imbecile away from me."

"Are you sure you don't want your scarf?" Jolene held out the scrunched yellow ball.

"Oh, sweetie. Miss Swan is more concerned with her arm and leg," Helen said, ushering Jolene away from the adjudicator. "I don't think she is worried about her hair."

The audience members who had followed the actors down the aisle pushed their way forward. They gawked at the sight, whispered to each other, and pointed at the frizzy white-haired woman sprawled at the bottom of the stairs.

"What the hell happened to her hair?" asked a muscular, balding man.

"I don't know." giggled a stout, middle-aged woman. "But do you see what she's wearing?"

"I know bloomers. Who wears bloomers?" chortled a severe-looking woman dressed in a red and black floral dress.

"Stand aside, make room," commanded Connie as she and Harvey forced their way through the crowd that was cramming the aisle.

"I'm going to sue you and your nasty little town," screamed Mandy as she levered herself into a sitting position. "I hate this horrible place. First, my car is rear-ended. And I have whiplash. Now my leg and my arm are broken."

"No, no. Probably not broken," the mayor said, backing hurriedly away.

"What the hell do you know? Are you a doctor?" she shrieked.

"No, no, sorry, I'm not. But Harvey and Connie are coming." Mayor Hamilton turned and hollered, "Hey, you people, get out of the way! Let Connie and Harvey through." He turned to the injured woman lying at the foot of the stairs. "I'm so very, very sorry about this unfortunate accident." He apologized. "I feel just terrible." He leaned down to whisper in his wife's ear. "Remind me to check the town's liability insurance."

Harvey knelt to examine Mandy as his partner opened her medical kit.

"Stand back, give us some room," commanded Connie.

The mayor turned to the inquisitive onlookers and ordered in a strong voice, "Please, everyone, either go back to your seats or go home. The show is over. We must let Harvey and Connie do their job." Muttering and murmuring, the crowd slowly left. But the Glenhaven cast, the Kegworth Players and the actors from the other drama clubs remained firmly in place, watching with curiosity as the paramedics examined the injured woman.

Standing beside Mayor Hamilton and his wife, Violet murmured, "It's lucky the paramedics are here and prepared."

"There is no luck about it. I told you it was good planning on my part. They don't call me Mr. Fixit for nothing," bragged the mayor.

"So clever of you, Mr. Mayor," Helen said.

The mayor leaned down and whispered. "I gave them both free tickets."

"Oh, I see. Well, it was a good thing you did."

"What happened to the lights?" Tommy asked, peeking over Mike's shoulder.

"I wish I knew," muttered the mayor. "Yesterday, the furnace went on the fritz in the hall. Now these damn lights. We never had problems with the lights in here before."

Harvey stood and announced, "We're taking Miss Swan to the emergency at the Kipling hospital."

"About time; you took long enough," Mandy snarled.

"Well, we're hooped. That's it for the festival. What an absolute disaster," wailed Gloria, throwing up her hands.

"No, I shall still adjudicate your festival. My broken limbs won't prevent me from honouring my obligations. The show must go on."

"Oh, my gosh, thank you, thank you, Miss Swan," gushed Gloria. "I knew from the moment I laid eyes on you that you were a truly good and generous person. And now I see what a trooper you are. Your bravery just makes me want to weep." Gloria covered her eyes with her hands and sniffed.

"Yes, I am," Mandy said stoutly. "I will adjudicate this festival. That is, if I'm not confined to the hospital."

"Even if your arm or leg is broken, they won't keep you in the hospital," Violet said.

"For Pete's sake, would everyone stop saying broken," snapped the mayor.

"And if I'm not kept in the hospital, how the heck am I supposed to get back here? Who is going to bring me back? I obviously can't drive, and even if I could. I can't, thanks to that goon who rear-ended me this afternoon. My car is damaged. God, what a town."

Taking down her hands, her eyes dry, Gloria smiled cheerfully and offered. "No worries, my dear Miss Swan. I'll bring you back to Mary's Bed and Breakfast." Then she turned to the actors, grouped behind her, and said, "My dear wonderful thespians. I'm so sorry. I'm afraid I will have to cancel the party I was hosting tonight for all of you lovely people. I was so looking forward to entertaining you." She looked at her husband and instructed, "Make sure those girls I've hired put the food away. Especially the perishables, those need to be refrigerated."

"Don't worry, darling, I'll take care of everything. You just look after our dear Miss Swan."

"No food? I'm starving," complained Martin.

"Yeah, I could eat a horse," agreed Sam, his arm draped over Martin's shoulders.

"Me too," voiced an actor from the Maryland Drama group. "The Last Chance Motel where we are staying doesn't even have a restaurant."

The mayor looked at his wife and then back at the actors. "Oh, well, maybe we can have the party—"

"No, we are absolutely not hosting a party tonight. Not while poor dear Miss Swan is in the emergency with God knows what is broken."

Her husband gritted his teeth. "Would you stop saying broken? We don't know if Miss Swan has broken anything. Maybe she is just bruised."

"Regardless. Forget about your stomachs. It's poor dear Miss Swan that is important now," snapped Gloria. She shot her husband a warning look before strutting off to follow the paramedics, who were carrying the adjudicator to the door.

"My darling wife is right. And Pam and Ally's café is downtown. They might still be open. And there is the burger place out by the highway," suggested the mayor.

"Thanks a bunch," snorted a Berryman actor. "Welcome to the great town of Glenhaven."

"My wife and I are so sorry that we must cancel the party tonight. But as my beloved wife pointed out, having a party after Miss Swan's unfortunate accident would be very disrespectful. We just can not celebrate while Miss Swan is, well, perhaps, in the hospital. Which, of course, we all hope is not the case," the mayor finished hurriedly.

"Not much to celebrate tonight anyway," grumbled Craig, giving Martin a dirty look.

Mabel saw Martin return Craig's look with a shamed face. At least the boy had sobered up and realized he'd ruined their play. She looked over at Sam; he, too, seemed to be sobering up. Sam denied he was drunk. If he wasn't, why had he acted so out of character?

The mayor, clapping his hands, said, "But I promise you tomorrow night, after the awards and the cup are presented, there will be a big party at our house. A proper celebration."

Gloria stopped mid-step. She spun rapidly around, glowering at her husband. "At our house? You're inviting everyone to our house?"

"Darling, we have all that delicious food you've had prepared. What else would we do with it? And a party will be a great way to celebrate the finish of your successful drama festival." Mayor Hamilton smiled at the actors gathered around him. "And I'm sure all the clubs will want to celebrate the winners in a spirit of camaraderie."

Mabel, who had been eavesdropping on Gloria, recalled the mayor's wife's lament and grinned. What was it Gloria said? Something about hosting horrible little people. Mabel's eyes sparkling with mischief, said, "What a good idea. Thank you, Mayor Hamilton. We know how much you and Gloria are looking forward to hosting us."

Scowling, Gloria slammed the door and left the building.

"I could do with a beer. Anyone want to join me?" asked Grant Middleman, the shaven-headed actor from the Maryland Musers.

There was a chorus of yeses from the other drama groups.

"Yeah, and I wanna propose the first toast to that frizzy white witch's trip down those stairs. It couldn't happen to a better person," Mike boomed.

"Mike, please, that isn't nice," admonished Helen. "Mandy Swan isn't my favourite person. But she fell. And she could have broken more—"

"Yeah, she could have broken her neck," muttered Mike, lumbering out the door.

Chapter Twenty-Two

Mabel cradled her cream-coloured wall phone receiver against her shoulder as she waited for Violet to answer. She took a dishcloth and wiped the toast crumbs off her red laminated countertop. The long cord from the telephone dragged on the floor behind her.

"Why don't you ever use your cell phone?"

Mabel wrinkled her nose at Violet's response. "Why don't you ever answer your phone with a hello? And how do you know I'm not?"

"I do have call-display. Unlike some people I know, namely you."

"I do too. So there." Mabel tossed her dishcloth into her sink and pulled a chair from her chrome kitchen table. She nudged her orange cat, Gertrude, off the chair and sat down. Gertrude stretched and then leapt back up onto Mabel's lap. "Regardless, have you heard any news?"

"Yes, I have. Gloria phoned me; she told me she has her hands full with Mandy Swan."

Mabel smirked. "Those two deserve each other."

"I'm not too fond of Mandy, but Gloria means well. She is just a little, well, you know."

"You mean a little full of herself?" Mabel pulled another red leatherette kitchen chair out from the kitchen table and put her feet on it. "Did she break her leg?"

"You mean Mandy?"

Mabel's lips twitched into a broad smile as she scratched Gertrude behind the ear. Her best friend, Violet, was always so literal. "Yes, I mean Mandy."

"Gloria told me Mandy has a small foot fracture, and she has a sprained wrist. And Mathew is very upset. He is worried about a lawsuit."

"No doubt. A broken foot to go along with her whiplash isn't exactly good advertising for tourism."

"Gloria said she had to listen to Mandy rant all the way home. Then, when she took her to Mary's B&B, Gloria had to help Mandy get undressed and into bed."

"I wonder what the trendy Miss Swan wears to bed." Mabel chuckled. "A long flannel nightgown? Did you see her white bloomers? Who wears bloomers?"

"Everyone has their own style," Violet said kindly. "And, of course, I didn't ask what she wore to bed. Anyway, this morning, Gloria has to return to the B&B and help Mandy get dressed. And poor Gloria isn't too happy about that. Her words to me were. '*The woman only sprained her wrist.*' But she will do it because she needs Mandy to adjudicate tonight."

Mabel grinned; the mayor's wife wouldn't like being anyone's servant. And certainly not for Mandy Swan.

"Gloria suggested that one of us from the festival committee would be better able to help Mandy get dressed. But when she mentioned that to Mandy. Mandy was adamant Gloria had to do it."

"Last night, I overheard her complaining to her husband about Mandy. This must be really grating on Gloria's nerves."

"I expect so. It's hard to see Gloria acting like a lady's maid." Violet chuckled. "But the good news is that even though Mandy has suffered all these injuries. The show, as they say, will go on. She will adjudicate this evening's performances. But there will be no acting workshop this morning."

"I'm good with that. Although we certainly could do with some help. We all had a hand in our bomb."

"I still can't figure out how that cocktail glass got miss-placed."

"Oh, Violet, forget about that silly glass. That was the least of the screw-ups."

"I don't care. I'm sort of a methodical person. And it irked me that I might have misplaced that glass."

Mabel nodded. "Sort of? You are the most organized person I know. But stuff happens. Forget it."

"Well, as it turns out. I don't think I miss-placed the darn thing. After our play was over, I searched for that cocktail glass backstage. And I found the glass lying behind the backdrop underneath a script. And the script was of our play."

"Under the script from our play? That's strange."

"I know, weird, right? The script was Gloria's prompting script. Remember, she had the wrong script."

"I remember all right. Jolene missed most of her cues. Oh, and speaking of Jolene. I overheard her telling her grandmother she did Mandy's hair. Did you see that woman's weird hair?"

"Yes, of course I did. The poor woman's hair looks like a white Brillo pad."

"What the heck did Jolene do? I've had my hair cut there. Is that where you go to get your hair dyed?"

"Yes, I do. As you know, I'm very fussy about how my hair looks. I've never had a problem at Flo's salon."

Mabel smiled; Violet was very proud of her red hair.

"It's no wonder Mandy wore that turban. She would certainly not be happy. I remember she had her lovely, long blonde hair done up in a kind of braid when she came to the welcome ceremonies. I wonder why Mandy decided to change her hairdo on the festival's opening day?"

Mabel frowned. "I don't know."

"Do you think Mandy's adjudication has anything to do with the bad hairdo?"

"It probably didn't help." Mabel sighed and bit her bottom lip. "But we shot ourselves in the foot. The only consistent actor was Rudy. And dear Miss Swan didn't even mention him."

"Maybe Rudy will get the best actor award."

"But she didn't like his fisticuff fight with Sam."

"I guess. How about Ned? She didn't mention him either."

"Seriously, old hotfoot Ned. Remember him cackling his crazy laugh every time Jolene missed a line? Just because she didn't include him in her critique doesn't mean she liked or approved of his acting. But she didn't miss me, and she sure didn't like my costume or my accent,"

"Well, maybe the mustache was a bit much."

"Yeah, maybe," agreed Mabel reluctantly. "And much as I hate to admit it. We all deserved Mandy's negative critique. Except for Helen, I feel sorry for her. I guess she wasn't the best director. She is a timid soul. But what happened onstage wasn't her fault. Sam went completely off the rails. His crazy, out-of-control performance was the worst. He was the tipping point. I can't understand what got into him."

"What got into him was alcohol. Nerves, I guess," suggested Violet.

"And he wasn't the only one who tossed back a few. The figure skating hockey player Martin must have also hoisted a few. Anyway, are you doing anything this morning? Like, are you conferring with the festival committee?"

"No, the committee members are pretty much leaving everything up to Gloria now. She has sort of, well, she has sort of alienated most of the ladies."

"Except you."

"Someone has to help her."

"Violet, you are way too nice."

"I feel sorry for her. She has to look after Mandy. And Mandy is distraught. Of course, she has good reason because of everything that has happened to her."

"Maybe someone is trying to sabotage the drama festival."

"Sabotage the drama festival?"

"Yes, our missing prop. You never mislay anything, and you found that cocktail glass under Gloria's missing script. How or who put the glass there? And Gloria just didn't lose her script. She had a script from another play. Who switched Gloria's script? I admit all that is minor. But there's Sherman's so-called accident, which was definitely not minor. The poor guy died. And if you think about it, the banister breaking and him falling down those stairs was a very strange accident. And then..." Mabel didn't finish. Her thoughts went back to that night. A car almost ran her down. Was it on purpose? Or was she being paranoid?

"Oh, Mabel, don't go there. Strange or not, the railing broke. It was an accident."

"Okay, but what about the rear-ending of Mandy's car? Was that an accident, too?"

"Hence the word accident. Anyway, why would anyone deliberately rear-end Mandy's car? That's just silly."

"It's not all that silly. There would be no drama festival if Mandy couldn't adjudicate. When the car accident failed, they tried something else. Think about it. The lights went out at the precise moment Mandy was coming down the stairs."

"Oh, for God's sake, not everything is a conspiracy. Sometimes things just happen."

"I never said it was a conspiracy," defended Mabel. "I said sabotage."

"Whatever."

"It wouldn't hurt to find that cell phone of Sherman's. Someone called him, and he went out on the landing. And we know what happened then."

"And if we do find his phone. What will that prove? How would the caller know Sherman would leave the stage and go onto the landing? And lean on the railing? They wouldn't."

"Hum, okay," Mabel reluctantly agreed. "But if he hadn't gone out onto the basement landing to take that call, he wouldn't have fallen. And maybe it wasn't a call. Perhaps it was a text that he got. We heard an alert on his phone. We don't know if it was a call or a text. If it was a text, it could lead us to—"

"For goodness' sake, that old railing was faulty. I know the screw discrepancy is odd. But any one of us could have fallen. I don't think Sherman was a target. We all used the stairs to go to the basement."

The memory of the speeding car flashed through Mabel's mind. "Aha, right, sabotage. Faulty is the keyword. I think someone tampered with the railing. Maybe it didn't matter who fell as long as someone did. Maybe they only wanted to hurt someone. Not kill them. If the Glenhaven drama group had to pull out of the festival, the festival would've been cancelled."

"But we didn't pull out of the festival. And the festival wasn't cancelled," Violet said.

"The saboteur wouldn't know that."

"Saboteur, really! That's a little farfetched. Who would hate the festival so much they would risk killing someone?"

"I don't know, but irregardless, I'm going to the theatre to look for Sherman's phone."

"Not, irregardless. Regardless," corrected Violet.

"Right, regardless, and I know the phone may not tell us anything. But I'm going to the theatre to look for it. And besides, Crystal Sherman's girlfriend wants it. I want to get the phone for her. I kind of feel guilty going to visit her to offer my condolence under false pretences."

"You mean snooping."

"Call it what you may, I say, investigating. Regardless, do you want to come with me? I can pick you up?"

"Okay, I guess," Violet reluctantly agreed. "I guess it wouldn't hurt to look. If your theory is right, Sherman was. Hum, what do they call it?"

"Collateral damage," supplied Mabel.

Chapter Twenty-Three

The warm morning sun glinting off the windshield of a battered old white Jaguar momentarily blinded Mabel as she parked her old purple Pontiac next to a blue van.

"I don't know why I let you talk me into this," Violet muttered as she got out of the car.

"Yes, you do. You can deny it all you like, but you know you love a good mystery as much as I do." Mabel shut her car door and momentarily stood, looking at all the vehicles parked in the theatre parking lot. Rehearsals were taking place for the evening's performance. She walked to a silver Subaru and leaned down, scanning the front of the car. "Are you thinking of buying one? It's about time you pensioned off your purple princess."

"There is nothing wrong with my car; besides, I don't think I could drive any of these new models. All the electronic gadgets in these new cars scare the life out of me. I don't know how you stand it: your car beeps, dings, tweets, and talks to you. I don't need some so-called new smart car. I turn the key on, and my faithful old car starts. I'm happy with my old purple princess, as you like to call it, the princess runs like a top. And it never talks back to me," Mabel said, moving on to check out a late-model white Ford truck.

"Then why are you interested in these cars?"

"Someone rear-ended Mandy's car. Their vehicle would have suffered some damage, too. I'm checking to see if someone from one of these drama clubs was the culprit."

"Seriously? Do you think the only person capable of rear-ending Mandy's car is an actor? The culprit could easily be anyone from Glenhaven. Or even someone who was passing through town."

"I suppose you're right." Mabel went down the row of cars, peering at the bumpers. "But don't you think it's suspicious, or at least interesting, that someone crashed into her car?"

"I think it's a criminal offence. Poor Mandy suffered whiplash."

"And don't forget, I almost got knocked down the other night by a car when I walked home after rehearsals."

"That was definitely a hit-and-run. Well, an almost hit-and-run," Violet said, following Mabel. "Thank goodness that idiot never hit you." She stopped as Mabel knelt, examining another car. "You should have reported it."

"Looking back on things now, maybe I should have. First, poor Sherman fell through that railing to his death. And the same night, that car careened up on the sidewalk, nearly hitting me. Then, someone rear-ended Mandy's car. And last night the lights went out, and she fell off the stage. Coincidence, I wonder. Or is someone trying to stop the festival.

Violet folded her arms across her chest and looked down at her friend. "So your theory is the car that nearly hit you and the one that rammed into Mandy's car is the same."

"Well, it could be. But it's not any of these," Mabel said as she scanned the bumper of the last vehicle in the parking lot.

"I told you."

"You told me what?"

"That the culprit driving that car is not an actor from the drama festival."

"Maybe all the actors don't have their cars here. Maybe someone caught a ride, because their car is in the shop, getting their fender repaired." Smiling, Mabel wiggled her eyebrows up and down. "And my spidey instincts tell me that I'm right, and the car that tried to run me down is the same car that rear-ended Mandy's car."

"There you go, jumping to conclusions." Violet shook her head. "And this absurd idea you have that someone is out to stop the drama festival." Mabel started to speak. Violet held up her hand. "And even if you are right. Which I highly doubt. Why would someone who is in the drama festival want to stop the festival?"

"You know you aren't a very good Watson to my Sherlock. You are always putting a damper on my ideas."

Violet's eyes twinkled as she chuckled. "Sherlock? Oh, I don't think so. Anyway, you need me. I'm the voice of reason."

"Whatever."

"Come on, let's nip down to the basement and take a look for that phone while the rehearsals are going on."

Mabel laughed. "Ah-ha, I knew you were just as interested as I am."

"Interested doesn't mean I suspect foul play."

"Don't say foul play. It reminds me of our play last night."

They mounted the cement steps entering the theatre through the large wooden main doors. The lobby's walls were decorated with old, faded theatre posters from the past. A counter with a glass front displaying chocolate bars and chips ran along one wall. A modern, shiny soda-pop vending dispenser hummed beside an old-fashioned popcorn machine. A yellowed sign propped up on top of the machine read. *'Out of order.'* Across the lobby, facing the front doors, was a raised wooden booth with a plexiglass window.

Behind the window set a tall padded stool. A small, curved opening in the plexiglass allowed the patrons to pay for their tickets to the performances. On either side of the booth, green wooden doors led to the theatre proper.

Mabel and Violet circled the little booth. As they entered through the small green door, they could hear voices. Rehearsals were well underway. The Maryland Musers were onstage. Violet started down the aisle, only to have Mabel tap her on the shoulder and grab her arm, pulling her back.

"What?" Violet asked softly.

"Follow me." Mabel led Violet along the back wall of the theatre, behind the middle row of theatre seats. She stopped under the stairs that led up to the sound booth. "Take a look," Mabel said, pointing to a black electrical breaker box on the wall.

"Okay, I get what you're showing me," Violet whispered.

"Look, there's no lock on the breaker box door," Mabel whispered back and opened the small door.

"But how would someone know which switch to turn off? There are no labels. Oh, no." Violet brought her hand to her mouth, looking horrified. "It has to be Mike or Tommy. No one else would know which switch to turn off."

"Not necessarily. Watch." Mabel swiped across all the little black switches, and all the lights in the hall went off.

There were yells and curses from the stage as Mabel hurriedly swiped the switches to the on position.

"What the heck do you think you're playing at?" yelled Sheeran Maier, the director of the Maryland Musers. The frumpy woman marched up to the apron of the stage, peering out. "Who's out there? What are you doing here?"

"Oh, sorry, it's just us," Mabel yelled back.

"Us who?" shouted Sheeran, her hand above her eyes, peering out.

"I'm Violet Ficher, and this is Mabel Havelock, my friend. We didn't mean to cause any trouble. We just ah." Violet bit her lip.

"We just happen to bump into the breaker box. And somehow, the lights went out," Mabel said, trotting down the aisle toward the stage. Violet, looking embarrassed, followed.

The four actors who had been sitting in a semi-circle on stage joined their director at the front of the apron.

"You have no business in here. We're rehearsing." Magdalen Kaminski, the tall, auburn-haired girl, had a script in her hand, which she shook at Violet and Mabel.

"Magdalen is right. We're mid-rehearsal. We don't need this interruption. Did you turn out the lights?" Sheeran, the director, scowled down at them.

"What play are you doing?" asked Mabel, trying to divert their attention from the sudden blackout.

"We are performing the play *Not Again*. It's about a self-help group of divorcees. Now, please leave so we can get back to rehearsing."

"You're doing the same play as the Berryman club?"

"No, we are not. The Berryman drama club is doing *Never Again*. Their play is about two people who are getting a divorce. It's completely different," sniffed Sheeran contemptuously.

"Hey, are they allowed to watch?" asked Levi, the square-jawed man leaning over the director's shoulder.

"We haven't come to watch. We're headed to the basement," assured Mabel.

"If you are going to the basement, what are you doing sneaking around at the back of the hall shutting the lights off?" asked the short pot belly man, Adam Kaminski.

Mabel remembered he was Magdalen's father. He called himself the fixer. "We were trying to be quiet. We were going to come down the side of the hall so we wouldn't disturb you," Mabel said. "And, and we accidentally bumped into the breaker box."

"Well, you damn well did disturb us." Adam's face flushed with anger. "How the hell could you shut off the lights by bumping into a breaker box? I smell a rat."

"I don't know what you're smelling, my good man." Mabel crossed her arms over her chest and looked up at him over her wire-framed glasses. "The breaker box door was open, and Violet tripped on my foot, stumbled back and hit a switch. As soon as we saw the lights go out, we flipped the switch back on," explained Mabel, her lips pursed.

Violet, breathing deeply, gave Mabel a hard look.

"Oh, don't worry about them. These two are from the Glenhaven Players, and they've already performed. They probably just want to watch us rehearse," the shaven-headed man called out, taking his place in the circle.

"We told you we didn't come to watch," Violet said.

"Yeah, I guess Grant is right. It won't make any difference if they come to watch. And they might learn a thing or two about acting," Magdalen chuckled.

"She must be mic'd up," Mabel murmured to Violet as they walked toward the small stairs leading to the stage. "I remember her having a very low voice."

"They certainly could use some acting classes. Too bad the acting workshop had to be cancelled." Magdalen smiled smugly, "I hope you don't mind me telling you. But you guys were terrible. You performed like a bunch of bumbling clowns."

Mabel stopped mid-step. "I can't wait for your play. I sure hope your microphone keeps working."

"Mabel," scolded Violet in a hushed tone.

"What?" Magdalen yelled, putting her hands on her hips; she glared down at Mabel. "Are you threatening me?"

"What are you talking about? I never threatened you."

"Mabel didn't mean anything," assured Violet.

"I didn't threaten her," defended Mabel as Violet ushered her up the side stairs to the stage.

Pushing Mabel onstage, Violet urged, "Come on, let's go down to the basement."

Adam, double chin quivering, snarled, "I don't think you came to watch. You came to sabotage us."

"Seriously! Sabotage your silly play. That's just nuts."

Magdalen curled her lip. "Our play is not silly. Not like your stupid play."

"Whatever, we didn't come to watch or sabotage. We are just passing through to the basement."

"I think these two are up to something," Adam said, arms folded over his chest.

"Did you listen to the last bit? We're not up to anything. We are just passing through to the basement."

"Oh yeah? How come the lights suddenly went out? Just like they did last night. I bet you were responsible for that, too."

"Are you out of your mind?" Mabel bristled. "We were sitting in the second row. How could we?" She threw up her hands. "Use your head and stop hurling accusations at us. You do realize this is a little country drama festival. Not the Academy Awards."

"Mabel's right. We didn't do anything. Why would we? You're being silly."

"Yes, please calm down, Adam," cautioned the director. "This is getting us nowhere. Everyone, back to your places."

"Fine, but she'd better not interfere with Magdalen's microphone," Adam said, eyeing Mabel. "I'll be watching you."

"Fine, watch all you like. I have no intentions of doing anything to your daughter's microphone."

"Well, you better not," Magdalen snarled.

"Magdalen, please sit down. We're here to rehearse, not get into a war of words with this woman," reprimanded Sheeran. The director then turned to Mabel. "And you ladies. Please leave the stage. Go about whatever business you have in the basement."

"Let's go." Violet tugged Mabel's arm, urging her forward.

The director and the actors silently watched as they crossed in front of them, exiting stage right.

Chapter Twenty-Four

Mabel stomped down the steps, muttering, "What the heck was that about?"

"We should have told the truth," Violet said as she began to rummage through a box of old clothes beside the stairs. "We should have told them you turned off the breaker switches."

"What? And add to Adam's nasty suspicions, he already thinks I'm going to mess with his daughter's microphone system. Like I would have a clue how to do that."

"He's suspicious because the lights went out the same way they did last night. He put two and two together."

"And came up with six." Mabel stood glaring back up the stairs.

Violet grinned. "If it was you up on stage, and the lights went out twice in a row, would you think it was a coincidence, or would you be suspicious?"

Mabel thought for a minute. "Yeah, I guess."

"You guess? You know you would be suspicious with a capital 'S.' It's no wonder Adam is skeptical about our reasons for being in the hall. He is very protective of his daughter."

"But to accuse me of sabotage, that's a leap." Mabel tramped over to another box containing old Christmas tree decorations and dumped them out, pawing through the brightly coloured ornaments.

"Oh, you mean he jumped to a conclusion? I wonder who that reminds me of? And by the way, that remark about Magdalen needing a microphone didn't help matters. No wonder Adam and

Magdalen got all bent out of shape." Violet stuffed the old clothes back into the box and wiped her hands on the seat of her jeans.

"Okay, maybe I shouldn't have said anything. But I just said the truth. She needs a microphone."

"I think you made that snide remark because Magdalen insulted the Glenhaven Player's acting."

"Yes, probably you're right," Mabel said, scooping up the ornaments and putting them back in the box.

"Probably?"

"Okay, so do you think I should go back upstairs to apologize for my unkind remarks and tell them my suspicions?"

Violet thought for a moment, sighed and said, "No, we already lied about bumping into the breaker box. I think we will either look like paranoid old women. Or liars. And I don't fancy being labelled either."

"Good, I wasn't looking forward to going another round with Adam."

"I suppose you should apologize to Magdalen. On the other hand, maybe you should let sleeping dogs lie."

Mabel paused on her way over to the dusty old grandfather clock. "You don't think I can make a convincing apology?"

"The point of an apology is that you mean it."

Mabel, squeezing behind the clock, paused and wrinkled her forehead. "I'll apologize, but I'm not going up there now. They'd only complain I was disturbing their rehearsal." She knelt, peeking under the clock. "Anyway, we know how those lights went out. Someone deliberately did it. It's just, as I thought, sabotage. Someone is trying to derail the drama festival."

"Not necessarily. Someone could have bumped the switch," Violet said, looking under the makeup tables.

"No way, the little door to the box was shut. Whoever it was had to open the door to turn off the switches, just as Mandy stepped on those stairs." Mabel climbed up on the bench, looking behind the Player piano.

"I'm just glad we cleared Mike and Tommy of that stupid stunt," Violet said, dusting off her hands.

"Not necessarily. It could still be. Mike was really angry when Mandy critiqued Helen's directing. We all heard him yell. *'Don't talk about my wife.'*"

"Mike, never!" Violet shot Mabel a fiery look.

Mabel saw Violet's face and quickly added. "But it could have been anyone at the back of the hall. Anyone could have seen the box. It's not hidden."

"Well, neither Tommy nor Mike would want to derail the festival. That would make no sense whatsoever, especially not Mike. Helen is our director. And he's so proud of her."

"Yes, I guess," Mabel agreed. But she wasn't so sure. Mike adored his wife, but maybe he knew in his heart that Helen's directing would not stand up to the competition. Maybe he wanted to prevent Helen from being humiliated. First, he tried to stop the festival and tinkered with the railing. She was sure Mike wouldn't want to kill anyone, just injure someone so the Glenhaven Players would have to pull out of the festival. When that didn't work, he got angry and turned out the lights. She recalled his words. *'Stop belittling my wife. Or you'll be damn sorry.'* But she knew Mike. Mike might bluster. But he wasn't a violent man, was he? Mabel frowned. How well did one ever know what went on in someone's mind?

"And I still don't understand why anyone would try to stop the drama festival. What possible motive would they have? There is nothing for anyone to gain by shutting the festival down." Violet stood, stretching her back. "I'm going to check the dressing rooms. Maybe the phone somehow slid in there."

"All I know is that weird things are happening on stage and off. I'm going to find out what exactly is going on."

Violet poked her head out from behind a hanging bedsheet and chuckled. "Well, Mrs. Sherlock Holmes, be sure to let me know when you have figured it out."

"You might be laughing now. But much as I hate to agree with Magdalen and her dad. They are right. They think someone might want to interfere with their play. Except they think it's me. But I do think someone is meddling with the festival."

Violet came out from behind the bedsheets, chuckling, "Now you are siding with Adam."

"I most certainly am not siding with that tiresome man. But you see, there is more than just me who is suspicious of what's happening."

Violet, getting to her knees, crawled under the stairs. "If you say so. Where is that darn phone?"

Mabel lifted the damaged artificial Christmas tree. As she propped the tree against the wall, a piece of tangled garland and bits of tinsel fell to the floor. She kicked the scraggly decorations out of the way and examined the floor. Finding nothing. The women hunted silently, looking under the tickle trunks and into boxes. Searching until they had covered the entire area around and near the stairs.

"There is no phone down here," Violet said, taking an alcohol wipe from a packet in her pocket, wiping her hands, and offering one to Mabel.

"Yes, I guess you're right. But where the heck is the darn phone?"

"Hey, what are you two doing down here?" Looking down at them from the landing was Adam. The short man crossed his meaty arms over his potbelly and asked, "What are you two up to?"

"Nothing," answered Mabel. What was he doing? Checking up on them?

"You came down to the basement to do nothing?"

"We're looking for a cell phone," Violet said.

"A phone."

"We're looking for Sherman's phone. He was the man who fell down these stairs."

"To his death," added Mabel.

"Why do you want his phone?"

Mabel's spidey senses perked up. Why was Adam so interested? "His girlfriend wants it."

"I see, and did you find it?"

"No."

Mabel watched Adam as he eyed them intensely before returning to the stage. Was there a connection between Adam and Sherman? Was he the caller who brought Sherman out on the landing to his death? "Violet, do you remember the night Sherman died?"

Violet gave her a disgusted look.

"Sorry, of course you do. What I mean is when we came into the hall, we saw that the lights had been left on. Mike swore they shut them off. Why would he lie? I think someone gained access to the hall and tampered with the railing. The question is, who and why?"

Chapter Twenty-Five

It was the last night of the one-act drama festival. Mabel, sitting next to Violet, squirmed in her seat. "I'll be glad when this is all over."

"Shush, the curtain is going up."

The curtains rose, revealing the Berryman actors scrambling to take their places onstage. Vera Devon, the woman portraying the lawyer in the play, hurriedly took her place at the desk. But the audience could only see the back of her head. Her chair had been put on the wrong side of the desk. She was facing the back of the stage. The crowd twittered as Vera quickly rose from her chair, turned and sat on the desk, facing the audience. "Divorce is a messy business," she said. Her new position left Eric Ko and Ivy Fensten looking at Vera's back.

Ivy and Eric exchange puzzled looks. Then Eric picked up his chair. Casually, he walked to the right of the desk, placed the chair facing the audience and the desk at an angle and sat. A pale-faced Ivy remained seated behind the desk.

"Move, Ivy," Eric urgently whispered

Ivy shook her head. Her lips trembled, and she remained behind the desk.

Vera turned to pick up a file folder from her desk, shaking her head at Ivy. "For God's sake, Ivy, move," she whispered, then turned back to face the audience. "Indeed, a very messy business."

Ivy, the pasty face woman, groaned; putting her hand to her mouth, gagging, she raced offstage. Vera and Eric looked at each other in shocked silence as vomiting sounds came from off the stage. A man's voice from the crowd shouted, "Yep, divorce is a very messy business!" His buddy's raucous laughter followed his comment.

There was a long, awkward pause as the actors looked nervously stage left. Finally, the director Audrey Marson cautiously crept onstage. Her face was also pale, and she was sweating. "I'm sorry, but unfortunately, Ivy has the flu, and so do I. We'll have to cancel our performance. I'm so sorry." With her hand to her mouth, she hurried back off the stage. There was polite applause as the curtains fell.

The paramedics, Connie and Harvey, trooped down the aisle and up to the stage. Parting the curtains, they disappeared behind them. Mathew, the mayor, was hot on their heels. Gloria rose from her seat and hurried over to confer with the adjudicator. Mandy Swan sat at her small table, tapping her pencil on her notepad. "Good God, it just doesn't stop. This damned festival is cursed."

"I know; what's next?" Gloria moaned.

"What's next is the next play. Get up there and announce it."

"Why me, why me?" muttered Gloria as she sped up the steps to the stage to stand in front of the closed curtains. She composed herself and smiled. "On behalf of the festival committee, I'd like to apologize for the ah." Gloria looked up to the ceiling as if searching for inspiration. After a moment, she continued, "We'd like to apologize for the unfortunate, the failure, the interruption. I mean the way that the Berryman's play had to end. And we are all so very sorry for Ivy and the Berryman Drama Club. And we wish them a speedy recovery."

The crowd clapped politely. "Do I get my money back?" yelled the loudmouth man who had yelled divorce was a messy business.

Gloria glowered momentarily, then pasted a smile on her face. "There is no need to refund your money. The drama festival will continue." She looked down at the actors sitting in the second row beside the Glenhaven Players. She held a hand up and said, "Please bear with me for a moment." With a determined look on her face, Gloria hurried back down the stairs. She knelt on a seat in the front row, then, leaning over the back of the seat and looking at the director of The Moose Creek Little Theatre, asked, "Can you go on now?"

The director Romelu Abbott, a sharp-faced man with piercing blue eyes, looked at his actors. Heads bent, they went into a huddle. "Are you guys ready?" he asked. The actors looked at each other and then nodded. "Yes, no problem, but you will have to give us time to get the stage set and into costume."

Gloria sighed and smiled. "Absolutely, thank you." She rushed back up to the stage, clapping her hands to get the audience's attention and announced, "There is a great tradition in theatre. It's the show must go on. And the wonderful drama group from Moose Creek has agreed to go on next. Please help me give them a warm welcome." The crowd applauded as the Moose Creek actors, dressed in matching sweatshirts, with the big brown moose sitting on a director's chair holding a bullhorn, left their seats and trooped up to the stage. Gloria waited until the Moose Creek club disappeared behind the curtain, then announced, "We will now have a short intermission while the Moose Creek club gets ready." She parted the curtains and stepped behind them.

Tapping enthusiastically on Rudy's arm, Alice gleefully murmured, "The Berryman club has the flu that shoots them down. That leaves us in the running to win the trophy."

"I doubt it. I just hope they don't pass that damn flu on," Rudy replied, texting on his phone.

"See, another performance has gone down the tube," Mabel whispered to Violet. "Noticed how things have a habit of going wrong with each performance. Someone is sabotaging the plays."

"Really? That's silly. You think the flu is sabotage?" Violet scoffed.

"I'm not talking about the flu. Wouldn't you like to know who was running the curtains for the Berrymans? Whoever it was raised the curtains way before the Berryman Players were ready. We saw them scrambling to take their places."

"Yes, I saw them, but members from each drama club are helping each other. It was probably an honest mistake. They didn't know the Berryman actors weren't ready."

"How could they not know? And helping the Berryman Players? Or hindering them? You saw the desk and the chairs were facing the wrong way. There is no way anyone would make such an obvious mistake. The placement of the furniture was done on purpose."

The curtains parted, and the paramedics came out. Connie had an arm around Ivy, holding a wastepaper basket. Harvey followed, helping the sweating director down the stairs. The mayor rushed ahead, holding the side door open for them to exit. He then returned to his seat, followed by his wife. Gloria sank onto the theatre seats, moaning, said. "Things can't get much worse."

"It's a good thing I had Harvey and Connie here. They are taking the poor, sick women to the hospital in case it is something else."

"Like God forbid food poison."

"Damn it. Do not utter the phrase food poison. It had damn well better be the flu. This town doesn't need another lawsuit." The mayor glowered over at Mandy; she smiled back at him. Her arm was in a sling, her leg in a walking cast, and a neck brace around her neck.

Chapter Twenty-Six

The hall lights flickered, and the audience took their seats with bottles of soda pop, bags of chips, and chocolate bars in their hands. The curtains parted, and Romelu Abbott, the Moose Creek Little Theatre director, stepped out, bowed and announced, "Ladies and Gentlemen. The Moose Creek Little Theatre is pleased to introduce our one-act play. Please sit back and enjoy our farcical murder mystery, *Which Way*." As the audience clapped, the director ducked back behind the curtains.

Suspenseful music played as the house lights went down, and the stage lights came up. The curtains rose to reveal a small creamed-coloured settee near the front of the stage. Stage left; a tall brown wardrobe set at an angle facing the audience. Stage right, a square wooden table with four wooden chairs. The wooden table was covered with a white tablecloth. Sitting on the table was a tray with four long-stem wine glasses, plates, cutlery, and a brass candelabra minus the candles. Near the table was a three-legged side stand with a large picture of a man dressed in an old-fashioned striped suit, his hand stuffed into his vest, Napoleon style.

From offstage, a gunshot is heard, and seconds later, a man wearing a long tan trench coat and a black trilby hat, the brim pulled down, shading his eyes, staggered onstage. The man was Novak Simms, the actor with the Van Dyke beard. Gurgling and clutching his chest, he fell theatrically onto the sofa.

Adele Janssen, the tall woman with closely cropped black hair, entered onstage in a long green evening gown; she held a pistol in her white-gloved hand. Britney Riter, the middle-aged redhead, teetered onstage wearing bright red high-heel shoes. Like Adele, she was dressed in an evening gown, her gown a shimmering mosaic of reds and blues.

Britney delicately took Novak's wrist in her hand and then quickly dropped it. "He's dead," she said.

"I didn't mean to kill him," Adele said, her voice trembling.

"Then why did you shoot him? This man is Felix, our long-lost cousin."

As the women continued their dialogue, Novak slowly raised his hand and flopped it on his chest.

"It has been so long since I've seen Felix. I didn't recognize him. I thought he was a mugger, so I shot him, but I didn't mean to kill him." Adele paced in front of the dead man. She dropped the pistol and, with the toe of her shoe, pushed the gun toward the couch. The gun slid and then spun in one spot. Adele then kicked the gun. The gun slid under the settee and then out the other side, spinning across the floor and landing beside the cabinet with the man's picture. Trying to look nonchalant, Adele tottered across the stage in her green and black high-heeled shoes. Awkwardly kneeling in her form-fitting green gown. She picked up the gun and, teetering on her high-heeled shoes, wobbled back to the couch.

Britney looked down at the actor Novak spread out on the small sofa, lying at an awkward angle. His head rested at one end of the couch, his feet dangling off the other. "I'm not sorry Felix's dead. I'm glad you killed him."

"You're glad I killed him? Why would you want him dead?" Adele asked as she casually nudged the gun under the couch with the toe of her shoe.

"Because Felix was a nasty man." Novak's foot slowly slipped off the arm of the couch. "And he's the heir to Uncle Riley's millions. That selfish man doesn't deserve our uncle's money. He left home, leaving you to look after Uncle Riley."

"Felix is the heir? How do you know that?" Adele asked as she tottered over to the settee and pushed Novak's foot back onto the arm of the sofa.

"I was a witness when dear old Uncle Riley wrote out his will. And I know that now you've killed Felix. You're the next in line to inherit."

"I am? Really." Adele, turning to the audience, smiled a sly smile.

"But not if you go to jail for murder."

"Go to jail?" Adele asked, adjusting Novak's foot as it slid down.

"Felix was the heir, and you shot him dead. And now you inherit. The motive and the smoking gun."

"I don't care about the money."

"The police won't believe you didn't want Felix dead."

"But I didn't mean to kill Felix. This is just a tragic accident." Wobbling on her high-heeled shoes, Adele paced back and forth centre stage.

"A tragic accident?" Britney turned to the audience and smirked. "Yes, it was, and I don't want to go to jail. What do I do?"

"I don't know." Britney cupped her chin, looking pensive.

Adele crossed to Britney and, putting her arm around her shoulders, said, "Listen. No one knows Felix is here. What if we get rid of Felix? We could take his body and drop him in the lake."

Britney pulled away from Adele, bringing her hand up to her mouth, and uttered in a shocked voice, "Oh, I don't know if I could do that."

"Why won't you help me? You just said you were glad Felix was dead."

"I am, but if I help you, hide the body. I will be aiding and abetting in the murder of Felix."

"But I didn't murder Felix. I shot him by accident."

Looking at the audience, Britney raised her eyebrows with a knowing look. "Yes, of course, an accident."

"Please, if you help me, I'll share some of Uncle Riley's lovely money."

"If you want me to help you cover up this murder. I will expect to get half of our uncle's lovely money." Britney, turning back to the audience, smiled shrewdly.

"Okay, fine, I agree. I'll give you half, but we have to hurry. We don't have much time to get rid of Felix. Don't forget we have invited our aunts here for a dinner party. Our aunts are due here any minute." Adele pulled back her long glove and looked at her watch. "And soon, think of somewhere to hide the body."

At the sound of a doorbell ringing, Adele tottered to the stage right and looked offstage. "Quick, think of something. Our aunts are here."

Britney made a show of looking around the stage and said, "I have it. We put the body in the bureau for now. Then we can have dinner with the aunts. And when the old ladies leave. We take Felix's body and dump him in the lake."

The same suspenseful music at the play's opening played again as the stage lights went off. But the lights quickly came back on, just in time to see Adele and Britney hoist a dummy dressed in a trench coat and trilby hat from behind the couch and Novak in mid-crawl. As he ducked behind the sofa, raucous laughter came from the audience. Adele and Britney exchanged embarrassed looks and dropped the dummy onto the sofa. Novak's feet, clad in black oxfords, stuck out from behind the couch.

"Right, you take his feet."

More laughter erupted from the audience.

The women exchanged puzzled looks at the sound of the laughter. Adele picked up the dummy's feet while Britney grabbed it by the shoulders. Floundering on high heels, they huffed and puffed their way to the armoire as if they were carrying a heavy body. They lowered the phoney Felix to the floor. Britney turned the handle on the door, pulling. But nothing happened. The door did not open. Britney gave her fellow actor a puzzled look and tried again. But to no avail. The door remained closed, and they conferred in hush tones. Novak poking his head out from behind the couch, looked at the audience; then, with his head down, he crawled offstage, laughter from the crowd following him.

Britney and Adele carried the fake Felix to the table. The dummy's hat fell onto the floor, exposing its shiny bald head. The women shoved the mannequin underneath the table just as the two short, chubby, grey-haired twins entered. The little women were dressed in evening gowns, one twin in white, the other in black. The twins looked at the table, back at each other, then at Adele and Britney. "We rang, but you didn't answer. So, we came in," the twin in white said in a squeaky voice.

Teetering across the stage, Adele greeted the plump little ladies. "Sorry, we were getting, we were, we are so happy you are here."

Britney snatched up the hat, hiding it behind her back; she minced over to welcome the ladies. Puckering her lips, placing faux kisses on their cheeks. "Dear, dearest aunties, we are so happy you could come to our dinner party."

"Come and sit down at the table. I'll pour you some of Uncle Riley's fine wine," Adele said, putting an arm around the twin in black and ushering her across the stage.

"Our dearly beloved brother did have the best vineyard," the twin in the black sequin evening gown said as she waddled over to the table to sit.

The twin in the silky white gown followed; she pulled a chair away from the table. A leg of the chair caught on the manikin's trench coat. As she tugged on the chair, the dummy came along with it. And the bare-headed fake Felix poked out from under the table.

"Please take another chair," Britney said hurriedly, kicking the dummy back under the table with her foot and tossing the hat in after it.

The twin in the white gown sat, and the audience laughed.

"I'll pour us all some wine," Adele offered, tottering to the side table with the tray of wine glasses.

"Oh, yes, we should toast our dear Uncle Riley," Britney said, sitting beside the twin in white. Adele set the tray on the three-legged stand; her eyes widened, and she stared at the cabinet. She picked up the large picture of the man dressed in an old-fashioned striped suit. Adele set the picture back down and looked offstage. She paused, shrugged, and, with a nervous smile, pretended to pour wine from a phantom bottle. She picked up the tray of empty glasses, carrying it back to the table.

"Now, let us raise our glasses in a toast to dear Riley." The twin in white raised her empty wineglass.

The women held up their glasses. "To our dear departed brother, may he rest in peace," the twins said in unison.

The women put the glasses to their lips and pretended to drink. "A wonderful bouquet." Britney's voice faltered as the crowd chuckled.

"Dear Riley, we miss him so." With a lace hanky, the white twin dabbed her eyes.

"Oh, did we tell you dear Felix has come home for his father's funeral?" asked the twin in black. "We have invited the dear boy to join us. I hope you don't mind?"

Adele and Britney exchange guilty looks.

"No, not at all," replied Adele.

From offstage, a doorbell sounded.

"That's probably the dear boy now," said the twin in the sparkly black gown.

"Excuse me; I'll just see who is at the door." Britney exited stage right and quickly returned with Novak, now dressed as a police officer. His blue Jacket and hat did not match his slacks. His trousers were tan.

"Your neighbours have reported a gunshot," Novak said, standing centre stage.

"We didn't hear any gunshot, officer," Britney said, wobbling over to the bureau; she stood spread eagle in front of the cupboard door.

Novak, stroking his Van Dyke beard, turned to the audience. "Suspicious, don't you think?"

"Don't pay any attention to my neighbours; they are crazy," Adele said, running across the stage toward Britney. A heel on her high-heeled shoes snapped off. "Those people are always imagining weird things." Adele limped the last few steps to stand beside Britney.

Novak looked at Adele and giggled.

"There is nothing to see here, officer," Adele said, frowning at Novak.

"Stand aside." Chuckling, he strong-armed the women away from the bureau.

"No," shouted Adele as she kicked off both shoes.

One high-heeled shoe sailed across the stage and landed beside the aunt in white. The aunt looked at the shoe and then at her sister. Her chubby sister shrugged. The twin in white stood, and, taking careful aim, she kicked the shoe under the table. The green high-heel shoe landed in the middle of the dummy's chest.

"The neighbour saw you hide a body," Novak said, taking hold of the doorknob and yanking. The door didn't budge. He grimaced and pulled again, and the door flew open, revealing an empty cupboard. "Aha, just as I thought, I, I —." His eyes darted to Adele and Britney.

The twin, dressed in black, putting her hands on either side of her chubby cheeks, screamed, "Oh no, poor Felix is dead."

Novak, spying the dummy under the table, pointed. "Just as I thought, this man has been shot in the chest."

The play continued without further mishap, but the damage was done, and the actors knew it. The play ends with Adele's character being arrested for the murder of Felix. Britney's character was intent on inheriting the uncle's money. But she was foiled when Adele revealed Britney helped her hide the body. The audience was left to surmise the aunts were the ones who would benefit from their brother's death.

As the actors came out in front of the closed curtains to take their bows to the audience's generous applause, a voice was heard from backstage, yelling, "Who the hell nailed that cabinet door shut?"

Clapping along with the crowd, Mabel leaned over to Violet and said, "Somebody definitely sabotaged their play. I'm sure that was the director's voice coming from behind the curtains."

"Yes, that was Romelu swearing. I recognized his voice," agreed Violet. "I feel so bad for the actors. Everything that could go wrong did. Poor Novak was so surprised that the bureau was empty. And the lights came back on way too quick. We saw the Novak and the dummy exchange. Maybe you are right about the early curtain with the Berryman's play."

"See, I told you so," Mabel said." But I have to say they weren't very good, even before the debacle with the props."

"Yeah, that's true. I hate to think what Mandy will say."

"I'm betting Romelu is on the same page as I am. The jammed cabinet and missing wine bottle were not accidents." Mabel's thoughts went back to Sherman's death, the near miss with the car and the accidents that befell Mandy Swan. "Somebody hates this festival."

Violet nodded. "You are right; someone is messing around with the props. That same person messed with our play, the Berrymans, and now the Moose Creek play." She paused and pressed her lips. "But even if someone hates this drama festival, The festival is still going on. So what do they have to gain by messing with the club's props?"

"I don't know. Revenge? Maybe someone tried out for a part and didn't get it? And wants to get back at everyone who is acting in a play? Or perhaps it's just someone's sick humour."

"I sure hope nothing goes wrong with the Maryland play," Violet said.

"Somehow, we need to get backstage so that no one can interfere with the play."

Chapter Twenty-Seven

Gloria clapped her hands as she strode across the stage and stopped. Standing at the centre stage in front of the closed curtains, she beamed a wide smile. "The Moose Creek Little Theatre group certainly entertained us. Wouldn't you agree?" she asked. Loud, enthusiastic applause followed her question. Mandy Swan looked up from her table, her face showing no enjoyment. "And now, last but certainly not least, are The Maryland Musers. With their play *Not Again*. And I believe the Kegworth director wrote this play."

"No, I most certainly did not," Max Woodard, the director of the Kegworth Players, stood and shouted. "I wrote *Hockey is Life*. Why the hell would I write a play for Maryland?"

"Please watch your language," Gloria, red-faced, scolded, then issuing a harsh laugh, said, "Yes, of course, you are the author of *Life is Playing Hockey*."

"*Hockey is Life*." Max blew out a long, loud sigh, threw up his hands, and dropped back into his seat.

Pasting a fake smile on her flushed face, Gloria said, "Anyway, I'm so looking forward to The Maryland Musers's performance. Ladies and gentlemen, please put your hands together for The Maryland Musers performing their play, *Not Again*." The house lights suddenly went down. "Put those damn lights back on!" she shouted. "For God's sake, wait until I'm seated." The house lights came back on, and Gloria strutted offstage to sit beside her husband. "Lord, you would think whoever is running the lights would be more careful after Mandy Swan fell down those darn stairs," she fumed. The mayor patted her hand, and Gloria moaned. "And now we have to sit through another dreadfully acted and unimaginative drivel. I can't wait for this fiasco to be over."

"Yes, sweetheart," the mayor said, putting an arm around her shoulders. "But wasn't this drama festival your idea?"

Gloria sighed and growled, "Don't remind me."

The house lights went out, and the stage lights came on. Sheeran Maier, the frumpy Maryland director, dressed in a long, drab navy dress, parted the curtains and stepped out. "There will be a slight delay. Our promised volunteers have not come up to help us backstage." Her eyes blazed with anger as she looked down at Gloria.

Gloria slapped a hand to her forehead, exhaled a big breath, and looked at Mabel and Violet. "You two backstage now," she ordered.

"I guess we could," Mabel said, rising from her seat. Gloria glared.

"She's just kidding. We're only too happy to help." Violet led the way up the side stairs onto the stage.

Mabel followed, and they ducked behind the curtains.

"Hurry up," hissed Sheeran, urgently ushering them offstage.

Adam Kaminski, the short tubby Mr. Fixit for the Maryland Musers, stomped over to stand beside the director. He had a script in his hand, which he waved in the faces of the women. "There better not be any shenanigans. I've seen what's happened to the other groups. And I'm warning you, it better not happen to our play."

"Not now, Adam. We don't have time for this. Go back to your prompting stool and get ready. We will be on as soon as I get these ladies at the window."

Adam eyed the women and said, "Remember, I'll be watching you." With that, he strode stage left and climbed up on a stool.

"I don't have to worry about you two, do I?" Sheeran asked, frowning at them.

"Oh, my goodness, no," replied Violet. "We had some strange things happen to our play, too. We certainly don't want anything to go wrong with yours, and we will be on the lookout for any strange goings-on backstage. So, no worries."

"I'm glad to hear that. Adam has a strange idea that someone is interfering with the props backstage. I personally think it's the drama clubs who are just plain sloppy. Now hurry up and follow me. Adam has already set up the stepladder behind the backdrop. And bring these bags with you." She handed them three large, clear plastic bags filled with white flakes.

Mabel took one bag, and Violet took the other two. "What is this stuff?" Mabel asked, following Violet and the director behind the stage.

Sheeran stopped beside a stepladder. "Here is your post," she said, showing them a fake window cut out of the muslin backdrop. "The bags contain instant potato flakes. One of you will shake the flakes over the window when given the cue. Here is the script. The cues for the potato flake shaking are highlighted. These flakes are snow. Our play takes place during a winter storm, so be sure to shake lots. Any questions?"

"No, it's pretty straightforward. Shake potato flakes, easy peasey," replied Mabel, opening her bag of flakes.

"Good, please don't mess this up."

"No problem. I don't see how anything can go wrong," Mabel assured her.

The director nodded and hurried away, leaving Mabel and Violet with the stepladder and the potato flakes. Setting two bags of the white flakes beside her, Violet took the script and opened it, scanning for the yellow highlighted cues. Mabel put her foot on the first step of the stepladder, holding the big plastic bag of instant potato flakes in her hand. Mabel was excited. Adam was right to be suspicious, just not of them. Now that she was backstage, she might just catch the backstage perpetrator or perpetrators who were playing the nasty little tricks.

Chapter Twenty-Eight

Long introductory music of *Candle in the Wind* by Elton John played, and slowly, the curtains rose. Revealing a bare set with five chairs in a semi-circle facing the front of the stage. The music faded, and Magdalen Kaminski, the tall, auburn-haired girl, entered, wearing a blue ski jacket. She sighed theatrically, took off her coat and scarf, and draped the garments over the back of a chair. Looking sadly at the audience, she sat.

Behind the scene, Violet pointed to Mabel and whispered, "Go." Mabel hurried up the stepladder to shake potato flakes over the window. "Stay up on the ladder," whispered Violet. "I'll tap you on your foot. That will be your signal to drop potato flakes."

"Right," Mabel whispered back.

Levi Sindanoi, the attractive man in his mid-forties, was the next actor to enter onstage. "Where is everyone?" he boomed. "I thought I would be the last one here. But I guess this terrible weather is stopping people from coming." Violet tapped Mabel on her foot. Mabel took a handful of potato flakes, vigorously shaking flakes over the window.

"Just look at that snow," he said, taking off his parka and slinging the jacket over the back of a chair. He smiled at Magdalen. "Maybe there will just be the two of us."

Looking back at the window as potato flakes continued to fall, Magdalen sighed, "I hope we don't get snowed in. Maybe I shouldn't have come."

"Oh no, I'm so glad you came. We need this group; divorce is a messy business."

An audience member hooted and burst out into raucous laughter. And a man's voice yelled, "Wait for it. It could get a whole lot messier." Some people in the crowd joined in chuckling, remembering the messy business from the Berryman's performance. Other audience members issued commands to hush up and be quiet.

Giving the crowd a puzzled look, Levi waited until they settled down and said, "This self-help group is helping me. Isn't it you? You had a bad breakup. I remember you telling us about that at the last session."

"I did; my husband Andy cheated on me." Magdalen's shoulders shook, and hiding her face in her hands, she made soft mewing sounds.

"Please don't cry." Levi jumped from his chair, hurriedly sitting beside her, putting his arm around her. Magdalen laid her head on his shoulder and sniffed.

Grant Middleman, wearing a black padded parka with the hood up, entered, pulling the hood of his jacket down. Magdalen moved away from Levi.

"Nasty night," said Grant, the shaven head man, as he stomped his feet and rubbed his hands together. "It's a heck of a winter storm out there. I almost didn't come. I wonder if Leonard, our mediator, will make it?" Mabel, taking another handful of flakes, sprinkled the flakes over the window.

Grant was followed onstage by Daryna Melnyk, garbed in a bright green parka. The young red-headed woman peeled off her gloves and sat beside Grant. "Nasty night out there." More flakes fell behind the fake window. "I wouldn't have come, but I need to tell you all something. Well, maybe it is more to get it off my chest. My ex-husband is getting married. Can you believe that?"

"Yeah. What's wrong with that?" Grant asked, shedding his parka. "We have to move on. Isn't that why we have this group?"

Daryna turned her chair. Facing away from the group, she threw her parka to the floor and shouted, "You insensitive moron. If Leonard were here, you wouldn't be saying such unkind things." Daryna covered her face with her hands and made the same soft, mewing sounds Magdalen had.

Mabel, standing on the top step of the ladder, groaned softly. She thought the play was boring. The play progressed with the group taking sides. Grant and Levi took turns defending Daryna's ex-husband, with Magdalen siding with Daryna. Violet, following the script, tapped Mable's foot, and Mabel dutifully grabbed another handful of potato flakes and shook the flakes over the fake window.

Daryna, the redhead actor, looking back at the window, moaned, "I wish this darn snow would stop. If it wasn't for this storm, I know Leonard would be here, and he wouldn't be siding with my ex-husband, Tom."

"That's not true. Leonard is a great believer in getting on with life after divorce." Levi said, smiling at Magdalen.

The long back-and-forth argument persisted. Violet sighed and handed Mabel another bag of potato flakes. Mabel dipped her hand in the bag just as a truce was called. The play progressed, with each actor complaining about their ex-partner and their divorces. Backstage, Violet continued to give Mabel her cue by tapping on her foot. And Mabel continued to shake the potato flakes.

During a long-drawn-out lamentation by Magdalen, Mabel climbed down the ladder and leaned against it, whispering to

Violet, "Lord, this is the most mind-numbing play ever. I'd take the figure skating hockey play over this one."

"Mabel, it's your cue," Violet whispered urgently.

Mabel hurried back up the stepladder, her foot slipping on the top step; as she dipped her hand into the plastic bag, taking a handful of potato flakes, she shook the flakes over the window. Wobbling, she reached for another handful of flakes, losing her balance. Screaming, Mabel tumbled onto the muslin backdrop. The backdrop ripped, and Mabel, still screaming, fell, taking a large portion of the backdrop with her. A loud collective gasp came from the audience as Mabel and the ladder lay on the stage floor.

The Maryland actors looked dumbfounded at Mabel, covered in white potato flakes. Violet leapt through the gap in the backdrop and knelt beside Mabel. "Are you okay? Are you hurt?"

Mabel, sitting up, brushed the white flakes off her face and out of her hair. "No, I don't think so." She looked in dismay at the astonished cast, then at the audience. Scrambling to her feet, she dashed offstage, potato flakes falling in her wake.

Violet picked up the ladder and the broken bag of flakes. "Sorry," she whispered to the cast; ducking her head, Violet raced offstage.

"Yep, what did I tell you? A messy business," hollered a male voice from the crowd. As the audience roared with laughter, the actors exchanged bewildered looks.

Magdalen suddenly jumped up. Donning her ski jacket, she said, "It's hard to get good help. Those workmen have just destroyed the wall. It's getting cold in here."

Levi, following Magdalen's improvisation, put on his coat. "Workwomen, but yeah, you are right. It's getting cold."

"They shouldn't be working during this winter snowstorm," Daryna said, picking her parka up off the floor.

Zipping up his jacket, Grant added, "Yeah, now we will have to find a new place for our meetings. This old place is getting too drafty. But we should finish the meeting. We can't let a little cold weather stop us."

The ad-lib exchange between the actors brought enthusiastic applause from the crowd. The actors moved their chairs closer to the front of the stage and continued where they had left off before the sudden appearance of Mabel and the ladder.

Mabel and Violet hurried backstage to stand by the opening in the backdrop, tossing potato flakes across the gap in the muslin backdrop. Mabel had to admire the actor's ability to perform after the scenery disaster. But in her mind, the play was still boring. The characters continue to complain about their ex-spouses and their divorces. At the play's end, Magdalen and Grant's characters reveal they are in love and plan to marry.

The actors lined up to take their bows. The audience, who had lost interest after Mabel's unexpected entrance, were yawning and stretching. But they applauded politely. Mabel and Violet, brushing potato flakes off their hands, crept away from the backdrop. An outraged Adam stomped up to them. "You did it. I didn't think you would, but you did it," he snarled.

"I'm sorry, but it was an accident," Mabel apologized, combing flakes from her hair with her fingers.

"You almost brought our play to a standstill with your antics. And you would have if it wasn't for my talented daughter's inspired improvisation."

"You can't think I fell intentionally."

With one last scathing look at the women, Adam turned on his heel and sped back to congratulate the Maryland Musers on their performance.

"Well, I guess that shoots down your theory. There's no sabotage," Violet murmured into Mabel's ear.

Mabel grimaced. She knew Violet was right; single-handedly, she'd almost ruined the Maryland play. She didn't fall deliberately, but just the same, she didn't blame Adam for being angry with her. Avoiding eye contact with the Maryland Musers, she and Violet joined their fellow actors in the front row.

Chapter Twenty-Nine

All the actors from the drama clubs waited impatiently for Mandy Swan to finish writing in her notepad. Finally, the adjudicator closed her notebook, nodded and waved her good hand in the air. Immediately, the music of *Pomp and Circumstance* blared out from the loudspeakers, and a smiling Gloria proudly holding the drama trophy paraded down the aisle. Stage side, she held the trophy up to the crowd, who enthusiastically applauded. She then placed the trophy on Mandy's small table.

Mandy gave Gloria a patronizing smile and rose from her chair. "My cane, please," she requested, indicating a rosewood cane with a decorative brass handle beside her table.

Mabel watched Mandy, who was wearing a scarlet turban stand. She looked like the walking wounded. Mandy's arm was in a sling, her foot was in a walking cast, and she had a neck brace. She guessed Mandy's fuzzy white hair was the least of her worries.

"If you want, you can adjudicate from here," suggested Gloria.

"In the great tradition of show business, I shall carry on. My cane, please."

"Yes, of course." Gloria handed Mandy her cane and stood to the side.

Mandy laboriously crossed the floor to the small set of stairs that led to the stage. She stopped and beckoned Gloria. "Come here, please." Gloria hurried over. "You may fetch my notes and bring them to me onstage."

At the word 'fetch,' Gloria tightened her lips; strutting to the table, she grabbed Mandy's notes. Mandy, struggling, made her way up the stairs, one painstaking step at a time, moaning with each step. When Mandy reached the stage, she paused. Receiving a huge round of applause, she nodded, smiling at the crowd. She looked down at Gloria, standing with her notebook in her hand. "My dear woman, the notes aren't doing me any good down there." Mandy made an impatient come here motion with her fingers. Gloria flushed, gritted her teeth, and climbed the stairs with Mandy's notes.

Mandy leaned heavily on her cane and asked, "Would someone be kind enough to bring me a chair?"

The mayor quickly stood, but before he could offer a chair. Adam grabbed one and bounded up to the stage. Holding the chair over his head, he rushed past Gloria. Gloria's nostrils flared as Adam set the chair on the stage, making a dusting motion on the chair's seat with his hands. "Here you go," he said, helping Mandy to sit. "They don't call me Mr. Fixit for nothing," he boasted, grinning.

The mayor scowled and sat back down.

Gloria handed the adjudicator her notes. Mandy, barely acknowledging Gloria, accepted her notebook, waved her away, and looked at Adam questionably. "Thank you?"

"I am Adam Kaminski. The proud father of Magdalen, the actress who saved the day."

"Saved the day?" Mandy looked down at her notes.

"The Maryland Musers. *Not Again.*"

"Yes?"

"After that terrible woman destroyed the set. Magdalen's brilliant improvisations saved the play. Because of her superb inventiveness, she got all her fellow actors back on track," bragged Adam.

Sitting in the second row, Magdalen beamed at her father while Grant, Levi and Daryna exchanged resentful looks. Mabel dropped her head and looked at her hands. Adam was right; she had destroyed the set.

"Yes, of course. Thank you for bringing me the chair. You may go," the adjudicator said, dismissing Gloria and Adam with a flick of her hand. They returned to their seats. As Adam's eyes gleamed with satisfaction, Gloria's brows knitted in a scowl.

"First, before I begin my adjudication. And hand out the award for best play. Best actor and best director. I want to offer my sympathies to the Berryman Drama Club. I hope for a speedy recovery for your fellow actor."

"And our director," shouted Eric Ko, the lead actor from the Berryman club. "Our director is sick, too."

"Of course, and a speedy recovery for him as well."

"Her recovery. Audrey Marson is our director," corrected Eric.

Mandy arched an eyebrow; her lips formed a quick smile. "Yes, and of course, my sympathies to Audrey. But, because one of your actors took sick." She paused and looked down at Eric. "You couldn't continue your play. So, unfortunately, I can not critique your performance. But I can judge the next two." She flipped open her notebook.

With a sly smile, Gloria stood and turned to the crowd. "Before Miss Swan gives her critiques, I would like to thank my wonderful festival committee." A round of applause accompanied her announcement. As Mandy glowered, Gloria smirked. "And, of course, acknowledge all the drama clubs who participated in Glenhaven's Municipal One Act Drama Festival. Please, my dear actors and directors," Gloria emphasized the word 'director.' "Please stand where you are and take a bow." The club members rose to thunderous applause. When the applause died down, and the actors sat. Gloria turned to Mandy, who sat sullenly onstage. "You may now continue, Miss Swan." Smiling smugly, she sat down beside her husband, who was grinning.

"Thank you, Gloria," Mandy said with a forced smile. "You stole my thunder, as I always thank the clubs at the end of my adjudication. But you were well-meaning."

Gloria rolled her eyes, her lips curling into a self-satisfied smile.

"Now, back to the job at hand." Mandy consulted her notes. "I was hoping for redemption for the festival performances this evening. But alas, that was not to be." She sighed and looked down at the Moose Creek actors sitting in the front row. "Moose Creek, I know you didn't have much time to prepare because the Berryman cast had, or have the flu. But you were shoddy. Yes, you had props that malfunctioned. But the Maryland Musers also had a malfunction. And they handled their malfunction much better than you."

As the Maryland Musers gave each other broad smiles, The Moose Creek actors sat, arms folded, with sullen looks on their faces. Mandy continued to critique The Moose Creek's performance, giving no leniency for the prop's mishaps.

The Maryland Musers were next to be adjudicated. "Your audience was yawning and fidgeting. They were bored. But that was not all your fault. Your director should have known who your audience was. This community isn't cosmopolitan, to say the least."

"Oh yeah? Who do you think you are?" shouted a man's voice from the audience. Boos directed at the adjudicator followed his outburst.

Mayor Hamilton jumped to his feet, turning to the crowd. He raised his hands. "Please, remember you are the good people of Glenhaven. This lady may not appreciate our culture. But let us show her our good manners." The mayor waited until the crowd settled down and returned to his seat. Gloria squeezed his hand, smiling proudly at him.

Mandy looked skyward, sighed, and continued. "But my dear Musers, you can't blame the audience for being bored. I have to tell you, Maryland Musers, your performance was lacklustre."

The crowd nodded approvingly and clapped.

Mandy waited for the applause to die down and continued. "But I commend you on your ability to bounce back after the calamity of the scenery crashing down around your ears. And for that reason, and that reason alone. I am awarding you the..." She consulted her notes again. "You are the winners of this year's Municipal One Act Drama Festival."

With loud, enthusiastic shouts of joy, the Maryland Musers rose from their seats. Cheering and laughing, they ran up the stairs and onto the stage. The rest of the drama clubs applauded politely while the crowd clapped enthusiastically as the actors stood onstage, raising their arms in the air in a victory salute.

"And the best actor award goes to." Mandy Swan paused. The actors onstage and the actors sitting below all waited with bated breath. Mandy looked down at her notebook and said, "The best actor in this year's Municipal One Act Drama Festival is." Mandy smiled and theatrically announced, "Is Magdalen Kaminski."

The drama clubs courteously clapped as the crowd heartily applauded. A loud cheer went up from the Maryland Musers. Magdalen, laughing and crying, bowed. She sped across the stage and curtsied to the adjudicator. Mandy, seated on her chair using her uninjured hand, shook hands with the happy girl and gave her a rolled-up scroll of parchment paper tied with a red ribbon.

Magdalen, grinning from ear to ear, undid the ribbon, unrolled the parchment, and read aloud, "It says me." She laid a hand over her heart, her eyes glistening with happiness. "It says Magdalen Kaminski, best actor."

Mandy sighed impatiently. "Time to move on. And as much as I don't want to. I have to award the best director. There wasn't much choice. Even though I thought the performance was dull and plodding. I have to give the best director award to Sheeran Maier. The director of the Maryland Musers."

"Oh my gosh, oh my gosh, I'm so happy." Beaming from ear to ear, Sheeran rushed across the stage to receive her parchment scroll. "Thank you so much," she said, shaking Mandy's good hand.

"Congratulations," Mandy said, snatching her hand back. "I will now present the trophy for best play to the Maryland Musers. That is if someone will please just bring the trophy to me?"

Mayor Hamilton leapt from his seat to grab the trophy. But Adam beat him to it. The happy man cheered, shouting, "We did it, we did it!" The small man carried the big silver goblet over his head onto the stage, ignoring Mandy Swan, who had risen from her chair. Adam awarded the trophy to his daughter and the rest of the Maryland Musers, who were laughing and cheering.

Chapter Thirty

Violet pulled her car to the curb, parking behind a white van on the street. "There is no room to park in the Hamilton's driveway," she remarked. "It looks like most of the participants in the drama festival are already here."

"If we didn't stay behind to shut out the lights and lock the theatre doors, we wouldn't be the last ones here," replied Mabel. Gravel crunched underfoot as they walked up the long circular driveway lit by tall black coach lights. Small shrubs bordered the gravelled driveway; tiny green buds were bravely popping out on the bare branches.

"The drama festival committee is responsible for closing up the theatre," explained Violet. "I don't mind. Gloria is hosting the celebration party tonight. It's the least I could do."

"Gloria is very lucky she has you. I'm wondering what kind of party this will be. Everything that could go wrong with this drama festival did. I'm not sure if this gathering will be a celebration or a wake," mused Mabel.

"Definitely a celebration, at least for the Maryland Musers."

"Yes, they certainly do have a reason to celebrate."

"But I'm a little nervous. What kind of reception do you think we will get? We destroyed Maryland's backdrop. Magdalen's dad was furious," fretted Violet.

"You don't have to worry. It was all me. Not one bit of that disaster is your fault. And I'm not worried about Adam. Remember what Mandy said? The Maryland Musers kind of won the best play trophy award because of me. Old Adam has to be happy with that."

Violet laughed. "Because of you, seriously."

"Yes, she liked their improvisation when I sort of crashed the party."

"Sort of?"

"Whatever. Anyway, falling through that backdrop was an accident. Who cares what Adam thinks? Not me. And after this wind-up party, we will never see him again. I just hope Gloria has lots of food. I'm starved."

Mathew and Gloria Hamilton's big two-story house was at the end of the driveway. Mabel thought that even Mandy Swan would find the Hamilton's residence impressive. It was a big white clapboard house that dated back to the early 1900s. Its wide, black-painted wooden steps led up to a glass-enclosed veranda. They opened a frosted glass door, stomping their feet on a big grey welcome mat. Inside the porch were two small white wrought-iron tables with small matching chairs on either side of a tall green cedar in a big black pot. They walked across the black-painted wooden plank flooring to a big burgundy door with a brass doorknocker. Mabel raised her hand to the knocker. But before she could knock, the door opened.

"Hi, oops, sorry. Gloria instructed me to say good evening." Giggled Sally Nesbeth, a small black-haired girl dressed in a black maid's uniform with a frilly white apron. Alice, Mabel thought, would be jealous of the girl's apron.

"You're working for Gloria? I thought you were going to university?" Violet asked as they stepped through the door into a spacious vestibule with white vaulted ceilings and dark red walls. A large gold-gilded frame mirror hung over a black padded bench.

"Oh, I am going to university in Saskatoon. I'm just home for the weekend. Gloria hired Fanny and me to cater for her this evening."

Mabel's eyes flickered with amusement. Gloria never did anything by halves, hiring two local girls to serve her guests.

Sally opened a closet door and took out a coat hanger. "I can take your jackets. Everyone is already downstairs."

Handing their jackets to Sally, they thanked her and descended the wide curved stairway leading to the basement. The Hamiltons had decorated the basement to resemble an English pub. Fake wooden beams crossed the ceiling, and small domed lights hung down.

The Kegworth actors lounged on black leather couches that faced a giant screen TV. The big screen displayed a picture of logs burning in a fireplace. On the opposite wall hung a dartboard; the darts on the board circled the bullseye. At the end of the red and gold carpeted room, two Berryman actors leaned against a wall, laughing and chatting with the Moose Creek club. Everyone had drinks in their hands. Helen, Glenhaven's nervous director, was visiting with Max, the director of the Kegworth Players. She waved a friendly welcome. Sitting at the bar, on black leatherette stools, the actors from the Maryland Musers; on the floor beside them was the big silver drama trophy. The actors and their director were all in good spirits, laughing, talking and taking turns taking selfies with the drama trophy. Behind the counter was a long mirror reflecting liquor bottles lined up on a shelf, where the mayor happily poured beer from a tap and chatted with the Maryland actors.

Tommy was carrying a tall, frosted glass of beer. He gave the mug to Jolene. Accepting it, she gave the skinny, white-blond-headed boy a friendly smile and then turned away to talk to Magdalen. Tommy stood awkwardly, smiling shyly at her back. Standing in front of the dartboard, Rudy hoisted a mug of beer to his lips as he listened to Sam. The tall raw-boned farmer was red in the face, jabbing the air with his finger as if making a point.

Mabel spotted Gloria. Gloria reminded Mabel of a butterfly as she flitted from group to group, smiling and exchanging a few words with a polite laugh, then moving on to the next group of actors. Mabel noted she seemed to be ignoring the adjudicator, Mandy Swan. The adjudicator was enthroned on a green and brown tweed recliner chair. She and the chair looked out of place. The neck brace woman held a cocktail glass in her right hand. Her left wrist, wrapped in a tensor bandage, lay on her lap. The leg in the walking cast was stretched out on the recliner's footrest.

Perched beside Mandy on a black padded footstool was Alice, who was talking and motioning with her hands. The turban-head adjudicator had a bored look on her face.

Alone in the corner near the buffet table sat Crystal Harrison, Sherman's girlfriend. The attractive girl was nursing a drink. Mabel bit her bottom lip, remembering Crystal's scathing remarks about an insensitive creep taking Sherman's part. Did she know she'd taken Sherman's part of Jeeves in the play?

"Good, you are here at last," greeted Gloria. "Mathew, pour these women a drink." She called out, ushering them to the bar.

"At your service, dear ladies, what will you have? Beer? Wine? Or something stronger?"

Accepting a frosted mug of beer, Mabel and Violet turned to face the room. "I'm glad you invited Crystal," Violet said, sipping her beer.

"Yes, it is a nice gesture," agreed Gloria. "I thought it was only fitting, as dear departed Sherman was part of our troop. A sign of respect for Sherman. But I'm a little surprised she came. And I must confess, it was really Mathew's idea to invite her. He's worried about a lawsuit, which is utterly ridiculous. Hopefully, by showing the woman a little goodwill, we will stop any ideas about lawsuits and such. I suggest you ladies go over and talk to her. I think the woman feels out of place, and I certainly don't want that."

"Yes, I bet she does feel a little lost," agreed Violet. "She's so brave to come. It must be hard for her so soon after her boyfriend's death. Come on, Mabel."

Mabel nodded; she hoped she wouldn't get a frosty reception from Crystal.

Sally and Fanny appeared on the stairs with trays of dim sum, cocktail sausages, and taco salads for the hungry actors. Mike, Helen's husband and Adam, the jack of all trades from the Maryland Musers, were already filling their plates from the long buffet table ladened with plates and platters of mini quiches, scotch eggs, little pork pies, salads, bruschetta, and Mozzarella sticks. Mabel's tummy rumbled; she was starved.

"Is this leftover food from the welcome party that Gloria cancelled?" Ned asked as he set his drink down and picked up a plate.

The elderly twins from the Moose Creek drama were at the buffet table, following Mike and Adam. "Don't be fussy, dear," said one of the twins, her plate piled high with a spinach salad.

"Besides, it's free," said the other twin helping herself to a scotch egg.

"Yeah, who cares? I'm hungry," agreed Craig, the big actor from the Kegworth club who played the luckless goalie. He set his glass of beer on an end table, making a beeline for the buffet table.

"Get the hell away from me," shouted Martin, the figure skating hockey actor from the Kegworth Players.

Conversations ceased, and heads turned. Sally and Fanny, depositing the food trays onto the buffet table, looked at the two men who were standing toe-to-toe. Giggling, the girls ran up the stairs.

"You're a slimy little good-for-nothing snake," snarled Sam. He slammed Martin's shoulder with one big hand, pushing the man off balance.

Martin batted at Sam's hands. "What the hell is the matter with you? Leave me alone," he bellowed, moving away from the angry man.

Sam's face, flushed with anger, advanced toward Martin. Martin, backing away, his hands out in front of him, palms forward, warding off the angry man. "Hey, settle down, man; you're acting crazy."

"I'll teach you, you little weasel. It will be the last time you pull a stunt like this," Sam yelled, backing Martin across the room.

"I didn't do anything. Are you nuts? What's the matter with you? What the hell have I done?" Martin asked, backtracking across the carpet.

Quickly coming from behind the bar, Mathew raised his hands, shouting, "Gentlemen, gentlemen!"

"Please, this is a party. There's no room for jealous rivalry here," pleaded Gloria, rushing up to confront the two men standing toe-to-toe, glaring at each other.

Crystal, Sherman's girlfriend tugging Mabel's arm, asked, "What's this about?"

"I don't know. It sure can't be about who won the best actor award," answered Mabel.

"Or best play because that went to the Maryland Musers," Violet added.

"Jealous rivalry?" snorted Mandy. "What rivalry can these men have? Both these men were disgusting." She looked at the men with disdain. "Both of you jerks were so drunk and so unprofessional. Your performances were the most shameless display of overacting and scene-stealing I've ever had the misfortune to witness."

Alice, sitting on the ottoman, smirked.

"I wasn't drunk," shouted Sam. With the flat of his hand, he pushed Martin on the chest, shoving him up against the dartboard. Martin's head ricocheted against the board, dislodging a dart. The dart fell to the floor. "This loathsome animal left his weed-infested candy out to entice me. And like a fool, I ate it. I didn't know the candy was loaded with cannabis. But I knew something was wrong with me. But I didn't know what or why. Rudy just told me. The candy I ate backstage was made with cannabis. That was pure sabotage. I don't believe in drugs. I never have; drugs are plain evil. My nephew died from it."

"You think your nephew died from smoking weed?" Martin asked, astounded, he rubbed the back of his head. "That's just dumb."

"No, you ass. But cannabis is a gateway drug."

"Well, I don't think it is —"

"You, slimy little lowlife. You tried to get me hooked on drugs." Sam bunched the front of Martin's shirt and lifted the younger man off the floor.

"No, no, I didn't bring that stuff. I, too, ate that candy by mistake. I was high. Do you really think I wanted to make a fool of myself?" squeaked Martin, squirming out of Sam's grasp.

"Stop this ridiculousness right now. I don't care who ate what. This is my party. This is not the place for a common barroom brawl," yelled Gloria. "Mathew, do something."

"My wife is right. Gentlemen, let bygones be bygones. Let me pour you a drink," urged the mayor, scurrying back behind the bar.

Gloria, glowering at her husband, threw up her hands. She marched to stand beside Mandy, crossing her arms across her chest and tapping her toe angrily.

Magdalen, laughing, swung around on her barstool. "Cannabis gummy bunnies won't get you hooked on drugs."

"She's right," agreed Craig. Plunking his plate on the buffet table, he strode to the bar. "You've got the wrong person, Sam, hasn't he, Magdalen?"

"I don't know what you mean," sputtered Magdalen.

"Like you don't know," sneered Craig. "I think you planted those cannabis-infested gummy bunnies to damage our play."

"What? Why accuse me?" Magdalen laughed. "And it's infused, not infested."

"You're laughing now, but not for long. You did it. You're the one behind Martin's crazy performance." He turned to Martin. "I'm sorry, buddy, that I doubted you."

Martin straightened his wrinkled shirt, narrowed his eyes, and stared at Magdalen. "Yeah, no problem."

"Oh, because I laughed. That's your proof," jeered Magdalen, raising her glass. "Here's to the great detective. I laughed, so therefore, I gave everyone pot gummy bunnies."

"I didn't say everyone."

Rudy, standing beside Craig, snarled, "Well, someone did. Someone brought that pot-infused candy, and they got poor old Sam here as high as a kite."

"Have you got that, Sam?" Martin asked. "It wasn't me. I would never sabotage you, and I sure in the hell wouldn't damage our play. I was embarrassed by what happened."

"It was you!" exclaimed Sam as he turned to face Magdalen. "Why? Why did you want to drug me?"

"Get real," snapped Magdalen.

"Don't accuse my daughter," Adam yelled, setting his plate on the buffet table and coming to his daughter's defence.

Gloria angrily brushed aside Adam and sank onto a barstool at the end of the bar. "Who cares? You guys are ruining my party. Nobody else is interested in your stupid little feud."

"I don't know why you're looking at me. What do I have to do with your preference for recreational drugs?" Magdalen swung her stool to face the bar. Her back was to the room.

Craig grabbed her by the arm, turning her back around. "You, troublemaking little cheater."

"Hey, hey. Hands off, my daughter," Adam demanded.

Craig lifted his hands and shrugged as he looked down at Adam. "Sure, fine, sorry. But I think your daughter ruined our play. I knew Martin wouldn't have taken that stuff on purpose."

"Damn right, I wouldn't."

"Gentlemen, gentleman. Stop this. This is no way to conduct yourselves." Mayor Hamilton stepped in front of Craig. "These unfounded accusations do not help anyone.

"Unfounded?" Craig dismissed the mayor with a wave of his hand and turned his back to him.

The mayor sputtered ineffectively, "Hey, hey." Then returned to his place behind the bar.

Gloria sighed. "Way to fix it, Mayor Fixit."

Not meeting his wife's eyes, the mayor poured himself a beer.

Craig, ignoring the mayor, put one arm on the bar; leaning toward Magdalen, he asked, "How come the best actress here knew the candies were the gummy bunnies laced with cannabis? No one here knew the pot candies were gummy bunnies. Except for the guys who ate them. Sam and Martin."

"Well, I guess I knew, but I didn't say anything to anyone," Rudy said. "I saw the dish of gummy bunnies. And I ate one, and I felt the effects. But I sure in the hell didn't put them there. You know I would never do that to you ever, Sam."

"Yeah, I know. And I'm sorry, Martin, I shouldn't have jumped to conclusions," Sam said, dropping down on a chair beside Ned.

Ned was munching on a cocktail sausage. He, like the twins, kept eating and watching the confrontation as if watching a tennis match.

Magdalen sniffed, sighed and said, "And you guys are all jumping to conclusions accusing me. Why me?"

"Because you knew they ate cannabis gummy bunnies," Mabel said.

"Oh, for God's sake, we all helped backstage. Magdalen saw the gummy bunnies, just like Rudy," defended Adam, putting his arm around his daughter's shoulders.

"You're making excuses because you don't want to admit your daughter and your play won by default," stormed Max, the director of the Kegworth players. "The play I wrote was a hell of a lot better than your stupid drama about a bunch of whiners."

"People, people. What's done is done. There is food, there are drinks. Please, everyone, let's enjoy this evening," urged the mayor.

"But someone did it," Mabel said, ignoring the mayor's request. "Someone planted those gummy candies there for an actor to eat. Either for a joke or to disrupt the performances."

"Yeah, she's right," insisted Martin.

"And it's not just those gummy guys. Some jerk messed with our props. The missing wine bottle, Adele was sure she put that wine bottle on the cabinet," declared Novak Simms, the Van Dyke bearded actor from the Moose Creek players.

"Hey, don't forget our armoire door was jammed shut." Romelu Abbott came to join the group in the centre of the room. "The damn thing didn't just stick. It was jammed. Some ass used small nails to tack it shut."

"And the poor Berryman Drama Club's food poisoning," Alice voiced.

"You don't know it was food poisoning," disputed the mayor hurriedly.

"It might have been food poisoning; we don't know," said Eric Ko, the actor from the Berryman Club. His co-actor, Vera Devon, nodded in agreement.

"Right, it's sabotage," Mabel exclaimed.

"Welcome to the witch hunt," muttered Gloria.

"You damn right there was sabotage. Our scenery came crashing down. And we all know who did that." Adam looked at Mabel and Violet. "I'd say the mystery of the gummy bunnies lay at your feet," he accused.

"Mabel and me planting cannabis gummy bunnies. That's ridiculous."

"You're all being ridiculous; this is all sour grapes," sneered Mandy Swan. "I judged you how I saw your performances onstage. Blaming some phantom is a cop-out. Let me tell you how I saw it. The worst case of scene-stealing award goes to." Mandy raised her cocktail glass in her one good hand, pointing the glass at Martin, spilling drops of her cocktail onto her lap. "The figure skating hockey player. What a pathetic spectacle you made of yourself."

"That was not my fault. I was high. Weren't you listening?" Martin spat.

"Oh, I was listening. Your disgraceful performance onstage was all your fault. I don't care what you ate."

Martin gave the adjudicator a scathing look; stomping to the bar, he picked up his beer mug.

"And the award for the worst play was a toss-up between Glenhaven and Moose Creek. But I'll give this coveted award to Glenhaven. Your director couldn't direct you out of a paper bag."

"Hey, hey," shouts from the Glenhaven actors filled the room. Helen bit her bottom lip and looked down at her hands.

"Lady, you had better stop belittling my wife. Or you'll be damn sorry," threatened Mike, crossing over to stand with his wife and patting her shoulder; he glared at Mandy.

Mandy gave Mike a dismissive look and continued. "And the worst bad acting award goes to." She paused and did a little drum roll with her fingers on her cast. "Ta-da, ta-da. To Jolene. I would say, Jolene, don't quit your day job. But as you can see." Mandy ripped off her turban, revealing her frizzy white hair. "You will not have a day job. Maybe the women in this hayseed town don't mind having their hair ruined by some incompetent little twit. But I do, and I will make sure you're fired."

Jolene's eyes filled with tears. She jumped off her barstool and crept over to her grandmother, who put her arms around her. Tommy rose, his face flushed; he slammed his drink down on the bar, storming up the stairs.

"Enough, you've said enough; leave poor Jolene alone," scolded Helen.

"Please, everyone, try to get along," Gloria pleaded. "This is an evening for celebrating. It's the end of the drama festival, and we had sell-out crowds every night."

"They probably came to see what disaster would happen onstage," snorted Mandy. "I need another drink."

Gloria glared at the woman sprawled out in the recliner and sighed. "Mathew, pour this disagreeable woman another drink.'

"Well, we certainly weren't a disaster. We won the best play and best actress," asserted Sheeran, the Maryland director.

"There was very little competition. I didn't have much to choose from," Mandy mocked. "This is the worst drama festival I've ever had the misfortune to attend. As an actor or as an adjudicator."

The actors and directors who were at odds before now were universally united, disputing Mandy's accusations.

Gloria shoved a mug of beer in Mandy's face. "Here."

"I don't like beer."

"That's no surprise. You've disliked everything here in Glenhaven. So, drink your darn beer or hobble on out of here."

Mandy sat back in her chair, shocked. "Well, I never," she said. The actors, laughing, held up their drinks in a salute.

Gloria preened. "I admit the plays did not come off as planned. But, honestly, what more could I do? I overcame Sherman's unfortunate death and carried on."

"You overcame Sherman's unfortunate death!" Mabel said, glancing at Crystal, Sherman's girlfriend.

Crystal sucked in a deep breath; her eyes grew wide. She opened her mouth to speak, but Gloria carried on. "Yes. It was up to me to coordinate this festival. I had Mike and Tommy help the other drama clubs with the lights and sound. And I arranged for each club to help backstage when they weren't performing. That's organization. Which you, Miss Swan, do not seem to appreciate!"

Mabel lifted an eyebrow. "Yes, you did. And in doing so, you gave someone the perfect opportunity to sabotage the plays."

"Sabotage, sabotage. I'm sick of that word. And I don't care who did what," muttered Gloria, slumping down on a barstool. "Mathew, I need a drink. Something stronger than beer."

"Right, and we all know who that is. It's you," accused Magdalen, pointing at Mabel. "Everyone saw you destroy our backdrop. It was you who put out those gummy bunnies. You stole the props and jimmied the cabinet door. I bet you even caused the Berryman's food poisoning."

Gloria, looking up at the ceiling, sighed. "I give up. You people are impossible."

The twins nodded in agreement as they circled the buffet table, topping up their plates with little pork pies.

"That is absurd. Mabel did no such thing. The backdrop falling was an accident," defended Violet, jumping up, her face flushed, her eyes flashing in anger. "She did not sabotage your play."

"Oh, she tried. But despite her best efforts, we won the best play.'

"Actually, because of the falling scenery, you won the best play," disputed Mabel.

"Mabel," warned Violet. "Leave it be."

"And you were probably in on all these horrible tricks," accused Magdalen. "You two did it because your play sucked, and you wanted to ruin everyone else's performances. And you succeeded. Except for ours."

"Ha, you were the best of the worst," Mandy mocked, then taking a sip of beer, she screwed up her lips.

"You just can't shut up, can you?" snarled Adam.

Mabel stepped into the centre of the room. "I'm sure there was a saboteur. But not me or Violet. Okay, I destroyed the backdrop. But that was an accident."

"Yeah, right," sneered Adam.

"Oh, for God's sake," pleaded Gloria. "Let's not get into this again. Mabel, just go sit down and eat. Do something you are good at, like eating. And everyone, please have another drink. And have some of this wonderful food I've had prepared for you."

"I agree; this is silly." Magdalen held up her empty glass. "Same again, please, Mr. Mayor."

"That's the spirit. Is anyone else ready for another drink?" asked Mayor Hamilton. Returning behind the bar, he began mixing a drink for Magdalen.

"What happened to the other plays was sneaky, the gummy bunnies, the missing props. The desk and chairs that faced the wrong way. The jammed cabinet. Who was lurking backstage when they had no business being there?" Mabel asked.

"I don't know about who was backstage with the others. But I did see someone not lurking exactly, but Magdalen was backstage before our performance." Jolene said.

Magdalen turned to Jolene. "I was helping."

"Helping with what? We were the only club that did not need extra backstage help. Why were you there?" Mabel asked, her arms crossed over her chest, staring at the girl suspiciously.

"I was helping my dad put our costumes and props downstairs." She turned to the Kegworth director. "Notice I was not backstage for the Kegworth ridiculous play. I sat down with the rest of the cast, watching you crash and burn. That shoots down this stupid woman's theory. Let's eat some of this delicious food Gloria, our gracious hostess, has provided for us."

"Maybe you weren't, but your dad was," Martin said.

"If there was any sabotage. The sabotage was against me." Mandy interrupted. "Look at me. My leg's broken, and my wrist has suffered a nasty sprain. My car is totalled, and I've got whiplash. And to top it off, my hair is ruined."

Tommy tromped down the stairs holding a shotgun. He pointed it at Mandy, screaming, "It's time you got yours, you nasty old bag. You're going to pay and pay big."

Chapter Thirty-One

Issuing a piercing, terrified scream, Mandy recoiled in her chair, her face white. She held up her good hand, spilling her beer on her lap.

The actors and the directors scattered, yelling and screaming. They hid behind tables and chairs. Magdalen ducked behind the big, shiny drama trophy. Crouching in a corner, Rudy took out his phone. This time, he wasn't texting; he was recording. Alice jumped behind Ned, knocking the scrawny little man head over heels; he crashed into the large trophy. The cup toppled over, sending Magdalen down on her bum. Her purse flew out of her hands, flipping across the floor, the purse landed on Ned's lap. Gloria leapt off her stool, quickly scrambling behind the bar beside her husband, whose head bobbed up and down, peeking over the counter at Tommy. The twins scrunched behind the buffet table, plates still in hand.

Mabel began crawling under the buffet table to join Violet and Crystal, who were already crouched there. She stopped in mid-crawl and turned to look at Tommy.

The tall, skinny boy's hands trembled as he stood over Mandy, waving the shotgun at her face. He looked as scared as Mandy, who was whimpering, "Please, please, what have I ever done to you?"

Mabel stood and walked purposely toward Tommy. "Tommy, you don't want to do this."

Violet shouted from under the buffet table, "Mabel, get away from him."

Mabel, ignoring Violet's warning, continued her march. "Put that gun down, Tommy. This won't solve anything. I don't know why you're mad. Maybe you have a good reason. But this will only make things worse."

"I hate this nasty old crow, and this time, I mean business," his voice quaked.

Mandy screamed, "Help, help. Please, somebody, please."

"I am not fond of her either, Tommy. But this is not the way. Put the gun down this instant."

Sam, stomping past Mabel, ripped the gun out of Tommy's hands.

"Call the cops," screamed Mandy. "Call the cops."

"Now, you sit down, young man, and behave yourself," Mabel said as Sam pushed Tommy down onto a footstool.

Disheartened, Tommy looked up at Sam.

"Call the cops, call the cops," Mandy screamed again.

"Tommy, what the heck has gotten into you?" Mabel placed a hand on the skinny man's shoulder.

Dejected, Tommy stared down at his hands.

"Look at me, please."

Reluctantly, Tommy raised his eyes.

"What on earth did you think you were doing?" Mabel asked.

"Call the cops."

"Just be quiet and let us get to the bottom of this," snapped Sam.

"Call the—"

"I said be quiet; we will deal with Tommy."

"Be quiet? Is this a regular occurrence in your hillbilly town? Do lunatics go around threatening innocent women with guns with no consequences?"

"Ma'am, please, for the last time, be quiet."

"Or what? Are you threatening me?"

"What? Threaten you? I just saved your ass. We will deal with this, don't worry. Tommy won't get away with this."

Mandy clamped her mouth shut; her eyes narrowed. Satisfied, Sam took the shotgun and leaned the gun against a wall by the buffet table.

"Tommy, Tommy. You scared poor Miss Swan," scolded Helen, rising from behind Mandy's large chair.

Mike, lumbering over to stand beside his wife, looked down at Tommy. "You made an ass of yourself, kid," he said.

The actors and directors emerged from their hiding places.

The mayor pushed through the actors, who were forming a circle around Tommy and Mandy. "Alright, now, Tommy, what the hell is this about?" he demanded.

Gloria elbowed her husband aside. "I thought this party couldn't get any worse. But I was wrong. How could you, Tommy? You've ruined my party with this ridiculous spectacle."

"Ruined your party!" Mandy howled, outraged. "What about me? This imbecile was going to shoot me."

"I'm so sorry; he scared you, Miss Swan. But Tommy wouldn't hurt a flea," assured Helen.

"He had a gun," Mandy said, suspiciously eyeing Tommy.

"Well, there is that," conceded Helen.

"Why on earth would you come here with a gun? What were you thinking?" asked Mabel.

"Yeah, if anybody has a reason to off the high and mighty old lady Swan, it's one of us actors," joked Martin.

Mandy glowered at Martin. "That is not even remotely funny."

"...e's a nasty old witch," Tommy said, casting a defiant look in Mandy's direction. "I've had it up to here. That old bag keeps mocking poor Jolene and, and she threatened her."

"Did you rear-end her car downtown?" asked Mabel suspiciously, looking down at Tommy sitting on the hassock

"Yeah, she said she was going to get Jolene fired."

"Oh, Tommy," Jolene said. Rushing over, she knelt, hugging the skinny young man. "That's so sweet."

"Sweet," shrieked Mandy. "You call running into my car, sweet?"

"Don't you worry, Miss Swan, we will deal with Tommy," Sam said.

"Really? Somehow, I doubt it. You clodhoppers stick together."

"Lady, I would be quiet if I was you," cautioned Sam.

Mandy pressed her lips together, looking slitty-eyed at Tommy.

Violet joined the circle of actors and asked, "Tommy, did you, by chance, ah, accidentally turn out the lights when Mandy fell?"

"Yeah, sorry, but it wasn't accidentally. I turned off the lights. But I didn't think she'd get a broken leg or anything like that. I just wanted to pay her back for the horrible things she said about Jolene. Jolene is a wonderful actress."

Jolene squeezed beside Tommy on the stool. "Oh, Tommy," she gushed, planting a kiss on his cheek.

Flushing, Tommy blinked his long white lashes, smiling shyly back at her.

"I suppose you think my broken leg is sweet, too," snarled Mandy.

"Oh, Tommy, what were you thinking? That was a terrible thing to do," scolded Helen.

"I guess sometimes I do get a little carried away. One night after rehearsals, I sort of tried to scare Mabel."

"Sort of? You mean you tried to run me down," Mabel said, shocked. "Why on earth did you want to kill me?"

"No, no, I didn't want to kill you. I was just. I just wanted to scare you. You were so mean to Jolene that night. Saying all those nasty things."

"I'm sorry, I don't remember being mean, but I do remember being scared stiff. Tommy, you need therapy. You need to take anger management."

"Anger management? He should go to jail," Mandy snarled.

"Was it you who interfered with the plays?" asked Violet.

"Oh, Tommy, please tell me it wasn't you who meddled with the props and the sets," pleaded Helen.

"You put the gummy candies out for Martin and me. Why did you do that? That is the worst." Sam stomped back to sit at the bar, shaking his head. "I'm so disappointed in you, boy."

"No, no. Sam, I didn't do that. I wouldn't do anything to hurt you, Sam. I just hate this evil woman. I didn't do any of the other stuff."

"Well, looky, looky here," Ned laughed shrilly. "Look what came out of this purse." He held up Magdalen's purse and a handful of gummy bunnies.

"You crazy old goat. Give me my purse," Magdalen yelled, snatching her purse out of Ned's hands.

Ned uttered a screechy laugh, taunting her; he held up the handful of gummy bunnies.

"I knew it," crowed Craig. "I knew it. I was right all along. She's the cheater."

"No, somebody is framing me. I have no idea how those gummy bunnies got into my purse. Someone put them there. I had nothing to do with it."

All the directors and actors' eyes turned to Magdalen.

"Tell me you didn't do what they are accusing you of," pleaded the Maryland Muser director, Sheeran.

Adam spread out his hands. "It's no use, Magdalen, honey. We might as well come clean."

"I can't believe you would do such a thing?" Sheeran looked at the father and daughter. Then, at the other Maryland cast members. "Were you people in on this?"

"What? No way," exclaimed Levi and Grant.

"Not me either." Daryna took a step back from Magdalen and Adam.

Adam crossed his arms over his chest, taking a defiant stance. "What's the big deal? So, my daughter and I devised a few tricks. I don't know why you're getting so upset about it."

"A few tricks! That was more than tricks. Drugging me, turning me into a drug addict," shouted Sam, lunging at Adam.

"Steady, steady," Rudy said as he and Craig pulled the irate man away from Adam.

"Let me at him," Sam cried, trying to free himself.

"You're okay, Sam. You're fine; you're not going to become a drug addict."

Sam sunk onto a chair, his head in his hands. "My nephew died from an overdose," he moaned.

Mabel put a comforting hand on his shoulder. "It's okay, Sam. Rudy's right." She turned back to face Adam and Magdalen. "Regardless, that was a nasty thing to do. You interfered with the plays, and you have traumatized poor Sam."

Magdalen bit her bottom lip but looked unrepentant.

"It was harmless, just a few tricks. My daughter wanted to win. The Maryland Musers have lost to Glenhaven for the last three years. I just wanted to make her happy. Sorry, Sam, we didn't plan on anyone in particular. And we didn't know how bad your Glenhaven club was. We didn't even need to do the gummy bunny thing. I guess we should have just given the cannabis candy to Martin."

"We weren't that bad," denied Alice.

"Oh, yes, you were," Mandy said, plucking at her damp dress.

"You, cheater," snarled Martin. Grabbing Adam by the arm, he spun the small man around.

Craig pulled Martin away. "Leave it, Martin. Maryland's reputation is shot. It's ruined, thanks to these two."

The Maryland actors and their director, Sheeran Maier, exchanged shocked looks, backing away from Adam and his daughter.

"You disgusting slimeball. You deliberately put the desk and the chairs the wrong way around. And you poisoned poor Ivy and Audrey." Eric Ko strode up to confront Adam.

"No, what kind of monsters do you think we are? We just played a few tricks. We didn't poison anyone. No one got hurt. Besides, it's only Little Theatre."

Chapter Thirty-Two

"Only Little Theatre!" the actors shouted in unison.

"No one got hurt? What about Sherman? Did you rig the banister on the basement stairs?" Mabel asked.

"What! No way. I said we only played tricks," denied Adam.

"Some tricks," snapped Martin, grabbing his beer mug; he glared at Adam and his daughter, who sat with a mutinous look on her face.

"Those tricks didn't make all that much difference. You were all awful. Maryland just happens to be the least of the bad," Mandy said.

Magdalen's lips twisted in a scowl.

The actors and directors milling around the room gave Adam and his daughter a wide berth. The Moose Creek Club and Kegworth Players joined the Berryman group, muttering and casting angry looks at Magdalen and her father. The director and the actors from the Maryland Musers were also giving the father and daughter team the cold shoulder. Mike, Sam, and Helen sat on a couch. Helen, looking weary, raised a glass of wine to her lips. The confrontation over, Mabel followed Ned, Alice, and the twins back to the buffet table. Her tummy rumbled as she surveyed the variety of food. Poor Gloria, her party was a bomb, but at least there was still plenty of food.

Sitting next to Crystal, Violet said, "I'm so sorry you had to suffer through all this. I think you are so brave to have come here tonight."

Crystal, looking sorrowful, replied, "The shenanigans at least took my mind off of my beloved Sherman, at least for a while."

Rudy, sticking his phone in his pocket, leaned on the bar. "Pour me another beer, please," he requested.

Mayor Hamilton brought a frosted mug from a cooler. "My dear boy, the correct term is pull a pint. As you can see, I have a proper tap," he said proudly.

"Mathew, just give the man a beer," said Gloria, plunking down on a stool beside Rudy. "And pour or pull one for me, too. The only good thing about this evening. Is that it can't get any worse."

Mandy, plucking at her damp dress, suspiciously eyed Tommy.

Tommy was smiling shyly at Jolene. "Oh, I still have Sherman's phone," he said. "It works. Do you want it?"

Jolene smiled sweetly back at him. "No, thanks, you keep it."

Putting a pork pie on her plate, Mabel turned and asked, "You found Sherman's phone?"

"Yep, It's a pretty good brand. Someone should get some use out of it. Do you want it? It just needs a new screen."

"You can't give that phone away. It doesn't belong to you. That phone was Sherman's. Give it to me," demanded Crystal.

"Sure, if you like."

"I like." Crystal marched over to Tommy, her hand outstretched.

"And I'd like to know who the last caller on Sherman's phone is," Mabel said, setting her plate down on the table.

"Give me the phone, and I'll tell you.'

Grinning, Tommy said, "I could tell you the phone was easy to unlock. And I know who was the last. There was a text."

"Did you read it?" Mabel asked, striding across the carpet to stand beside Crystal.

"You had better not have read Sherman's messages. That is disrespectful. And an invasion of privacy."

"Well." Tommy, embarrassed, ducked his head.

"Give me the phone," instructed Crystal.

Chapter Thirty-Three

M abel quickly stepped around Crystal, preventing her from snatching the phone from Tommy's hand. "You seem very intent on getting Sherman's phone. Do you have something to hide? Is there something incriminating on that phone?"

"Incriminating! What rubbish. Of course, I've got nothing to hide. What Sherman and I text is private and is nobody's business."

"Did you lure Sherman out onto that landing? And ultimately to his death."

"What? That's ridiculous. I didn't lure Sherman anywhere. Sure, I texted him that night, but I often texted Sherman. I loved him. I was going to be his wife."

"You told me you didn't call Sherman that night."

"Texting isn't calling."

"I think I'd like to hear what you text to Sherman. Tommy, please read out the last text to Sherman."

"Mabel, what are you suggesting? This is unacceptable. Miss Harrison is our guest. Stop harassing this poor woman," ordered Mayor Hamilton in a raised voice. The drama guests stopped talking and looked at the mayor, then at Mabel, Crystal, and Tommy, who was clutching the phone firmly in his hand.

"Listen to your mayor. Don't you dare betray the confidential texts between my fiancé and me." Crystal sidestepped around Mabel.

Tommy jumped up from the ottoman with the phone in his hand and sprinted behind Mandy's chair.

Mabel turned to Tommy. "Tommy, please read the text aloud," she requested again.

"Tommy, you will do no such thing. Give the phone to Crystal," ordered the mayor again, coming out from behind the bar. The actors and directors now gathered to watch the struggle of wills between Mabel and Crystal and the mayor.

Tommy's eyes darted from Mabel to the mayor and back to Crystal. Mabel smiled at Tommy, crossed her arms, and nodded.

Taking a deep breath, the skinny young man began. "The text is from this lady." He looked at Crystal.

Her face flushed, eyes blazing; Crystal stood with fists clenched at her side.

"The text starts with, '*It's time to leave the stage, sweetie,*'" Tommy read, looking up at Crystal. He gulped and continued. "There are some hearts and laughing emojis. Then the text says *I love you*." Tommy blushed and stammered, "There, there is another heart, and then, the text says, *I'm waiting.* More hearts and hugging emojis. Then the text ends with a; *just go and do it.* With another thumbs up and a heart emoji."

Mabel frowned. "And?"

"Sherman texted back. *I'm ready. Here I go.* And three thumbs up emojis and a heart."

Crystal smiled. "Right, now that's settled, and everyone's morbid curiosity is satisfied. Give me the damn phone; as you heard, these texts mean nothing."

"Mabel, go back to the buffet," Gloria called wearily. "We have had enough accusations, real and false, for one night."

Mabel's eyes narrowed; looking defiant, she said, "I'm not sure what these texts mean. Why did you tell him to leave the stage? Maybe promising to show him some sexy pictures?"

"Don't be disgusting," snorted Crystal.

"Whatever incentive you promised, you got him offstage, and you hoped or knew he would lean on the banister and fall to his death."

"Mabel," warned the mayor. "Stop this harassment right now. These are ridiculous accusations."

"Ridiculous accusations? I don't think so. And what I do know is that Sherman leaned on that railing and fell to his death. And his so-called accidental death has something to do with his girlfriend."

"Mabel, my party is ruined already. Don't make it any worse," moaned Gloria.

Mabel took the phone from Tommy's hand, scrolling through the texts. "What else will we find on this phone?"

"Nothing, that's what. The old railing just happened to break when Sherman leaned on it. And now that the banister has been repaired. You can't prove anything." Crystal reached for the phone.

Mabel batted her hand away. "Prove anything? That's a curious term to use. And by the way. We know the handrail just didn't happen to break. It was tampered with. I saw that some of the screws in the support structure were ripped out of the wood. I also saw screw holes that had no splintering or tearing. Those screws were taken out. Alice has photos on her phone to prove it," she lied. "When I pointed out the discrepancy, she took pictures. And she shared them with the RCMP. Right Alice?"

"Ah, maybe, yeah, yeah, I do, did," Alice sputtered.

"Really?" Crystal asked skeptically.

"If Alice doesn't have pictures, I sure do," Rudy said. His phone was in his hand, and the record button was on. "I videoed everything."

Crystal arched an eyebrow. "Seriously?"

"Yeah, I did. I have a YouTube channel. Check it out. '*Rudy Goes and Rudy Knows.*' I have almost a thousand followers," boasted Rudy.

Mabel cast her thoughts back to the night of Sherman's death. She recalled Rudy constantly texting. She didn't remember him videoing the damage to the railing. But it didn't matter if Crystal thought he did.

"I don't care what you have. I didn't do anything to damage that old railing or whatever it was that broke. I never even saw the damage. I can't even bear to go to the theatre." Her voice trembled. "So, I don't even know what you are talking about."

"Really? You keep saying old railing. If you have never been to the theatre, how would you know the railing was old?" asked Mabel.

"It's an old building."

"An old building that was renovated."

"Whatever, a figure of speech. I guess the railing was old. I've never been to the theatre."

"Well," squeaked Ned. "I did see your flashy car in the theatre parking lot late one night. And I know which night it was, too. Because it was the night before the rehearsal when poor old Sherman did his nosedive."

"Aha, that's when you snuck into the theatre and took the screws out of the railing," accused Mabel. "You left just enough screws in the wood so the banister would look normal to Sherman and to us. And then you called Sherman and lured him out on the landing with some kind of promise. Sherman leaned on the railing. And then fell to his death."

"How would I know Sherman would lean on that railing? Anyway. The car this crazy old guy saw wasn't my car."

"I may be old," cackled Ned. "But I'm not crazy. I know a Porsche when I see one. The car was dirty, but there was no mistaking that car. That car was a Porsche. A red Porsche."

"There's only one red Porsche in town, and I saw it in your driveway. Besides, Ned took a picture of the licence plate just in case someone vandalized the theatre," Mabel said, lying again.

"Yep, you can't be too careful nowadays," Ned said, giving Mabel a big, gap-tooth smile.

"If you have a picture of the licence plate, then you know it wasn't me."

Mabel was perplexed. The girl seemed unfazed by Ned's surprise revelation. But it had to be her. Okay, they didn't have a picture of the licence plate. But Crystal didn't know that. Anyway, the car Ned saw in the parking lot was proof positive, at least in her book. Mabel took in a breath and continued with her accusations. "The evidence is mounting against you. Sherman's phone with your text urging him to go out to the landing and the picture of your licence plate. Why did you murder Sherman? Was he unfaithful?"

Crystal moaned, collapsing onto a chair. "Sherman did it," she wailed. "It was all Sherman's idea; it was his plan. He wasn't supposed to die. Only fake an injury. But it all went hideously wrong."

"Why the heck would he do something as weird as that?"

Crystal wiped her hands on her slacks. "Insurance, accident insurance."

"Ah-ha, I'm right. The oldest motive in the book. Greed. And you're the beneficiary," accused Mabel.

"I told you I didn't do it. Sherman did." Crystal began to cry. "One night after rehearsals, he went back to the theatre and loosened a few screws on the railing. The plan was that I would call

Sherman so he would have an excuse to go out on the landing. He would break off a piece of the handrail and then go downstairs, lie on the floor, and call for help. He was going to fake an injury."

"That was not a very good plan," disputed Violet. "The doctors would soon find out nothing was broken."

"Sherman was going to fake a back injury. He said you can't x-ray pain. But his plan didn't work out. It all went oh so horribly, horribly wrong. I'll never forget his screams as he fell. His screams will haunt me until the day I die," Crystal moaned, crumpling in a heap, rocking; she covered her face with her hands, her shoulders shaking.

"You and Sherman cooked this up for insurance money?"

"Yes, we needed money. We owe everyone," Crystal said. She took her hands down and looked at the crowd of actors watching with fascination. Her voice broke; she took a deep breath and continued. "Our debt was out of control. We are behind on house payments. We had our final notice we were about to lose the house. And our cars were going to be repossessed. All of our credit cards are maxed out. And we were going to lose our vacation home down south. We were at our wit's end. We even took out a payday loan, and the interest skyrocketed. We were desperate. Sherman has, or rather, had accident insurance with our mining company. And we have private insurance as well. We figured we could get even more money from the town. Sherman found out that Glenhaven was responsible for the hall's maintenance. We were going to sue the town. But everything went wrong. Now my beloved Sherman, my best friend and the love of my life, is dead."

"Sue me. I mean, the town?" shouted the mayor in outrage. "I will make sure you go to jail for trying to defraud this beautiful little town."

"Oh, Mr. Mayor, I think this is way more than a mere fraud case," Mabel said. "Crystal killed Sherman. More than a couple of screws were taken out of the wood." She turned to confront Crystal. "You went there after Sherman did his dirty work. You snuck in and took the rest of the screws out of the bottom of the railing. So, when Sherman pushed on the railing, the railing gave out, and he plunged to his death. The money from an injury is not nearly as much as you will collect from accidental death. You wanted him dead."

"No, you're wrong. I loved Sherman." Crystal took a deep breath. "But I, I did kill him." Her voice broke into a sob. "I didn't think a fake back injury would work. I tried and tried to convince him. But he was so sure his plan would work. He wouldn't listen to me. So, I decided to make the accident more realistic. I Know, I know, it's all my fault Sherman is dead." She took another ragged breath. "You're right. I did go to the hall after Sherman, and I did loosen some screws on the railing. And I took some out. I really thought he would just fall and break a leg or an arm. But I...I took too many out." Tears streamed down her cheeks. "I never meant for Sherman to die."

The actors and directors stood in shocked silence as they listened to Crystal's confession. Mabel cocked an eyebrow. Crystal didn't mean for Sherman to die? Or was she a cold, calculating murderer? But that would be for a jury to decide.

"Call the cops," Mandy yelled, breaking the silence. "For God's sake, you people, do something. First, you let a crazy lunatic get away with threatening me with a gun. Now you're going to let this killer get away with murder? Call the cops."

Panicking, Crystal picked up the shotgun that was leaning against the wall by the buffet table. Waving the gun wildly, she pointed it at Mabel and the actors gathered in front of her. "I'm not going to jail," she screamed. "I can't go to jail. I didn't mean to kill Sherman. I loved him. Stay back. I don't want to hurt anyone, but I'm leaving."

"Crystal, don't be silly. You're only making things worse for yourself. Please put that gun down," urged Mabel.

Crystal backed toward the stairs, the gun pointing at Mabel. The actors and directors scrambled back to their hiding places. "Stay back, or I swear I'll shoot," screamed Crystal.

Tommy pushed past Mabel and grabbed the gun, wrenching it out from Crystal's hands.

Crystal slumped down on the bottom step, sobbing.

"Oh, Tommy, you're so brave," Jolene cried, clapping her hands.

"Ah, gosh, it was nothing. This shotgun isn't loaded. I wasn't ever going to hurt old lady Swan. I just wanted to scare the old bat." Pointing the gun at the big screen TV, Tommy pulled the trigger. There was a loud, deafening roar of the shotgun, and the TV shattered.

The End

Don't miss out!

Visit the website below and you can sign up to receive emails whenever Joan Havelange publishes a new book. There's no charge and no obligation.

https://books2read.com/r/B-A-CCKUC-WGVSF

Connecting independent readers to independent writers.

Did you love *Murder Exit Stage Right*? Then you should read *Wayward Shot*[1] by Joan Havelange!

When Mabel slices her golf ball into the town cemetery, she and her best friend Violet, think the worst that could happen would be a lost ball. Until they discover a dead body, and it isn't six feet under.

Mabel's ball lies in the middle of his forehead. It can't be murder, can it? The ladies take it upon themselves to solve the mystery of the dead body in the graveyard.

Using the information gleaned from Coffee Row, a collection of eccentric townspeople leads them to investigate golfers and

---

relatives of the deceased. Their investigation frustrates a newly appointed RCMP officer, who does his best to put a stop to their interference. But nothing stops the intrepid detectives. Not the RCMP, a stampede of cattle or even shots fired at them in the dark. They have an uncanny ability to find trouble and dead bodies.

Also by Joan Havelange

Mabel and Violet Mysteries
Wayward Shot
Death and Denial
The Trouble with Funerals
The Suspects
Murder Exit Stage Right